# OFF HIS GAME

## HOT RUGBY KNIGHTS — BOOK TWO

## COURTNEY CLARK MICHAELS

AUGUST PUBLISHING

**Off His Game**
**Hot Rugby Knights - Book Two**

by Courtney Clark Michaels

This book is a work of fiction. Names, characters, places and incidents are the product of the author's imagination or are used fictitiously. Any resemblance to actual events, locales, or persons living or dead is coincidental.



E book ISBN: 978-0-473-68738-0



Cover design: Melville Design

*To all my closest friends, who pissed themselves laughing when The Sprinkler Incident happened. Bitches.*

CONTENT ALERT

This book contains depiction of the following: parental infidelity, parental alcoholism, reference to drug use, death of a loved one (not on page, not main character), potential child abandonment and touch aversion, sex work. Every effort has been made by the author to handle this content with sensitivity, however please consider whether this may be upsetting for you as a reader and take care of yourself.

# CHAPTER 1

*I*t was the sprinkler that broke him.

Zac Fearon wasn't a guy to lose his shit over the small stuff. When you grew up with big stuff happening all around you, crying over spilled milk, or burnt toast, or whatever random kitchen disaster you could think of wouldn't do anything except leave you thirsty, hungry and pissed off.

But then his younger sister Frances had shown up on his doorstep, two kids in tow, fresh needle marks in her arm and a sob story about needing to go out of Auckland for a few weeks.

That was some big stuff.

And it came with lots of little stuff. All the little stuff that a five-year-old and a three-year-old needed. Not diapers, thank God, though he'd changed enough of them when the kids had been younger, but schoolbags and stuffed animals and those drink bottles that had a thousand fucking parts and needed to be handwashed every night. Puzzles and colouring pencils and cans of spaghetti with tiny meatballs in them because he'd tried to serve spaghetti without meatballs on the second night and the resulting tantrum had lasted over an hour and given him a migraine.

Zac loved his niblings. Otis and Hazel were the cutest kids he could imagine – funny and loving and mischievous. But they had seemed a bit more manageable when he was visiting on the weekends or stopping by for dinner occasionally. Not when he was trying to get them out the door to preschool and school on time before making it to training. Not when he was trying to manage bedtime, with both of them popping up like they were in a game of Whack-A-Mole, wanting extra stories, or apple slices, or another drink of water. And definitely not when he'd left them playing outside in the sprinkler and ducked into his bathroom to take a slash, only to return and find the goddamned sprinkler swirling around inside his living room, soaking his furniture, his carpets, his fucking television.

He lost his shit.

Now both the kids were in time out, the windows were open in the hopes that the warmth of the early New Zealand autumn sun would dry some of the worst spots, and Zac stood in the kitchen, rage-eating peanut butter toast.

He was out of his depth. He'd floundered for the last two weeks, trying to make it work. Every nanny service he'd called had a waiting list. He'd been late to training more times in the last fortnight than in the whole of his career. Through her closed bedroom door, he could hear Hazel wailing like the world was ending. He hadn't yelled at the kids. Hadn't smacked them. Hadn't done anything but have a stern word about outside toys and respecting people's property before shutting them in their rooms to think about what they'd done, but Hazel had a touch of the melodramatic about her.

He needed a solution before the neighbours called protective services.

Chest tight, he lifted his phone and dialled the number he'd avoided calling for the past fortnight.

"Fearon?"

"Hey Chalmers."

"What's going on?"

Zac winced. He wasn't really a friendly guy, everyone knew that, but he'd never had to call his captain outside of practice hours before. Mind you, Finn Chalmers was an astute guy. Zac had caught him looking at him recently, a little divot between his brows. If he hadn't called tonight, chances were good Finn would have sat him down for a chat soon enough.

"I need some help." It killed him to admit it. He should be able to take care of his family – all of them. God knows, he'd been doing it for long enough.

"With what?"

"I'm looking after my niece and nephew for a couple of weeks." Christ, he hoped it *was* only for a couple more weeks.

*If Frances ends up like Dad...*

He pushed the thought away. He couldn't help his sister right now. There was no way to reach her. He didn't even know what city she was in. She'd left her cellphone in Otis's overnight bag, and even if he could get someone to track her down, there was no guarantee she'd be in any state to come back to Auckland and take care of her kids. Failure weighed him down. He'd tried so hard to protect her, yet here they were, stuck in a time loop he'd worked his arse off to avoid. But he was fucked if he would let Otis and Hazel suffer the way he and Frances had growing up.

"You need a babysitter?" Finn's voice brought him back to the present.

"More like a nanny." Zac sighed into the phone. "I'm not handling it, man. It's impossible on top of training and the regular season starts next week. We're slated for a couple of out-of-town games early on. I've called a few agencies, but none can get to me until after Easter. I was wondering if maybe Cara knew someone who would be willing to step in for some casual work for a bit?" Finn's fiancée was an early childhood teacher.

"Hang on, I'll ask."

There was some murmuring on the other end of the line, and then Finn was back.

"She's got someone in mind."

Hope shot through Zac. "Yeah?"

"Her sister Izzy moved back from the UK last month. She's been working as an au pair overseas for a few years now."

Hope died a swift death. Isabel Holt hated him. Not without reason, but still, he'd have to have bigger problems than a fried TV to ask her for help. The chances of being smothered in his sleep were too high. He'd seen her at their preseason game last week and he'd barely survived the death glare she'd levelled at him. His own feelings about Izzy were more complicated – and decidedly more lust-filled – but since being murdered in his own house wasn't on his to-do list, he'd have to find an alternative solution.

"I don't think that will work," he hedged. "Is there anyone else? Anyone who's recently retired?"

Someone who didn't have honey-brown eyes, a smattering of freckles across their nose, and a burning desire to do him harm.

"Sorry," Finn sighed. "I know you and Izzy don't know each other well–" *We know each other better than you think*, Zac thought, trying to shake the image of Isabel's naked breasts from his mind "–but she's all Cara can think of. She's really good," he assured Zac when he didn't answer. "She was the live-in care for the Sultan of Brunei's cousin's kids a couple of years ago."

"Look, I'm sure she's very good at her job," Zac began stiffly, his mind searching for a way to extricate himself from this conversation that wouldn't make him look like an arsehole; or piss off Chalmers, who'd thought of Isabel as his honorary little sister for the past five years, "but the thing is..."

He didn't have a thing. At least not one he wanted to tell Chalmers. But then a voice came from behind him.

"Uncle?"

He turned, phone held to his ear. Otis stood in the kitchen, still in his swim trunks. "Hey, mate."

"I'm sorry about the sprinkler." Otis's eyes were brimming with tears. "I made you a card." He produced it from behind his back – a folded sheet of white paper with the word 'Sorry' in huge, red letters. Underneath was a picture of two misshapen figures that Zac recognised from Otis's previous canon of family portraits.

Squatting down, he looked into his nephew's eyes. "Is that you and me, mate?"

Otis nodded solemnly. Zac would be worried as fuck about how quiet his nephew had seemed since Frances had dumped them on his doorstep if Otis hadn't been this way since the first time he'd stared unsmilingly up at Zac as he held the newborn to his chest in the hospital.

*My serious little man*, Frances called him, and Zac hoped to God that Otis hadn't seen anything recently to make him even more serious.

"Why don't you put it on the fridge door?" Zac suggested. "Then go tell Hazel her timeout is over, and you can watch a movie in my room."

Otis brightened. "*Cars*?"

"Sure, mate." Both kids were obsessed with the film. He had no idea how much of the story they had picked up over regular rewatches, but he knew it would buy him a couple of hours to sort out the living room before they came racing out to skid their own toy cars in 'races' along the edge of the coffee table.

Otis cheered and whacked his picture onto the fridge with a Saturn shaped magnet, before running out of the kitchen towards the bedrooms. Zac watched him go, letting out a heavy breath.

*Fuck.*

These kids might drive him crazy, but he loved them beyond words. If that meant he had to put himself in an uncomfortable position for a couple of weeks...

"Chalmers? You still there?"

"I'm still here."

"Call Isabel. Set it up."

"No way."

"Come on," Isabel Holt's older sister, Cara, pleaded. "You're great at it."

"I'm great at lots of things," Izzy shrugged. "Baking. Charity runs. Blow jobs. I don't do those for just anyone, either."

"Zac isn't just anyone," Cara protested. "He's one of Finn's teammates!"

"He's an arsehole, is what he is."

The man in question cleared his throat. "I can hear you."

"I know," Izzy snapped. "That's why I said it."

He looked at her steadily and for about the thousandth time since she'd first laid eyes on him in an inner-city Auckland bar, she cursed him for being so good-looking. Dark hair, silver-grey eyes, tanned skin, an unshaven jaw that could cut glass or, even worse, melt her with a single rub of it against her neck.

Izzy's jaw clenched. It was a pretty package alright. Too bad it housed a raging arsewipe. Luckily, she'd never given *him* a blow job.

He hadn't hung around long enough.

"Look," he said, and she braced herself for some bullshit. "I wouldn't ask, but I'm desperate. These kids," he shook his head, his stony expression softening for a second, and she glimpsed the sweetness that had fooled her the first time around. "They're incredible. They're my favourite people in the world, and they're going through a hard time at the moment. From what Finn and Cara say, you're the best at what you do." He met her eyes and something tugged in her gut. "I'll be honest, I don't even need the best, but I do need someone, and I need them now. This season's travel starts next week and I can't leave these kids alone with someone they don't know. The idea of it..." He drew a deep breath and shook his head. "They need stability. The same person who's there every day until their mum gets back. My job is too erratic for that, and I need this job so I can provide for them. It won't be for long, maybe only a couple of weeks or so." His mercury eyes bored into hers. "Can we please put aside our differences for a fortnight?"

"What differences?" Cara mumbled beside her, but Izzy was saved from answering by Finn, who gaped at Zac.

"That's the most I've ever heard you say. Ever."

Zac didn't spare his captain a glance. "That's how important Otis and Hazel are to me."

*Damnit.*

She was going to fold like wet cardboard. Izzy had looked after other people's kids for pretty much her entire adult life. She knew too well how often parents and guardians tossed their kids to the mercy of staff with nary a care for their well-being. Zac Fearon actually cared. Enough to beg her for help, which was saying a lot considering their history. And if it had only been Zac at stake, she could have turned away, wished him the best of luck and carried on with her life without thinking twice. But those kids...

"What would the job entail?" Her voice was stiff, but Zac's shoulders dropped and he huffed out a sigh that sounded a lot like relief. He knew she was going to fold too.

"It'd need to be live-in." He shot her a look that a weaker woman might have called apologetic, but Izzy waved a hand for him to continue. "Getting the kids ready for school and preschool in the mornings and dropping them off. Picking them up afterwards. Getting dinner ready for them and putting them to bed sometimes if I've got a late practice or a work event."

"No cooking for you?"

"No."

"Cleaning?"

"The kids' laundry. I have a cleaning service for the house that comes twice a week."

"You'll be playing pretty much every weekend. What nights will I have off?"

"Sundays and Mondays probably work best with the season schedule, but we can negotiate."

"Pay?"

"What do you want?"

She named a figure that was fifty percent more than she'd made at her last position in London, including the exchange rate, and he nodded.

"Done."

*Ah, fuck.*

He wasn't even going to haggle. He *was* desperate and despite her personal, and extremely valid, dislike of him, Izzy wasn't the type of woman to leave someone lost at sea in the maelstrom of childcare. Her Achilles Heel was caring too much. It always had been, and with the desperation pouring off Zac in waves, all she could think about was how badly he needed her, how badly those *kids* needed her.

Plus, Cara had asked her to do it. Cara, who never asked her for anything. Izzy didn't care about disappointing the rest of her family, she was used to that, but she cared about disappointing Cara.

"A few weeks?"

Zac winced. "Maybe? Hopefully. I don't–" he cleared his throat, Adam's apple bobbing, "-I'm not sure when their mum will be back. We're not in touch right now."

Jeez, no wonder stress lines bracketed his mouth. Having kids dumped on you with no word from their parent on when they'd return would send most childless adults into a spin. Finn had mentioned before Zac arrived at the cafe that it had already been a couple of weeks. For a guy with his schedule, he'd done well to last this long before calling for reinforcements.

And by the pained look on his face when he'd walked into the cafe, he'd been as uncomfortable with who those reinforcements were turning out to be as she was.

"Fine," Izzy sighed. "I'll do it."

Zac's head sank, a heavy exhale rushing out of him. He rubbed one big, calloused hand across his mouth, fingers trembling, and guilt wormed its way into Izzy's stomach.

"I can only do three months, though," she warned. "I'm leaving New Zealand at the end of June. You'll need to find someone to replace me by then if their mum isn't back."

"What?" Cara's head snapped up, but Izzy ignored her. "Why so soon?"

Zac nodded fervently. "I will." His silver eyes met hers. "Thank you, Isabel."

She nodded curtly in return, sliding her gaze away. His gratitude was unpleasant, like a scratchy cape over bare skin, leaving her itchy and frustrated.

"I can start tomorrow." It was a public holiday and God knew she had nothing else going on. She was subletting Cara's bedroom in her old flat and doing casual work at nearby preschools with the odd catering shift thrown her way by one of her high school friends.

"That would be great. Around lunchtime? I can help you move any extra gear you have."

"I don't have any extra gear." She'd been living out of a single suitcase since she was seventeen. Any additional possessions she'd picked up since returning to Auckland a few weeks ago would fit in a sports bag. She'd ask Finn for one. He must have heaps.

"Well, I can pick you up tomorrow and take you out to the house. I'm in Devonport, so it saves you taking all your stuff on the ferry."

Ugh, did he have to be so gentlemanly? He certainly hadn't been the night they'd met. Speaking of, if they were going to be living together for an indeterminate amount of time, it was probably a good idea to get that conversation out of the way.

"Can you two give us a second?" she asked Cara and Finn, who acquiesced with curious looks. She would be answering questions later, that was for damn sure.

"Look," she said, when her sister and Zac's captain were out of earshot, "about Agatha's–"

Zac winced, his eyes on his coffee. "I don't want to talk about Agatha's."

"Well, we have to," Izzy snapped, the frayed cord of her patience pulled tight. "Whatever happened that night–" *when you left me half naked and on the edge of an orgasm in someone's office* "-we need to clear the air."

A muscle in Zac's jaw ticked, as though he found their topic of conversation offensive. Though how offended he could be when he wasn't the one left in the back room at his favourite bar, tits out, with his bra whipping around a ceiling fan she didn't know.

"You know you actually locked me in that room, right?" Izzy persisted. "You realise I had to bang on the door to be let out by the duty manager and that you took my underwear with you?"

Pink climbed Zac's cheeks. "It's not like it was a lot of underwear to begin with."

Izzy sucked in an outraged breath. "Quality over quantity," she replied tightly. "I don't suppose you still have them?"

The flush painting his cheeks turned to scarlet. "I apologise for what happened that night," Zac said stiffly, continuing to stare into his cappuccino like it offered salvation. Maybe not from life itself, but possibly from this conversation. Too bad. Roasted bean juice and frothy milk couldn't save him from this awkwardness. "It was a mistake. Obviously we didn't know who the other person was, that we'd be...seeing each other again." His eyes slid towards the counter, where Finn and Cara chatted, Cara waving her arms animatedly. "Nothing like that can ever happen again," he finished firmly.

Izzy snorted to cover the dregs of humiliation at being so roundly rejected – again. "As if you'd ever get another shot."

Zac had the gall to look relieved, the tight lines that bracketed his mouth relaxing as he nodded. "Good. I wouldn't want things to be uncomfortable."

*Uncomfortable.* That was one way to describe the situation.

"It'll be fine." She kept her voice breezy. "It's not like anything really happened. I'm sure we can mostly stay out of each other's way." She was lying, of course. No way she could avoid him when they'd be living together. "It's not like we need to have anything to do with each other outside of the kids."

Cara bounded over, face lit with delight. Finn trailed behind her, self-satisfaction showing in every line of his face. "Are you two finished being mysterious and weird yet?" Cara asked. "We've got news. Because you're leaving so soon, Izzy, we've decided to get married before you go."

"That sounds great!" Izzy smiled at her sister. Cara had been glowing since Izzy returned to New Zealand, the surety of love between her sister and Finn like an aura that settled around them both. "Are you going to do the courthouse thing?"

"Oh no," Cara laughed. "The whole big thing." Her smile expanded to include Zac. "We want the entire team involved, which means doing it in one of the two weeks in the season they don't have a game." She waved her phone in the air and Izzy caught sight of her calendar app open. "We're getting married in a month!"

# CHAPTER 2

Isabel Holt was in his house.

It didn't seem quite real – like a fever dream that blurred at the edges, pulling at the mind until you weren't sure of your own senses. Zac felt like he was floating outside his body as he watched her haul her battered purple suitcase into his hallway. She lifted it, rather than rolled it, and even in his disconnect he was grateful that he didn't have to worry about her scratching the polished kauri floorboards that he'd finished by hand.

The villa had been falling down when he bought it during his second season with the Knights, and even then the prime position overlooking the water in the seaside suburb of Devonport meant the purchase had almost bankrupted him. It had taken years to renovate, with Zac doing most of the work himself. He could sell for a healthy profit, but he wouldn't. This was his oasis.

He'd struggled growing up – part of a dysfunctional family in the middle of a small town where most people worked labour-intensive jobs – and the sense of peace he felt each morning when he sat on his porch was worth more than money. No matter the season, he brewed a cup of coffee from his cafe-quality espresso machine and sat on the swinging love seat, watching the light play across the rippling water of Auckland Harbour as the sun rose.

It was his haven. And right now, it was a complete shambles.

Otis and Hazel zipped past him on their way through the door, hollering at one another about a dinosaur. Mrs Purdy from next door, who'd been watching the kids while he drove into the city to pick up Isabel, had wasted no time in introducing herself to his new nanny, and Isabel was nodding along to a treatise on the proper climate for growing rhododendrons. She was perfectly polite, never taking her eyes off the elderly woman, but Zac could see the tight line of her arm, her knuckles whitening as she worked to keep her suitcase off the floor.

"Here," he grunted, reaching for it. "Give me that."

Isabel handed it over with a grateful look, and Zac's chest tightened. It was the first look she'd given him that wasn't laced with disgust since the night they'd met at Agatha's. He hefted the suitcase from her hands – Christ, it was heavy – and left her at the mercy of Mrs Purdy and his niblings while he transported it to the spare room.

It was a light and airy room. He'd taken out the boxy dark drapes that had originally framed the windows and replaced them with gauzy white ones. He'd made the bed with a terracotta linen comforter, loaded it with white pillows. There was a chestnut-coloured leather chair in the corner, and yesterday on his way home, he'd stopped and bought a peace lily from the garden shop to put on the wooden bedside table – a fresh sign of life to brighten the room up. Somewhere amid the renovations, when sawdust and plaster permanently scented the air, he'd fallen headfirst down the rabbit hole of interiors. He'd picked everything himself, loath to let some fancy schmancy designer poke around his home. His intention had been that this room with its big bay window would be for Frances to stay in, or his mother on the rare occasions she pulled herself away from the trainwreck of his father's life to visit.

The kids each had their own rooms towards the living areas. Hazel's had originally been the formal dining room, but his desire to have the kids stay far outweighed any desire to host large dinner parties, so it had been an easy decision to convert it to sleeping quarters and Hazel's face when she'd seen the four-poster princess bed had been priceless.

Speaking of Hazel... it was suspiciously quiet in the hallway. Dumping Isabel's suitcase on the bed, Zac strode out in time to catch Mrs Purdy examining his nanny's left hand.

"No ring. You're single?"

"I am." Isabel's face bore the tight smile of an impatient woman.

"Lovely," Mrs Purdy beamed at her. "It'll be nice for the kids to have someone stable here without worrying that they'll flit off on a whim to get married."

*I'm here*, Zac thought angrily. He hadn't dated in years, damnit. He was stable. Hell, he was so stable he might as well be stone.

"Oh." Isabel's smile was pained now. "I'm actually only here temporarily. I'm leaving in three months."

Otis wrapped his arms around Zac's leg and he automatically reached down to ruffle his nephew's dark hair.

"That's right," he agreed, Mrs Purdy looking up guiltily when she heard him. "We're very lucky to have Isabel with us while she's in New Zealand."

Otis tugged on Zac's shirt and he leaned down so the boy could whisper in his ear.

"I'm scared, Uncle Zac."

"Don't be scared, mate. She'll love you. Just act normal." He could have kicked himself the moment the words left his mouth.

*Just act normal.*

That had been his and Frances' battle cry growing up. A sort of family motto between the two of them as they faced down social welfare checks, concerned neighbours 'popping in to say hi' while their mother worked around the clock, the sympathetic eyes of the school librarian as they slunk in each morning to take advantage of the free breakfast the school provided. Over the years, it had devolved into a kind of sarcastic acknowledgement of their lived reality, the recognition that their family struggled in ways that their friends' families didn't.

He hoped like hell that these kids never knew what that felt like.

"This is Otis," he said, instead, nudging his nephew forward. Otis ducked his head and Zac let it go. The poor kid had enough on his plate without worrying about social niceties right now. "And there's Hazel," he continued, pointing at his niece, who had come to a stop near Isabel and was staring up at her.

"Hi Otis. Hi Hazel." Isabel smiled down at Hazel. "It's nice to meet you."

"*Meow*," Hazel said, and licked the back of her own hand.

*So much for normal.*

"Are you a cat?" Isabel dropped into a crouch, as Hazel nodded proudly. "Cool. I'm Izzy. Can you show me where the kitchen is please, Hazel-Cat?"

Hazel took Isabel's hand, nuzzled her face against it, and towed her new nanny past Zac towards the kitchen. Otis blinked after them, and then followed slowly, hovering at the door to the kitchen as Hazel's voice floated out, firmly educating Isabel on how many cookies they were allowed per day.

"She seems nice." Mrs Purdy had snuck up on him.

Zac grunted. Isabel probably *was* nice – God knew, he'd thought so at Agatha's – but all he could think about was how pretty she'd looked in jeans and a loose cropped tee, standing in a shaft of autumn sunlight on golden wooden floorboards, smiling at a three-year-old who identified as a feline.

"Zac, lovey, I've been meaning to ask. Do you think you might pop over and help Marvin stack this season's firewood? It got delivered yesterday, but we're supposed to get rain later in the week, so I'd like to get it away before then."

"Sure." Edith and Marvin Purdy had lived in the classic New Zealand-style villa next to Zac's since they'd married fifty years earlier. They'd been delighted to have him move in next door, and often invited him around for afternoon tea, neighbourhood gossip and unsolicited advice on his renovations. In return, Zac helped with odd jobs around their property. Marvin's arthritis had been acting up more and more in recent years and he knew they were too proud to ask their children for any additional help. In fact, Edith had whispered conspiratorially to Zac once that she'd quite like to move into one of those fancy aged care places with a library and exercise classes and a hairstylist who came weekly, but Marvin was dead against it.

Zac knew how he felt. The idea of being crammed into a social living situation with strangers gave him the willies. He had to force himself to socialise with his Auckland Knights teammates at least once a month to seem like he was making an effort. Teams didn't keep players who didn't gel with the others — it was a fact. And he needed to be in Auckland, to look out for Frances and the kids. He was the one who'd talked his sister into moving here after all. It was his responsibility to make sure she had a support network in place.

It'd be a lot easier if he knew *where the fuck she was*, though.

"I'll pop around shortly and get started," he told Mrs Purdy. "I need to help Isabel get settled in first."

"Of course." Mrs Purdy patted his arm. "You're a good boy, Zachary." She toddled off through the open front door, and Zac watched to make sure she made it down the wide wooden steps of the porch before he turned and headed towards the living area.

Isabel sat cross-legged on the floor by the built-in bookshelf, a battered copy of *Hairy Maclary's Dairy* in her hands. Children's books filled the entire bottom shelf, while Zac's own collection filled the rest. Everything from William Shakespeare and Jane

Austen to Lee Child and Kennedy Ryan. No Hemingway, though. After the way he'd grown up, Zac didn't have patience for alcoholics in his life, even if they could turn a decent phrase. He watched for a minute as Isabel finished reading the beloved children's story aloud to Hazel, who curled in a cat pose next to her on the Persian rug, and Otis, who perched on the brown Chesterfield couch, near enough to be part of the impromptu story time without getting too close.

Zac cleared his throat when she finished, and Isabel looked up from the book.

"Hi."

"Hi," he replied, then swallowed. "I, uh, I'm going to head over to the Purdys' place soon to give them a hand with their firewood. Will you be alright with the kids?"

"Sure." She smiled brightly, taking in all three of them with her warmth. Otis looked a little dazed, and Zac didn't blame him. His nephew wouldn't be the first Fearon to be taken aback by that smile.

"Do you want some lunch before I go?"

"I do, Uncle Zac!"

Zac grinned at Hazel. "I'm sure you do. I was asking Isabel, though."

"Izzy."

"Pardon?"

Whisky brown eyes met his and awareness zipped through Zac's blood.

"You might as well call me Izzy. Everyone else does." She turned to Hazel. "What should we have for lunch?"

Hazel pondered the question. "Marmite sandwiches."

"Yesterday you told me you hated Marmite," Zac

pointed out, and his niece shot him a scandalised look.

"Uncle Zac, I *love* Marmite. It's my favourite."

"Of course it is," Zac mumbled, moving towards the kitchen. There was a magnetic whiteboard stuck to the front of his refrigerator, the words 'Foods The Kids Won't Eat' scrawled across the top. Using his forefinger, he erased Marmite from the list below it.

The air moved and then Izzy was beside him.

"Spaghetti without meatballs, cucumber, mushrooms, pistachios, pesto, crunchy peanut butter," she read the remaining items aloud.

"It's a work in progress," Zac warned her. "We add and subtract new items every day, but these seem consistent."

She shot him a grin. "No worries. They like smooth peanut butter?"

"Can't get enough of it," he confirmed. "But crunchy will launch a nuclear level tantrum."

"I can work with this," she assured him, eyes sparkling.

"You don't have to have Marmite in your sandwich," he blurted, desperate to say something that would stop her looking at him like that. "I've got ham, tuna, sliced turkey. Or hummus, if you're vegetarian."

"I'm not. Marmite's fine," Izzy shrugged. "I might add some cheese to it, though. How do the kids go with hummus?"

"They like it on crackers, not on carrots."

"Ah, kids," she smiled again, and Zac pulled the refrigerator door open to block her from his peripheral view. She was so cheerful. How could she smile at him like that when he'd embarrassed her and forced her into this awkward living situation?

"They're only predictable in that you can't predict them. No allergies?"

He grunted a negative, pulling out the cheese, intending to make everyone sandwiches before heading to the Purdys. He needed the breathing room and the familiar burn of exercise. Isabel's smile, her eyes, her *presence* was too much right now. He'd get used to it, he knew that, but he was used to a slower, smoother process. This felt rushed, sudden, and it threw him. He didn't like rushed. Rushed meant panicked. It meant something had gone wrong. It had, of course.

He'd known Frances wasn't coping after the death of her husband, but to abandon her kids with him... Zac liked his world neat, orderly. The last two weeks had been the very antithesis of that, and to throw Izzy Holt, the mystery woman from Agatha's, into the mix seemed like a cruel cosmic joke. He needed time to adjust. He'd never lived with a woman he wasn't related to before, let alone one he'd fingerbanged in the back room of a bar before names were even exchanged.

It was going to be a difficult few weeks.

Izzy was in Zac Fearon's house.

It didn't seem real. She'd known who he was when they first locked eyes at Agatha's. He played on Finn's league team, and thanks to the glory of the Internet Izzy had missed very few of Finn's games over the last few years. She wasn't a jersey-chaser, didn't particularly like sports, but Finn was a good guy, almost like a brother except for the part where he was wildly in love with her sister, so she'd supported him in a vague sense by watching, and by watching, she'd seen Zac Fearon. Tall, dark, permanently scowling, but he had sure hands, could run a quick line, and scored the winning try for the Knights in the championship game the season before last. So yeah, she'd known who he was.

Had she known she'd end up living in his spare room though, she'd definitely have kept her bra on.

He'd stomped off earlier, muttering something about firewood, and she settled in with Otis and Hazel playing Candyland. They were cute kids, the kind that reminded her exactly why she was getting out of the nannying game. She'd au paired and nannied her way around the globe since the age of seventeen, and all it had done was break her heart, bit by bit. She'd fallen in love with kids, with entire families, only to be dismissed when her usefulness was at an end. The position with the Khans in London had been the final straw. Two years she'd spent raising Hamid, while his mum and dad flitted around the globe, only coming home most nights after she'd already tucked him in bed, arguing in front of him about which one of them would go to his school art show because they were both too busy to fit the inconvenience of being a parent into their packed work schedules.

Izzy had gone to the art show, though. She'd always gone. And then she'd come back from school drop off one day to find the Khans waiting for her, thanking her for her service and informing her they were moving to Abu Dhabi the following month and would no longer require her. Two weeks later she'd got a phone call from Finn telling her Cara had been attacked by a stalker, a day after that an email from her mother saying she was leaving Izzy's father, and Izzy had packed up her belongings, hugged Hamid tightly, told him she loved him, and boarded a plane home to Aotearoa New Zealand, her heart in tatters.

She'd decided on the flight back that she was done. No more long-term positions. She wasn't cut out for it. That was why she'd chosen cruise ships. Six weeks at the most with the same kids in the daycare facilities. Parents who dropped them off in the morning and picked them up in the afternoon, the odd babysitting gig while the parents went for dinner at one of the ship's fancier restaurants. No mess, no fuss. No chance to lose her heart to kids she couldn't keep, kids who wouldn't even remember her name in years to come. The Fearon job was a good transition to that. A limited contract, with no hope of extension. She'd already been accepted for the July intake for one of the larger cruise ship companies that ran out of Sydney. Otis and Hazel would be a pleasant career stopover, and the hefty wages Zac paid her would set her up financially for a while, considering all her savings had gone towards a short-notice flight from London to Auckland.

"Izzy? It's your turn."

Izzy smiled down at Otis. "Thanks, sweetie. What did you get?"

"Two yellows."

"Excellent." Izzy selected her own card from the pile. *Ugh, the peanut.* Back to the almost-beginning. Otis was a sweet kid, quiet. She got the sense that he didn't miss much though, and he was clearly protective of Hazel, who had personality and spirit in spades. Hazel needed protection about as much as a Tyrannosaurus Rex, but it didn't stop Otis from helping her carry her plate to the benchtop after lunch or making sure she got to roll the dice first in Candyland.

"Mrs Purdy said you don't have a boyfriend," Hazel announced.

"I don't," Izzy answered, although it hadn't been a question. She needed one, though, and fast. Not for the usual reasons a twenty-five-year-old woman might want a partner, but specifically for Cara's wedding. The date had been set - a Thursday in five weeks time, which Cara had informed Izzy met the dual requirements of being a bye week, meaning the Knights wouldn't be playing that weekend, and being far enough out from the previous game that most bruises should have healed adequately for the photos. The timeframe didn't give her much hope of finding a date. All her New Zealand connections had dried up since she left, save for her cooler older cousin, Andie. Izzy would have to brave the apps once more to keep her family off her back.

"You shouldn't get one," Otis said gravely. "They die."

*Woah.* That was dark.

"Who said that, sweetie?" Izzy kept her voice light as she nudged the pile of cards closer to Hazel for her turn.

"My mum." Otis fixed solemn dark eyes on Izzy. "She said boyfriends and daddies die sometimes and we can't do anything about it, but we need to remember they loved us very much."

Holy shit, what had she walked into here? And why on earth hadn't she been warned?

They finished up their third game of Candyland as Zac entered the living room, covered in sweat.

"What's wrong with her?" He pointed at Hazel,

who sat by the French doors, arms crossed, eyebrows drawn together in a stubborn line.

"She lost. She isn't taking it well. Can I speak to you in private, please?" Izzy brushed past him towards the hallway, catching the scent of fresh-split wood and something lighter, citrusy. It wasn't right that a man who looked that good also smelt so lickable. Zac followed her to her bedroom, leaning against her door frame with his arms crossed while she plopped on the bed.

"What's up?" He wasn't looking at her, instead studying the peace lily on her bedside table.

"Is there something I should know about the kids? Something about their family situation, perhaps?"

That got his attention, his eyes hardening to flint as he looked at her.

"What do you mean?"

Izzy took a deep breath. Families were complicated, but it paid to have all the information if there was something behind Otis's assertions. If the kids had been through a loss, it would colour their entire worldview and she'd need to take it into consideration while working with them.

"Otis mentioned something about boyfriends and daddies dying."

Zac blew out a harsh sigh. "Yeah. Yeah, the kids' dad died about a year back. Undiagnosed genetic heart failure. Came out of nowhere."

Izzy's stomach sank. "Oh, those poor kids."

Zac nodded, his eyes back on the floor. "Frances got pregnant with Otis at seventeen and moved up here with me. She met Ben when Otis was six months old. Love at first sight. They were engaged two months later." His voice softened. "He was a good guy – the best kind of guy. Never treated Otis and Hazel any different. It's no wonder Frances has struggled since. I've never seen two people so in love."

Izzy swallowed past the lump in her throat. "I'm sorry to hear that," she offered softly. "He sounds incredible."

Zac nodded, jaw tight. "He was. The kids are still coming right."

"I'll take that into consideration. Thank you for sharing that with me. It can't be easy letting someone into your family business like that."

He shrugged, but discomfort was etched into every line of his body.

"You asked," he responded gruffly.

"I know, but I still appreciate your honesty. It means I have the necessary information I need when I talk to the kids."

Horror passed across his face. "You're not going to talk to them about their dad?"

Izzy chose her words carefully. "I won't bring it up, but if they mention it, I'll be able to address it sensitively without dismissing their feelings."

"In that case, there's something else you should know." If possible, Zac looked even more uncomfortable. "There's a good chance their mother has gone on a bender."

"Booze?" Izzy asked. "Or..." She let her words trail off, and Zac nodded. She pressed her lips together. "I see. Again, I appreciate the context."

"Nobody else knows." He was looking at her now, eyes hard again, but she could see the toll it was taking on him to open up his messy, haunted family box of secrets and let the contents spill out in front of her. "If it gets out–"

"It won't," Izzy assured him hurriedly. She'd lived in London, the gossip rag capital of the world. Next door to Stella McCartney for a while, even. He didn't need to tell her how the press would chase a story like this if they got wind of it. It would be like vultures over a kitten's carcass. No mercy. And in the end, the kids would suffer most.

"I have training most mornings at eight," he said, obviously ready to move on. "Hazel goes to the preschool two streets across from eight thirty until three thirty, and Otis's school is next door. I'll send you the locations."

"They live in Devonport, too?" Izzy tried to hide her surprise. Devonport was a wealthy suburb, at the southernmost tip of Auckland's affluent North Shore. Not really the place she'd expected a twenty-two-year-old single mother to live.

Zac nodded. "Frances moved to an apartment here after Ben's death. I thought about living with the kids at their home, so their daily routine isn't so disrupted, but there's not enough space."

"They seem really comfortable here," she said, and the knot between his eyebrows loosened a little.

"Yeah, they are."

"You're a good uncle," Izzy assured him. He might have failed spectacularly as a lover, but there was no doubt he loved those kids. Otis and Hazel had given her a tour of their rooms, both set up to cater to their individual interests. Otis had a Lego building table and art desk set up in the corner, while Hazel's housed a princess bed, dress ups and a volcanic rock collection. The number of well-worn kids' books in the living room and the stacks of tinned spaghetti with meatballs in the pantry were even further proof of Zac's efforts to show the two little people in his life how much he cared. She opened her mouth to tell him so, but her phone rang in her pocket before she could get the words out.

"I'll leave you to it," Zac muttered, and then he was gone, coloured shafts of light from the stained glass panels in the front door decorating the door frame where he'd stood.

Izzy didn't bother looking at the Caller ID as she answered. Only half a dozen people had her New Zealand number.

"Hey."

"Hey yourself."

Izzy groaned. "Do we have to do this now?"

"Yes, we certainly do." Cara was using her Very Important Older Sister voice. "I've just worked out how much goes into planning a wedding. I'm trying to cram it into a month, Mum and Dad aren't speaking to each other and I'll have to buy my wedding dress off the rack. So I need to know what on Earth is going on with you and Zac Fearon. Are you there now?"

"All moved in," Izzy joked, patting her still-closed suitcase even though Cara couldn't see her.

"And how is it you met him?"

"You introduced us at the season opener last month."

"Try again."

Izzy winced. "I made out with him at Agatha's the first weekend I was back in NZ, and he left me high, dry, knickerless and locked in the back office when his phone rang seconds from an orgasm."

There was no response, and Izzy imagined her sister's face stricken with the pure horror the story deserved, until a high-pitched wheezing emitted from her phone.

Ah. Not horror, then. Hilarity.

"Yes, it's very funny," Izzy said dryly above Cara's increasingly loud howls of laughter. "Get your laughs in. I've never been more embarrassed."

"Never?" Cara asked, when she managed to calm herself. "Not when you called Hamlet a whiny little bitch in front of the representative of the Globe Theatre? Not when Mum and Dad were remodelling the bathroom, and you ended up having to take a dump in a bucket in the garage when the plumber was in there? Not when you broke that guy's banjo string during sex, fell off his hotel balcony in the dark trying to escape, fucked up your knee and then the housekeeper found him in a pool of his own blood the next day, and it ended up as a story on the radio?"

Izzy glowered at the phone. "Do you feel better now?"

Cara sighed happily. "Yeah, the banjo story always cheers me up."

"Good for you. I still have a scar on my knee from that night."

"Well, wear a dress that covers it for the wedding."

"You're not going to pick my dress for me? Is this how you tell me I'm not a bridesmaid?"

"I'm not having any bridesmaids. No wedding party. Finn and I will already be standing up there with our best friend – each other."

Izzy wrinkled her nose. "Cloying, but fair."

Twenty-four hours' worth of tension evaporated knowing she wouldn't be called on for hours of photos or a speech. Family weddings were the social equivalent of landmines for Izzy, her rural Taranaki family taking every opportunity to pick holes in her life choices and single status, making her feel like a pariah. An active role in the wedding would only have made it worse. She'd already revived her online dating profile from where it had lain dormant in Internet purgatory since she'd left London.

"We've booked out one of the Waiheke wineries." Cara's voice was excited now. "There's a house and a few little cottages on site to get ready at. Finn and I will take the house, but you can have one of the cottages. It'll save you getting the ferry home after the wedding, and we're having a breakfast at the winery restaurant the next morning."

"Sounds great." Izzy loved Waiheke Island. The small island in the Hauraki Gulf was a mishmash of artistic hippie-style community and multi-millionaire chic, famous for producing exceptional wines.

"And that way, if you decide to bring a date, you'll have some privacy." Cara's voice was deceptively light, tiptoeing around the bull in the Holt family china shop.

"Oh, don't worry," Izzy said darkly, her determination fighting off visions of great aunts pinching her cheeks and wondering aloud at her lack of feminine appeal. "I'll have a date for your wedding."

# CHAPTER 3

Izzy had been on some bad dates. Some really bad dates. There was the guy whose idea of romance was to take her from a restaurant directly to a ghetto in Toulon to buy weed, persisting even after Izzy told him she didn't smoke. There was the girl who'd seemed like a sweetheart right until she stole Izzy's purse and slipped out of the restaurant through the kitchen without paying. There was even the dude who'd abandoned her on the cliffs of Dubrovnik and she'd had to find her way back to her hotel, stumbling along unlit streets seeking directions with Croatian language skills limited to basic greetings and inquiring about bathroom facilities.

Izzy still harboured extremely dark feelings about that one.

But none of those compared to her date right now.

If she had to pick a word, Izzy mused, swirling her wineglass and watching the liquid wash the inside of the glass in a golden wave, it would be obnoxious.

*Deeply* obnoxious.

He'd tried to order for her. Scratch that – he'd tried to order a *salad* for her.

When that failed, he'd tried to change her drink order to match what he thought would go best with her lamb.

Now they were on dessert. Well, she was. He'd refrained, ordering a coffee instead with a pointed look at her waistline, which meant that Izzy was going to have to scarf down every bite of this chocolate cheesecake despite actually feeling pretty full.

Harvey, his name was, and he stretched the vowels when he said it, giving it a whiny quality that implied he thought he was more important than he actually was. *Haaar-veeeey.*

*Haaar-veeeey.*

Maybe the third glass of wine hadn't been a great idea.

*Nah, fuck it. Haaaarveeeey's paying.*

He'd seemed so normal on his profile. No topless mirror selfies. No pictures of him with giant fish. Nothing to imply that she'd be forced to spend an hour listening to his brain-numbing monologue on mortgage brokerage.

"It's such an *asset,*" he'd claimed, aghast at Izzy's earlier revelation that she wasn't looking to break into the home ownership market.

Izzy had smiled and nodded, and shoved a piece of bread into her mouth because he was objectively good looking and had a steady job and that was really all she was looking for in a wedding date.

But that was an hour and two glasses of Sauvignon Blanc ago, and Harvey was still stuck on her intrepid lifestyle.

"It's important to have a hobby, of course," he

said now. "And travel has its advantages, I suppose. But eventually you'll want to settle down."

"Will I?" Izzy asked, past a mouthful of cheesecake. "Why do you say that?"

"For the children, of course."

"What children?"

Harvey looked at her like she was a bit dim.

"Your children."

"I don't want children."

Horror passed across Harvey's face and Izzy gleefully shoved another bite of cheesecake into her mouth. She wasn't technically sure if that was true, but he looked so scandalised she was glad she'd said it.

"But who will look after you in your old age?" Harvey asked.

"Uh, the employees in my aged care facility?" Izzy shrugged. "Why? Who's going to look after you?"

"My children!" Harvey bellowed.

"What if they don't want to?" Izzy responded mildly. "What if they have their own lives, or they're living overseas, or they stopped talking to you when they left home?"

"Why would they do that?"

*Because you're a genuine fuck-knuckle.*

"Who knows why kids do what they do?" Izzy took another sip of wine.

"Indeed. Indeed. Unfathomable creatures," Harvey nodded, seemingly relieved at the sudden twist into sweeping theoretical statements. Izzy could relate. Theoretically, Harvey was a catch. It was the reality that was the problem. He was like Communism. Great on paper, but problematic as fuck when you tried to make a go of it.

"You've worked with kids so long," Harvey said, doing what was likely his best impression of an understanding nod. "It's natural you'd be ready for a break before you think about settling down and having your own. How old are you again?"

"Twenty-five," Izzy mumbled, and his gaze ran over her with the kind of assessment she'd seen her father make of bull calves at stock auctions.

*Ick.*

"Plenty of time," Harvey nodded again, decisively this time, though what he'd decided on she had no idea.

Goddamn it, she'd made an effort for this date. She wore a cropped black bustier and pencil skirt combo that made her look like a slutty librarian fantasy come to life. She'd even taken the time to curl her hair, something she only did about twice a year because of the ridiculous thickness of it, and she'd pulled out her best red lipstick - the one made by her London aesthetician in her bathroom sink and sold in sneaky cash transactions on the side.

She looked hot, she knew it, and she was wasting it on this absolute douche canoe.

She stabbed her fork into her cheesecake again. At least she was getting a free meal and a night out of the house. Sharing a space with Zac was even more painful than she'd anticipated. Izzy had always approached sexual encounters with the attitude that things were only as awkward as you made them. This approach had allowed her to remain on friendly terms with almost everyone she'd ever hooked up with.

It was different with Zac though. Perhaps it was the fact that they'd never made it all the way to orgasm-ville. Perhaps it was the way his eyes looked like molten silver when the light hit them. Perhaps it was that she was still very definitely, very inconveniently, into him. Given the chance, she'd ride him like a rodeo queen, and she was disgusted with herself for that. Surely, she had more self-respect than to jump on the dick of a man who'd already rejected her in a humiliatingly public way? Certainly, she had more common sense than to engage in sexual activities with her employer. But despite all the good, sound, logical reasons why she absolutely would not be shagging Zac Fearon, a distinct part of her still wanted to.

She wasn't happy about it.

One week of living with him had tuned her into the fact that Zac was a bona fide control freak. Although his cleaner came twice a week, he tried to keep his house ruthlessly tidy, and she could already see the impact of two young kids giving him an eye twitch every time he tripped over an abandoned shoe or stood on a stray piece of Lego.

He'd had his groceries delivered on Sunday and she'd unpacked them to be helpful, stunned at how boring they were. Bags of salad greens and cruciferous vegetables, seven fillets of salmon, seven plain chicken breasts, low fat milk, low fat yogurt, eggs, oatmeal, coffee beans and mixed nuts. That was basically it. She'd dug through the pantry and freezer to see if he kept decent food somewhere else, but aside from a half-eaten carton of ice cream from Motueka Creamery and a couple of cans of Sprite, she'd come up empty-handed. Everything else - chia seeds and hemp hearts and LSA and oodles of protein powders and potions - lined up as if they were in a dispensary rather than a home pantry. All the kids' food was relegated to one shelf, and even that suffered a dire lack of variety. He'd obviously found a few things Otis and Hazel would eat and bought in bulk.

Izzy had immediately whipped up a batch of carrot cake muffins and the kids had fallen on them like starving wolverines.

She and Zac were fundamentally ill-suited. And yet, even with the ghost of Agatha's hanging over them and his propensity to communicate in grunts, she'd rather endure another lesson in how to properly sanitise Zac's benchtop after cooking than waste her life and lipstick stuck across the table from the insufferable Harvey.

Harvey, who was looking at her expectantly.

"Pardon?" Izzy put down her fork, defeated by cheesecake. "Could you please repeat that?"

"I asked where your family is from."

"Oh, Taranaki." That was a sore point in itself, though she couldn't blame Harvey for that. Her feelings about her family and her parents' recent separation weren't first date material. "My sister lives here in Auckland and she's getting married soon, so I decided to stay and help her out while I'm in New Zealand."

"Loyalty," Harvey nodded approvingly. "That's a rare quality."

"Is it?" Izzy didn't even try to hide her sarcasm. There was nothing rare about loyalty in this world, despite her father's habit of sticking his dick where it didn't belong.

"And who is your sister marrying?"

It didn't escape Izzy's notice that he'd asked about Cara's fiancé, but not anything about Cara herself.

"Finn Chalmers," she answered through gritted

teeth, and Harvey's eyes lit up like he'd won the patriarchal lottery.

"Really? From the Knights?"

"Yup." Izzy drained the last of her wine.

"You know," Harvey said, looking at her with renewed interest. "I think there could be something here, Iris. You're not like other girls." He said it with a twinge of admiration and a truckload of smarm from someone who obviously had season tickets dancing in front of their eyes, and Izzy had had enough. She stood up, and he looked at her in surprise. "Do you need the bathroom?"

"No," she responded, plucking her bag from the back of her seat. "I'm leaving."

His froggy eyes almost bulged out of his head. "What?" he gaped, looking for all the world like she'd announced plans to harvest his organs. "Why?"

"Because I am like other girls, Harvey. I'm exactly like other girls. But the fact that you think that not being like them, like my mother and my sister and my friends, is something positive, says more about you than it does about me. And none of it's good. Also, you're a rude date and boring as fuck to boot."

"Iris–"

"Christ, man. That's not even my name."

She turned to leave. Behind her she heard him mutter 'bitch' under his breath, and she let the fantasy of turning and hurling her wine glass at his head wash over her like a lovely wave. In the end though, she settled for requesting another bottle of Sauvignon Blanc from the bar and telling them to put it on his tab as she stuffed it in her leather tote and headed out into the night air.

~

Zac was in the kitchen when Izzy stomped in. She headed straight to the walk-in pantry, pulled out a bag of chocolate chips she must have bought for baking, and stuffed a handful into her mouth.

"Huh," Zac offered. "Good night?"

Brown eyes glared at him as she shoved in another fistful of cooking chocolate.

He tried not to be affected by it – honestly he'd been thrilled she'd chosen to spend her night off out of the house. The less she was around the more he could relax – but goddamn she was pretty. She was stunning in workout pants and loose sweatshirts, but tonight tight black clothing hugged every inch of her lithe curves, offering a tempting peek at the toned golden skin of her midriff. Her legs looked like forever and her mouth was painted for sin.

*Fuck.*

He moved around the counter so he could adjust himself subtly behind the thick zipper of his jeans.

"Are you okay?" Now that his dick wasn't strangling itself he could think a little clearer and the more he thought, the less likely it seemed like Izzy busting in like a hurricane, dressed to kill, and mainlining low-quality cocoa products were good signs. "Were..." he cleared his throat. "Were you out with someone?"

She snorted. "You could say that."

"Did he–*they*–do something wrong?"

"You could say that as well. This isn't cutting it," Izzy mumbled, returning to the pantry and digging through the shelf he'd assigned her. She pushed aside crackers and chips, cans of black beans and a super-sized bottle of Thai sweet chilli sauce, clearly searching for something.

"Where's my dulce?"

"Your what?"

"My dulce de leche. It's like caramel."

Zac's stomach dropped. "Was it in a glass jar? Like a jam jar?"

Izzy stiffened, then turned. "Yes."

"I... might have given it to the kids on their ice-cream."

"You what?" She whisper-yelled the words, and Zac got the distinct feeling she would have yell-yelled them if it wasn't that Otis and Hazel were asleep in their rooms, separated only from the open plan kitchen and living area by a few thin sheets of drywall.

"It was on their shelf. I thought you'd bought it for them as a treat."

"It was a treat. For me." Izzy's face crumpled, and she heaved a sigh. "Never mind."

"I can buy you some more," Zac offered. He didn't know what was going on, why she looked like he'd killed her pet turtle over a little jar of caramel. Even as good as it had been – fine, maybe he'd polished it off after the kids had their share – it was only a fancy sauce.

Izzy shook her head, resignation in every line of her face. "No, you can't. I bought it from a small family farm in Uruguay. I started with six jars. That was the last one."

"Oh," Zac said. He felt like dirt, a hollow, sick feeling scooping out his stomach. The way he felt whenever he let people down. "Were you saving it?"

"Yeah," Izzy breathed, eyes closed. A few seconds later she opened them, and Zac watched as she blinked the hurt away, the disappointment lifting from her eyes like a veil, and he wondered why on Earth a girl like Isabel Holt had needed to learn how to do that.

"I mean, we could try..." Why was he still talking? Why hadn't he faded away yet, leaving Izzy, her hair and her eyes and her big, bright personality to the room and retreated to his bedroom so that her light didn't spill across him and reveal every broken piece he'd stitched together to survive? Zac didn't spend time with people as a matter of course. He didn't give interviews, or go to nightclubs, and he had to force himself to attend some kind of gathering with his teammates once a month. Spending time with people was an invitation for them to poke around in your life, open up the dark areas you kept shut off and covered up. For them to ask uncomfortable questions like why and what and how. Zac had grown up in a small town and he'd been the subject of gossip the whole time thanks to his father's choices. It had been a blessing to be sent to boarding school at the age of fourteen. He could live out his weeks free from the concerned whispers and prying eyes, only needing to suffer through them on weekends when he returned to Motueka, to his mother and Frances. That guilt had weighed on him too, the way they were left to the murmurings of the town without him to protect them Monday through Friday. Not enough to stop him taking the scholarship he was offered, to keep his eyes on the light at the end of the tunnel.

Rugby league, he had known from a very young age, was his way out. *Their* way out. His mother might still be in Motueka, married to the rum-soaked bum who'd donated half of their DNA, but he and Frances were free, and they maintained that freedom through his job. So no, he'd never had a woman's magazine through his house to photograph his new kitchen, never posed in his undies like Chalmers, or MC'd a charity auction like Dominic McQueen.

Once people thought they knew you, they got curious. And Zac wasn't going to let anyone's curiosity drag his family through the mud of their past. Especially not now that Otis and Hazel would be part of it.

Izzy Holt might live in his house for now, but she wasn't part of his life. Which meant he needed to leave this kitchen right now, before she focused all that brightness on him and saw the cracks.

"I'll go then," Zac croaked, and she shot him a small smile, slinging her handbag onto the countertop. It landed with an unexpectedly heavy clunk.

"Okay. I'll see you in the morning." She rounded the counter, and he took a hurried step back, pressing himself against the wall to avoid her brushing against him. "I might stay up and watch a bit of TV–" her voice cut off abruptly and Zac cursed under his breath, knowing what was coming. "You watch *Bridgerton*?"

Zac shuffled his feet. "Yeah."

Izzy's eyes narrowed. "Which season is your favourite?" she asked suspiciously.

"Kate and Anthony."

"Oh my gosh, me too," she squealed, all signs of her dulce-based despair gone. "Kanthony forever. That sexual tension..." she let out a dreamy sigh. "It's flawless. I didn't pick you for a fan though."

His jaw tightened.

"I'm not stupid, you know."

"Pardon?"

"People think I'm dumb sometimes, because of my job, but I majored in English lit."

"I don't think you're stupid, Zac." She was looking at him properly now, and the intensity of her attention made him hot, his skin feeling a size too small as she peered at him. "You're a professional athlete at the top of his game. That takes more than skill on the field. You must do well in other areas too. But actually," she continued, "I figured you for more of a season one fan."

"Simon and Daphne?" He screwed up his face. "Bite your tongue."

Izzy giggled evilly, and his heart lifted. "Not a fan of the good Duke of Hastings then?"

"He's so repressed," Zac groaned, and she laughed out loud.

"Oh yes, men who repress their feelings and brood darkly in the corner at parties. Definitely don't know any like that."

"Shut up," he muttered, but his mouth twitched.

"The horror," she gasped, as she strode to the couch and plopped down on it, still laughing at him. He didn't mind with her though. Somehow Izzy laughing at him didn't make him feel like a pitied specimen under a microscope. Her joy was infectious, wrapping around him and tugging him closer until he sat on the couch next to her. "What kind of loser would do that?"

Zac sighed heavily. "Start the damn episode, Isabel."

"As you wish, Your Grace."

# CHAPTER 4

*L*ong fingers of golden sunlight reached across the painted boards of Zac's porch and wrapped themselves around the corner of his blanket, bathing it in light. Zac pulled it back into the shadows, tucking it tighter around his legs as he cradled his coffee to his chest and watched the same light dance across the water.

This view was why he'd bought this house. He wasn't the only player on the team to live on the North Shore – Finn was in some fancy-schmancy gated community that backed onto the estuary – but Zac was the only one in Devonport. A haven for vertically-upwardly mobile families and wealthy retirees, it wasn't the place anyone expected a bachelor to buy a house, but he'd wanted something private, something out of the way, and then he'd seen this view. Directly across the street from his front porch was a small reserve, no more than a strip of meticulously manicured lawn and a few pohutukawa trees, and beyond that, the harbour. From here, he couldn't see the way Auckland curved around, bustling and busy and bursting at the seams with its people and their problems. There was only the horizon, a thin line that hovered in the distance. Constant. Unchanging. Intangible. The endless possibilities stretched out between the ocean and Ranginui, the Sky Father. Something in Zac's fractured soul had soothed the first time he saw that view. Not healed entirely, but smoothed out, like brittle parchment under a gentle touch. It had been five years now, and every morning he was home, without fail, he fixed himself a cappuccino with his cafe-capacity espresso machine and sat in his porch swing, rain or shine, to watch dawn creep over the ocean.

It was the twenty minutes a day he could breathe freely.

Except today. Today, stress pinched at his shoulders, dark and thick, like storm clouds rolling in to disturb his peace. His agent had called last night.

"It's nothing to worry about," Scott Saunders had assured him over the phone, "but the Knights haven't confirmed that they'll be re-signing you for next season yet."

Of course it wasn't something for Scott to worry about. Scott represented half the Knights team. His investment in Zac's contract renewal had little to do with Zac and more to do with making the payments on his yacht. But for Zac? The contract was everything. Without it, his whole world was in question. He could get another contract somewhere else, sure. He wasn't at the end of his career yet, but that contract could be anywhere. The South Island. Australia. He could even head to the UK, join the Super League. They'd pay well, probably a damn sight better than the Knights. But Zac's motivation regarding money had always been about making enough to support his family. And since Frances had followed him to Auckland when she was seventeen, supporting her in other ways too. More tangible ways. Ways that were impossible to achieve from the bowels of the British Super League.

Jesus, he'd barely been able to help her from the same suburb.

No, he needed to re-sign with the Knights. The money was good enough, and it meant he could be here for Otis and Hazel as they grew up. They needed him now more than ever. There were no other options for him. Auckland was it.

Determination skated across his skin with the ocean breeze and he took another fortifying sip of coffee as he stared out at the rising sun.

*A new day. Another chance.* He wouldn't waste it. Now that he knew for sure that his job wasn't rock-solidly secure, he needed to be more focused than ever on succeeding on the field.

Thank god for Isabel Holt. Even with the hot awareness that pulsed through him every time she walked into a room, she was the answer to all his problems. Finn and Cara had been right. She was fantastic with the kids. Knowing they were in good hands, that they were taken care of, he could funnel his attention onto the game and guarantee a contract extension offer.

As if his thoughts had summoned her, Izzy appeared below him on the street, turning onto the little bricked driveway that ran down to the garage under the villa. Zac watched in silence as she let herself in through the white picket gate at the side of the driveway and bounced up the wide wooden steps leading to the porch.

"Oh." She stopped still when she saw him sitting

on the porch swing. Reaching up, she pulled her ear buds out. "I didn't see you there."

He didn't know how to respond. Should he apologise? For sitting on his own porch? In the end, he grunted.

"It's a beautiful view," she offered, ignoring his social gaffe. "You must love waking up to this each morning."

"It's why I bought the place," he offered, his voice rusted. Clearing his throat, he tried again. "I like to watch the sun rise in the morning."

The smile she gave him rivalled the light flooding the sky. "Me too," she confessed. "That's why I run in the mornings. It's like by the time I'm finished, the day is starting. Also," she added practically, "it's the time that parents and guardians are most likely to be home in case their kids wake up."

Zac nodded, throat thickening again. "Right. Well, speaking of..." he let his voice trail off and he saw the instant she realised what he was saying.

"Yes! Right! Okay, I'll go and get started on the kids' lunches." She bustled past him and he pulled his feet back under the porch swing like they were on fire to avoid her touching them. It was too much, the sun turning her hair the colour of liquid honey, the black sports bra and leggings moulded to her body, leaving tanned swathes of it exposed. The brightness in her eyes when she looked at him. The black ink of a tattoo peeking out above her sock. He felt fifteen and foolish, tongue-tied and tripping over his too-big feet when she looked at him, the shame of Agatha's warring with the memory of her nipple in his mouth. She was his employee, for God's sake. She was off limits. He couldn't have anything messing up his home dynamic, not while the kids were here, and he needed to focus on playing.

It wasn't like she'd be interested anyway. As far as he could tell, Izzy wasn't in the habit of giving second chances. She'd been on several dates since the night they'd watched *Bridgerton* together. Not that she'd told him, but he couldn't help but notice when she left the house in dresses or tight jeans and nice tops, hair styled and lips glistening. It was a far cry from the athletic gear and messy buns she lived in when she was working or hanging out at home. And from the meagre information he'd gleaned listening to Finn sing her praises in the locker room, none of those dates were with the same person.

Why was she dating so ferociously? He had no idea, but he'd started keeping a little tally on the whiteboard on the refrigerator. A tiny checkmark for each time she came home dressed to kill and threw herself on the couch with a frustrated sigh. He couldn't say why he did it. Maybe it helped his ego to know he wasn't the only man out there who'd blown his chance with Isabel Holt. There were four of them so far, not including himself. Four poor bastards who'd let sunlight slip through their fingers, and he couldn't help the sliver of satisfaction that settled in his chest at that. He might have fucked up. Hell, he *knew* he'd fucked up, but he wasn't the only one. The difference between those poor bastards and Zac was that he had to see her again, in all her bright, funny glory.

Izzy would only be a memory to those men one day, a 'what if'. She'd be a memory to Zac too, but a stronger one. He'd see her every time Otis or Hazel took their plates up to the bench after their meals, each time he lost to his nephew at Kings and Jokers, which she'd taught Otis the week before. That was why he needed to keep his distance, to keep her from getting too close, because when she left, she wouldn't be leaving him, she'd be leaving the kids as well. And failing at being Isabel Holt's lover was nothing compared to failing at being Isabel Holt's employer, not when the happiness and well-being of his niblings hung in the balance.

As far as he was concerned, she was here to do a job. Leaving her to do that job left him free to focus on his.

That was all that mattered.

~

"Otis! Shut your car door!" Izzy hollered, scooping Hazel out of her car seat with the arm that wasn't laden with grocery bags.

Otis gave a long-suffering sigh. Never had a young man been so maligned as he stomped back towards Zac's Volvo and slammed the SUV's door shut. Izzy was eternally grateful for the loan of Zac's vehicle. He'd leased himself another, identical, one after he hired her, citing the kids' safety as the reason for his selection, but he only used it to get to training or games and back. It had been a fortnight and Izzy was yet to see him drive for any other reason. If it wasn't rugby league or his niblings, Zac Fearon wasn't interested. There was always the possibility of course that he'd start partying when the season kicked off in earnest - the Knights' first away game was tomorrow night - but somehow she couldn't picture her dark, brooding employer in a club. Even at Agatha's, under the cocktail lounge's glinting gold lamplight, he'd looked out of place.

"Izzy!" Otis yelled. "I need the keys!"

"I'm coming!"

Hazel yanked on the raw-cut amethyst hanging around Izzy's neck. Her head was pulled forward, colliding with the toddler's, who let out a high-pitched scream.

"Are you alright there?"

Izzy turned, grocery bag handles cutting into the flesh of her forearm as she cradled Hazel's head to her chest and tried to comfort the child.

"I'm fine, thanks," she lied.

The slim brunette looked unconvinced. Behind Izzy a rhythmic thump echoed as Otis started kicking the front door.

"Do you need a hand with the groceries? I'm sure Zac–" the stranger dragged his name out, almost purring it "-would feel better knowing his nanny wasn't wrangling the children like monkeys in the driveway, right out on the street."

*Wow.* Izzy was no stranger to bitchy subtext – she'd worked for too many wealthy families for her to be naive about that – but this woman had brass balls. If Izzy wasn't so pissed off, she'd be impressed.

"Izzy! There you are, lovey. I've been waiting for you to get home." Out of nowhere, Mrs Purdy appeared, bustling over and hoisting Hazel out of Izzy's arms. The girl curled into the elderly woman's arms, sniffling into her cardigan. "Ready for our meeting?"

"Ah, sure," Izzy floundered. She was ninety-eight percent positive she hadn't agreed to a meeting with Mrs Purdy, but she was eager to get the kids inside and remove herself from the triumphant laser-like eyeline of the strange woman, who suddenly looked like she'd bitten a lemon.

"Wonderful," Mrs Purdy beamed. "Otis, sweet pea, come get these keys and see if you can unlock that door yourself! You're getting so big and independent!"

Izzy gratefully relinquished the keys to Otis, who smiled shyly at Mrs Purdy before scampering off to unlock the front door.

"I see you've met Annabel Sampson," Mrs Purdy continued, gesturing at the brunette. "She lives next door on the other side. Don't you Annabel? A real star of Devonport," she confided in Izzy, without waiting for the other woman to speak. "She runs our Arts Festival every year. Such a champion effort! We're lucky to have you, dearie," she told Annabelle. "But I'm afraid we must be off inside, as Izzy and I have some very important matters to discuss."

Izzy allowed herself to be led by the elbow up the villa steps and through the front door, which Otis had left swinging open. Mrs Purdy deposited Hazel safely on the hallway floor and sent her running to the kitchen with instructions to find some nice biscuits for afternoon tea before shutting the door behind them.

"Phew. That woman," Mrs Purdy sighed. "She's a shark."

"She seemed... invested," Izzy hedged, swapping her grocery bags to her other hand. Zac had ordered groceries to be delivered last Sunday, but before collecting the kids from school, she'd picked up a few extra items she was keen to test out with them.

"She's invested in trying to scare you away." Mrs Purdy toddled down the hall, leaving Izzy to follow. "She and her husband divorced two years ago, and she's spent the entire time trying to land Zachary. Poor man is terrified of her."

They entered the kitchen to find Otis in the pantry, balancing on a bar stool he'd dragged from the counter while he handed a Tupperware container of chocolate coconut cookies to Hazel, who waited eagerly below.

"Hop down off there, Otis," Izzy sighed, dumping her paper bags on the counter.

Mrs Purdy shook her head. "Friday. The little ones are all burnt out by the time it rolls around." The elderly neighbour fished a delicately patterned china plate out from a cupboard and loaded it with fruit, raisins, and a few of the cookies from Hazel's container. "Here we go, lovies. Let's pop this in the living room and you can watch a bit of TV before your uncle gets home."

Otis and Hazel cheered, rounding the counter to throw themselves bodily on the couch while Mrs Purdy set the plate on the coffee table in front of them and fiddled with the remote.

At a loss for anything else to do, Izzy flicked the kettle on and pulled a couple of mugs from the cabinet.

"Tea, Mrs Purdy?"

"Ooh, please. That'd be lovely." The older woman took a seat at the counter. "Call me Edith. Where are you from, originally, dear?"

Izzy plonked a couple of teabags in the mugs and turned towards the fridge to grab the milk.

"Taranaki. My parents – my mother, sorry – owns a farm down there." Since Linda Holt had kicked Izzy and Cara's dad out a month or so ago, she'd run the farm independently. Izzy had offered to help when she returned to New Zealand, but her mother had told Izzy in no uncertain terms that it was her job to take care of it. She'd hired a farm manager and put him up in the extra living quarters a couple of paddocks over from the main house, and seemed to be thriving, based on the video calls Izzy and Cara had received.

Meanwhile, her estranged husband Steve was holed up in some rental in New Plymouth, apparently telling people Linda's farm – the farm she'd grown up on, that had been in her family for generations – would be nothing without him.

Even thinking about her father, his arrogance and infidelity, made Izzy's blood boil. She'd travelled all over the world and the one defining factor she'd seen, from country to country, culture to culture, was women giving up their dreams. She wasn't naive enough to think her own family was exempt, but seeing her mother flourish in the role that should have been rightfully hers from the beginning, not to mention Izzy's own recollections of Cara sacrificing everything – extracurriculars, her burgeoning hockey career – to take care of Izzy when they were younger, grated. That was one reason she was here, in the house of a man she lusted after but didn't like, because Cara had asked her to. And Cara had never, not once, asked Izzy for help. Her older sister had shouldered every burden alone, from her knowledge of their father's infidelity, to her attempts to make their mother's life easier by taking on a maternal role with Izzy. It warmed Izzy's heart to see the way Cara leaned on Finn, the way they leaned on each other, supported one another, but if Cara asked Izzy for a favour, Izzy was sure as shit granting it. Years had skewed the scales of sisterhood far too heavily in one direction for Izzy's comfort, and although she was only in the country for a short time – she'd be damned if she was going to be one of those women who gave up their dreams – she'd do anything she could to tip them back towards balanced.

Mrs Purdy exclaimed in delight and launched into a story about starting her teaching career in Taranaki, while Izzy fixed tea and slid one mug across the counter to the older woman. Edith Purdy was clearly warm, intelligent and bored out of her tree in retirement.

By the time the front door slammed shut, heralding Zac's arrival, the women had moved onto a bottle of wine.

He arrived in the kitchen like an avenging angel, dark eyes stormy as he took in the scene. The kids were colouring while soothing images of coral reef life and classical music played on the giant TV – Izzy had called time on cartoons after thirty minutes – a curry she'd prepared earlier in the day simmering away in the slow cooker, and two glasses of the Sauvignon Blanc she'd liberated after her date with Harvey shining golden in the patch of late afternoon sun that filled the kitchen.

"Having a good time?"

"Yeah, thanks." Izzy toasted him with her glass and even through the dark scruff that covered the lower half of his face, she saw a muscle in his jaw pop.

"Let's ask Zachary," Edith suggested. "Zachary! Marvin is still refusing to move into assisted living with me. Should I go ahead and do it without him?"

"No," Zac said shortly, and Edith booed.

"You're no fun. What do you think, Izzy?"

"I think you should do whatever makes you

happy," Izzy replied and clinked their wine glasses together. "To happiness!"

"To happiness!" Edith crowed, and Izzy laughed. Mrs Purdy was a delight when she relaxed. They'd already discussed the education system, youth justice, local politicians and Annabel Sampson's divorce.

Zac's frown deepened. "Should you be drinking on your heart medication?"

"Pssh," Edith waved a hand. "You're as bad as Marvin."

"It's only her second glass," Izzy assured him. "And this is my first. I know we didn't discuss alcohol when you hired me–"

"I didn't think we needed to." Zac's lips pressed together in a thin line. "You're working. Do you often drink when you work?"

Izzy straightened on her stool, surprise flaring through her at the hard edge to his words. "I do on occasion, yes. One glass of wine while I get dinner ready. Is that going to be a problem?"

"No," Zac ground out, clearly lying.

*Huh.* Well, that was a conversation for later. For now, she needed to get the kids fed anyway. The mild yellow pumpkin and chicken curry was a risk, but Otis and Hazel hadn't been as resistant as she'd expected to Wednesday night's stir fry so she was giving it a go.

"Do you want dinner?" She didn't look directly at Zac as she hopped down from her stool and rounded the kitchen counter. "I know you said I didn't need to cook for you, but there's plenty if you're hungry."

"No," Zac said again, and when she glanced at him, exasperated – didn't he know any other words?

– his face softened slightly. "I'm flying out tomorrow morning for Sunday's game in Sydney," he elaborated. "The nutritionist has a meal plan I'm supposed to follow before international flights for peak performance."

Something shifted in Izzy, but she brushed it aside. It didn't matter if he ate her food or not. Better that he didn't actually, and then there'd be more for her for lunch tomorrow.

"Sounds good," she offered lightly, pulling a bag of rice from the pantry.

He cleared his throat. "I'll be home late Monday morning."

"Fine."

"Uncle Zac, will you bring me a present?" Hazel was at his knee suddenly, imploring him with big, brown eyes.

"Of course." Zac dropped so he was eye level with his niece. "What would you like?"

Hazel thought for a moment, her tiny brow puckered in concentration. "A unicorn," she finally declared.

"I'll see what I can do," Zac promised, tugging the end of one of her pigtails.

"What a lovely boy," Edith sighed. "Isabel, isn't Zachary lovely?"

Izzy eyed Zac, who glowered at her over Hazel's tiny shoulder.

"The loveliest," she lied flatly.

# CHAPTER 5

Zac dropped his bag inside his bedroom door, placed his box of airport donuts on top and flung himself onto his bed. He let out an almighty groan as the familiar mattress moulded around his body like an embrace. The Knights had eked out a win last night in Sydney, but it was a close thing, a game dominated by the kind of messy, scrappy play that signified the start of the international season. Their set pieces had been sloppy, leaving Zac exposed on the wing more than once, and his body felt every hit this morning after the stiffness set in and the flight back to Auckland took its toll.

He'd avoided the team celebrations in the hotel bar last night, locking himself in his room with a couple of ice packs and a Nalini Singh thriller. He'd been restless though, unable to concentrate on the story, and eventually he'd ended up in the one place he usually tried his hardest to avoid. Social media.

He'd meant to look up Izzy's travel pics from Uruguay, to see where it was she might have bought the dulce de leche he'd inadvertently eaten. He'd found the little farm she'd talked about easily, seen pictures of her bottle-feeding baby goats and posing with an armful of the little jars filled with caramel-coloured spread. It had been relatively simple to order a case of it online, but before he knew it, he was miles down her profile rabbit hole. She'd been everywhere. There were pictures of her in Egypt and Brunei and Scotland, in the Czech Republic and the Caribbean. In pubs, and clubs, and fields of sunflowers, surrounded by ancient ruins and painted laneways. On mountains and in canyons, happiness beaming out of her in every picture. There was one video he'd watched too many times, a group of people inside a pub, clustered together, swaying, pints of beer in the air, singing along to a nineties Brit Rock anthem. In the middle of it all was Izzy, blonde hair a tangled mess over her shoulders, tight white tank top clinging to her skin as she smiled directly into the camera and belted out lyrics about how someone wasn't ever gonna burn her heart out.

She looked young. She looked free. And he'd watched until it hurt, because the young, free woman in that video was the last person he could ever have any kind of relationship with. Not with his life – his responsibilities – here. So, he'd watched until it hurt, and then he'd watched it again and again, until the pain, the *wanting*, ebbed, leaving numbness in its wake.

Isabel Holt belonged to the world. She would never be happy stuck in New Zealand. Alone in a sterile hotel room, watching her through time and a screen, it was the second-truest thing he'd ever known. The first was how much he belonged where he was. With Frances. With Otis and Hazel. He belonged in his world as much as she belonged outside of it, and the third truest thing Zac knew? That wishing something was different didn't make it so. So, he'd switched off his lamp, put his phone on Do Not Disturb, and pushed Isabel Holt to the far recesses of his mind, where she'd stayed until he walked through his front door and caught a whiff of the pear-scented candle she kept in her room.

*Fuck.*

"Zac?" Her voice echoed through the high-ceilinged hallway. "Is that you?"

He groaned a noise of affirmation into his pillow.

"Oh good," Izzy said, her voice clearer now. She must be standing in his doorway. "I thought you might be an intruder."

Zac rolled his head to the side so he could speak over the cool cotton of his pillowcase. "An intruder with a key?"

"I don't know who you give your keys to. With your hard-partying lifestyle, half of Auckland could have copies by now."

He cracked one eye open at her deadpan delivery and looked towards the door.

*Mistake.*

She wore another one of the sports bras she jogged in, electric blue this time, and navy leggings that might as well have been painted on. She grinned at him when his eyes met hers, and it felt like being bathed in warmth, the pain in his body floating away, except for the ache in his groin which sharpened and flared at the sight of her lounging against his open bedroom door. It didn't matter that she was making a joke at his expense. All that mattered was the way she smiled. At him.

"There you are. I worried you might not make it

back to us after a couple of those hits last night. It was a brutal game."

Zac managed a short, sharp nod. He knew from hearing Finn talk in the locker room that Izzy had invited Cara and Clare over to watch the game with her while the team was away. Finn and Manu had called their women from the locker room after the game, snippets of their conversations and low laughs drifting over to Zac as he dressed, his phone dark and silent beside his gear bag.

Izzy hadn't moved, and it hit him like a collapsed scrum that this was the first time she'd set foot in his bedroom. He watched as her eyes tracked left and right, taking in his bed, with its dark wood headboard and slate blue comforter, rumpled from the weight of his body; the bedside tables piled high with books, the framed photograph of Otis and Hazel on his wall, the open wardrobe where his clothes hung organised by colour. Her whole perusal took only a couple of seconds, but Zac had the distinct impression she missed nothing and it felt like someone standing in his brain and poking at it. He had a sudden desire to push his possessions aside, shove them under pillows and drawers, lest she see too much of him.

Izzy blinked then, and the moment passed, though discomfort still coated Zac like a second skin at having her too close. She looked at him again, and gave a little nod, as if she could see inside his head and he wondered if the contents pleased her or not.

He swallowed.

"Do you want a coffee?"

Zac perked up at that. "Please."

Izzy disappeared, taking her too-perceptive gaze

with her. Normally Zac insisted on making his own coffee. After his childhood, it was the only substance he had ever committed to. He'd bought a state-of-the-art machine, designed for cafes, and it sat proudly on his kitchen counter, the bells and whistles it possessed polished to a shine every day after he'd finished using it. It was the one kitchen item he truly loved.

Izzy, of course, had mastered using it in about two seconds. When he'd looked at her askance, she'd simply shrugged.

"Cafe work." Apparently, she'd mixed a few odd hospitality jobs in with her au pair work over the years.

Zac levered himself off the bed. He needed a shower. He probably smelled like stale aeroplane air and a cocktail of his teammates' aftershaves. God knows, he needed to get out of this suit. Shrugging his jacket off, he loosened his Knights' tie and threw it on the bed. He unbuttoned his shirt and opened his suitcase to pull out his toiletries bag. He'd have a shower and a coffee, then call his agent to enquire about the contract negotiations. Last night he hadn't played his best, but he'd still dotted down over the try line, putting four points on the board and assisting one of Rangi's tries as well. Nothing objectionable from the head office's perspective, especially given the jerky, unstructured pace of the game. He needed to know where he stood. He'd missed a call from Frances yesterday – deliberately, he suspected, since she'd called from an unknown number while he was on the pitch. She'd left a voicemail saying she was doing okay, and thanking him for looking after the kids. She'd signed off saying she missed them, and he'd almost thrown his phone across the locker room.

If she missed them, she should be here with them. Looking after them. *Parenting them*, for fuck's sake. Frances and Zac knew the difference between a parent who was there for their kids, and one who showed up to parent when it suited them. Zac did his best to give his sister the benefit of the doubt, but with no explanations, she was straying a little too close to that line for his comfort.

He'd called his mother after he'd calmed down, sending out feelers to see if she'd talked to Frances at all, but either Tui Fearon hadn't heard from her daughter recently or she was keeping mum.

Zac hated himself a little for his nagging suspicion it could be the latter. It certainly wouldn't be the first time Tui had done something like that, tried to protect him from the truth, but now there were innocent kids involved he wouldn't be as forgiving.

*There were innocent kids involved last time, too*, the voice in his head whispered, but he pushed it aside because last time *he'd* been one of the innocent kids and it was a long time since he'd felt that way.

He showered quickly, rinsing off the grime of the journey and letting the hot water spray against the tight muscles of his back. He watched the bubbles from his shower gel swirl down the drain in a thick, glistening foam, washing away the fatigue that had settled over his skin in the comedown from the match.

This was fine. He was fine. He only needed to get his routines back. The grocery delivery should have arrived yesterday, so that was sorted. He'd call Scott and get a line on his future employment before tomorrow's game tape session, and email the kids' teachers to make sure they were tracking okay at school and preschool despite the current turbulence of their home life. Yet something niggled in the back of his brain, something he was supposed to remember but couldn't. His life was as automated as it was possible to get. Bills and appointments were scheduled in advance, right down to his monthly hair trim. The cleaning service arrived like clockwork, incorporating his oven and windows into their schedule every twelve weeks without fail. Routine, that was the key. He knew what to expect when he had a routine. More importantly, the kids knew what to expect when they were here, too. Still, he couldn't help but feel he was missing something.

He stepped out of the shower, drying off quickly, wrapping his towel around his waist, lost in thought.

Opening the bathroom door, he almost collided with Izzy as she came into the hallway from the kitchen, directly to his right.

"Oh, shit." She jumped back, almost spilling the mug of coffee she held. "I thought–" She trailed off.

"You okay?" He'd grabbed her wrist to keep her from splashing scalding espresso everywhere and he used it to pull her in, his eyes raking her body for any signs the hot liquid had burnt her.

There were no stains on her clothing, no errant droplets anywhere he could see. Just miles and miles of soft lightly tanned skin, with a dusting of freckles across her shoulders. His grip loosened on her wrist, but he didn't let go, let his fingers rest there, the flutter of her pulse against his fingertips like butterfly wings.

They were so close he could hear her swallow.

"I'm okay," she murmured, husky and slow, and

he swept his gaze up her body to meet hers, eyes molten chocolate, pupils wide, as they stared at each other.

"You're sure?" He ran his thumb over the smooth inner skin of her wrist, noted the intake of her breath. His own breath caught in his chest.

"Sure." Then her hand was on his bare hip, resting above the thick cotton of his towel, searing him with her heat and her touch.

At that moment, he wanted to be branded. To be marked, owned, and known by Isabel Holt. Then her hand moved higher, gliding across his abdomen, and he flinched away from the unfamiliar sensation.

As swiftly as it had been created the moment was broken. Sharp and fast. Izzy stepped back, tugging her wrist from his hold, confusion and anger warring in her dark eyes.

Zac cursed low under his breath. "Izzy..."

He stepped towards her, and she moved back and to the side, a vicious cha-cha that put her out of arm's reach. He watched again, heart sinking as she pulled the emotions from her face, tucking them somewhere deep inside where he couldn't see them, couldn't watch them paint their way across her expression like perfect glimpses into her.

"Your coffee." Her voice was even. Clear. Controlled neutrality in every syllable. "I was bringing it to your room."

Zac cleared his throat. The memory of her touch seared into his brain, across his stomach. "Yeah, nah, the kitchen is fine. I'll–," he gestured to himself, discomfort forcing its way to the forefront of his brain as he realised he was loitering in the hallway wearing only a towel "–I'll get dressed and come out."

"Okay," she dipped her gaze briefly, but he felt her eyes, stroking across him, and beneath his towel his cock stirred.

"Isabel, I–" he started, but the doorbell rang, and she moved past him, careful to keep her distance.

"You get dressed," she threw over her shoulder, still clutching his coffee. "I'll get the door."

Zac did as he was told, ducking into his bedroom. In the hallway the front door chain rattled as Izzy unlatched it, and he remembered what had been nagging at the depths of his subconscious.

"Izzy, no!" The words exploded out of him, and he dashed back into the hallway, towel clutched to his hips for dignity's sake, but it was too late.

There, on the porch, stood Michaela.

~

"Hi."

"Hi." The woman on the porch smiled. She was gorgeous, Izzy thought, a little blinded by her beauty. Glossy dark hair, ruby painted lips, wide eyes made for winged liner. She wore a black silk blouse, wide legged trousers, and designer heels, looking cool and elegant. Sticky with dried sweat and repressed lust, standing there, Izzy kind of wanted to be her.

"Izzy, no!" Behind her, she heard Zac shout and she turned in time to see him barrel out of his room, clad only in her new favourite towel and a sheen of visible panic.

"Zac?" The woman on the porch sounded confused. "Is everything alright? It's the third Monday of the month, yes?"

"Yes, yeah. I...I..." Zac stammered, the tips of his

ears turning bright red. "I need to reschedule, Michaela. Sorry for the late notice."

"Telling me while I'm standing on your porch is a little more than late notice." The beautiful woman didn't sound angry though. If anything, her tone had morphed into amusement, and when Izzy turned back to face her, she caught Michaela eyeing her with interest.

"Of course," Zac still sounded winded. "You'll be compensated for your time, obviously."

"Obviously." Michaela finished studying Isabel, and focused on Zac, who was flushing an impressive shade of scarlet despite his tanned skin. "Shall we perhaps move to an ad hoc appointment schedule from this point onwards?"

Realisation hit Izzy like a bolt of lightning. The appointment. The gorgeous clothes. Zac's embarrassment. Oh, God. She'd opened the door to his sex worker. Mortification prickled against her skin. Here she'd been *fondling* the man's abdomen while he prepped for sex with someone else. She needed to leave. Immediately.

"If you'll excuse me," she chirped out. "I'm actually on my way out." She dumped Zac's coffee on the hallway table and squeezed past Michaela – *god, she smells good* – scooping up the running shoes she'd kicked off by the front door after her workout this morning. What the hell. Two runs in one day wouldn't kill her. Staying here, on this porch steeped in awkwardness, might though.

Izzy was very, very firmly pro sex workers. Of any and all genders. That being said, she'd never met one on the front doorstep of her current abode, here to fulfil a standing appointment with a man who'd openly rejected Izzy. No wonder her martini-slackened moves in the back room at Agatha's hadn't inspired Zac to carry through on the promises his dick hinted at, if he was used to professional treatment.

"Izzy," she heard him say behind her, but she waved him off without looking.

"Back in an hour. Or two! Probably two. Lovely to meet you," she told Michaela, shoving her feet into her sneakers. "Beautiful shoes."

"Thank you." Michaela smiled, a wry twist to her lips. "Lovely to meet you, too."

Izzy darted down the porch steps and through the gate leading to the driveway, jogging past a powder blue Mercedes that had to belong to Michaela.

*I wonder how I can make friends with her,* she mused, as she reached the street and pushed herself into a steady run. She'd left the house without her phone, her earbuds, her wallet, anything. She might as well exercise, she couldn't do anything else. And she had at least two hours to fill in.

She ran for about forty minutes, an impulsive, meandering loop that ended up at the beach. Not the one directly across the road from the house – that wouldn't have been creepy at all – but the main one at Devonport, where she sat on a bench near the playground watching the ferries to the city and various islands pull in and out until she got bored, then browsed the shops along the esplanade. Izzy fingered scarves and necklaces that shone under artificial lights, soaking up the rare, luxurious feeling of having nothing to do, nowhere to be, and no way of being contacted. She picked up a stunning pair of earrings, freshwater pearls twisted with jewellery wire to resemble vines.

*I wonder if Cara has her wedding jewellery yet.* She'd have to message when she got back to her phone and ask. They'd be perfect for a ceremony at a Waiheke winery, and they fit her sister's feminine, boho style to a tee. She flipped the tag to see the price and choked on her own spit.

*Maybe not.* She loved her sister, but these retailed for the same as a week's charge for passengers on the cruise ship line she was about to be employed by. Even with the obscene money Zac was paying her, they were exorbitant.

"Are you alright, there?" The shop assistant eyed Izzy warily. Probably worried she'd collapse holding the earrings, and they'd have to mark them down to fifty percent off as a result of prying them from her unconscious claws. Mind you, that would be the only way Izzy could afford them.

"I'm fine," she wheezed. "It's my asthma." Apparently, she was allergic to overpriced jewels. She dropped the earrings onto the display table as her smartwatch buzzed with the half hour reminder to leave for the school pickup run.

The Mercedes was gone from the driveway when she returned to the house, and gratitude sank into Izzy's bones at having missed the entirety of Zac's appointment with the stunning Michaela. His Volvo remained parked on the street, so she entered the garage through the driveway door, grabbing a hoodie she'd left in the back of the car and pulling it over her sports bra to combat the slight chill as the autumn sun dipped lower in the sky. The kids were tired when she picked them up, but excited to get home and see Zac. She'd let them stay up a little later last night to catch the first half of the Knights' game on TV, and they'd cheered like mad every time he appeared on screen. He might be a grumpy, taciturn sod when it came to her, but you couldn't fault him as an uncle. Otis and Hazel adored him, and it was obvious the feeling was reciprocated. Izzy had spent enough time around families where the adults clearly had little interest in the children, aside from their social capital, to recognise the genuine warmth and love between Zac and his niblings.

It was obvious in the way he scooped them up in a massive hug the instant the kids bowled into the kitchen, pressing kisses against their cheeks, and asking about their school day. Izzy trailed behind, studiously avoiding eye contact with Zac, even as he pulled out a box of donuts he'd bought for the kids at the airport.

"Donut, Izzy?"

"Hmmm?" She looked up. Zac looked almost pained, holding out the donut box. Something flashed in the mercury depths of his eyes – an apology? A warning? She was too flummoxed to try to decipher the eye signals of her batshit hot employer, who'd probably spent the afternoon getting his soul sucked out of him by the most glamourous woman Izzy had ever met, so she grabbed a glazed ring and shoved half of it in her mouth at once.

"Cheers," she mumbled, through crackly sugar and pastry. Unfortunately, Zac didn't physically recoil from her display of poor table manners, as she'd hoped. Instead, he moved closer, lowering his voice.

"About earlier–"

Izzy put a hand up. "Oh God, no. Zac, we don't need to talk about that. Ever," she emphasised.

"I, uh, forgot I was supposed to be meeting Michaela," Zac finally gave up the good fight for eye contact, his gaze fixing intently on his box of treats. "I'm not sure what you thought..." he trailed off.

"Well, I pretty much thought you had a standing appointment with a professional," Izzy said, glancing at the counter, where the kids sat, focused on their donuts. Otis was taking small, careful bites of his, and Hazel was in full cat-mode, licking all the cinnamon sugar off hers with small flicks of her pink tongue. "And that the courteous thing to do would be to leave and allow you to have that appointment."

Zac ground his jaw. "With my schedule, and the type of people who hang around the games–"

"You don't need to justify yourself." Izzy knew she was interrupting, but this exchange needed to end as soon as possible. Sweet Jesus, this was uncomfortable. Zac gave the impression of someone who'd repressed every emotion he'd felt since puberty. Why on earth couldn't he repress the need to have this conversation as well? "No judgement. Heaps of people use professionals to, uh, provide that service." Another check and the kids were still distracted by their donuts. "I'll make sure I'm out on the third Monday of next month."

"You don't have to do that."

"I don't know, Zac. I'm not trying to k-i-n-k shame anyone," she spelt out, "but hanging out across the hall from that kind of appointment blurs a few professional boundaries." Not to mention that as much as Michaela seemed like a nice woman, Izzy kind of wanted to scratch her eyes out for touching Zac. Which was ridiculous, of course. Zac *wanted* Michaela to touch him. He was literally *paying* her for it. A lot, if her clothes and car were anything to go by. Izzy hadn't been paid for sexual services since she flashed Sean Rogan for twenty bucks and a quarter bottle of vodka on New Year's Eve when she was seventeen. Jealousy sprouted inside her. It wasn't that she wanted Zac to pay her for services rendered – she'd be more than willing to perform them for free – but seeing cool, elegant Michaela on the porch this afternoon had driven home that Izzy was so far from Zac's type it was ridiculous. It felt like being rejected by him at Agatha's all over again. If only her stupid libido could catch up with her logical brain and stop dancing about, all lit up like Catherine Wheels every time she caught a whiff of the cedar and grapefruit shower gel he used. She'd taken to sniffing it every time she took her own shower, and as a result, she was operating like a horny Pavlovian dog. Which was the last thing in the world she needed when he'd made it perfectly clear he wasn't interested in her in that way.

She bet he didn't flinch away when *Michaela* put her hand on his stomach.

The thought depressed her so much she shoved the rest of her donut in her mouth and reached for a second one.

"I mean," Zac looked as though he would rather get shoulder charged into the ground than talk to her. Nevertheless, he persisted. Why God, why did he persist? "I've cancelled my appointments from now on."

"Oh," Izzy managed, struck dumb by his announcement. Was it the kids? The money? What if the money he paid her for nannying came from the account he used to pay Michaela? Or was the awkwardness of today's encounter enough that Zac had decided he'd rather stay celibate than risk another situation like today? Not that cancelling his appointments meant he would be celibate. A man who looked like that could have anyone in the city. Even if there was a chance he'd leave them worked up and disappear into the night before they could get their end away. Still, most people would consider a run at the try line with Zac Fearon worth it, even if they didn't end up scoring. "Okay."

He turned away, taking the box with him as he turned down the pleading for another pre-dinner donut from the kids, leaving Izzy more confused than she'd ever been about the man she now lived with.

# CHAPTER 6

*I*zzy bowled into the bridal shop fifteen minutes late and out of breath.

"Cara Holt?" she asked the woman behind the counter, who escorted her to the left, past rows of frothy dresses in various shades of white to a dressing area, where Cara stood on a small dais, encased in a dress constructed entirely of ruffles.

"Christ, no, not that one." Izzy flopped onto one of the pale pink velvet settees, next to her cousin Andie. Cara's friends Denise and Clare were perched on a similar one, everyone sipping champagne. Izzy accepted her own glass gratefully from an employee who took in her athletic attire and sweat-mussed hair with a pinched expression. "That's not the one you're choosing, is it?"

"Well, not *now*," Cara said, and a frisson of guilt ran through Izzy before her sister laughed. "No, we'd already vetoed this one before you arrived."

"How many have you done?"

"Just this one. We have another four in the changing room." Cara stepped down from the little stage. "I'll get the next one on." She disappeared into a small room with the judgy assistant, and Izzy smiled her greeting to the rest of the group.

"Sorry, I hope that wasn't anyone's favourite."

They shook their heads in unison, Clare looking forlornly at the door Cara had gone through.

"I didn't like the dress, but it made me hungry for lemon meringue pie," Cara's scientist friend mused. "I'm going to buy one on the way home."

"Oh God, me too." Denise licked her lips. "Great idea, Clare."

"How's your wedding planning going?" Izzy asked Denise, who was the manager of Cara's preschool and engaged to a lovely woman named Jodie. Izzy had joined them and Cara for dinner a couple of times since she'd been home.

"Still a pain in the arse," Denise responded cheerfully. "I can't believe Cara's trying to cram the whole thing into four weeks. It took us that long to decide on an invitation design."

The woman in question returned, wearing an off-the-shoulder gown with a full skirt in pure white.

"Pretty," Andie offered, and the others nodded.

"You think?" Cara twisted to look at the back of the dress in the mirror. "What do you guys think of the buttons?"

A row of gleaming pearls marched down the back of the dress to the floor.

"I like them," Izzy offered. "I'm not the one who has to undo them at the end of the night, though. Is Finn a patient man?"

They all knew he was. Finn and Cara had been best friends for five years before he'd declared his love for her – love he'd held inside the entire time.

Cara shot Izzy a wicked look. "Taking off the dress isn't essential, you know."

The women roared with laughter and the sales assistant pasted a smile under long-suffering eyes.

They ooh'd and aah'd over Cara as she turned this way and that in front of the mirror, holding her braid off her neck to give the illusion of an updo before retreating to try the next dress.

"How goes the hunt for a wedding date?" Denise took another sip of champagne. Izzy's diatribe about not showing up alone at the wedding the last time she joined Cara, Denise and Jodie for pizza had obviously not been forgotten.

"It goes," Izzy sighed. "I'm actually using Finn's name as a litmus test. Any time I get a vibe someone might be okay, I mention his name and see how they react. The last thing I want is to bring someone to Finn and Cara's special day who's going to fanboy-slash-girl out and ruin their event. So far, nobody's passed the test."

Her companions winced.

"What about one of the team?" Clare suggested. "That's a good way to avoid bringing a fan."

"Ooh!" Andie rounded on Izzy, eyes champagne-bright. "Aren't you living with Zac Fearon at the moment? Could you swing a little nanny-with-benefits action?"

"No way." Izzy shook her head emphatically. "Even if Zac liked me a little bit, even if he's hotter than the sun, I'm staying far away. I can guarantee that man has high school dick."

"What the hell does that mean?"

"It'll be long and hard, but it'll also result in emotional damage that will stick with me for life."

The other girls laughed, but Izzy was

determined. No matter how good a kisser Zac Fearon was, no matter that he looked like a god while wrapped in a towel, she got the feeling if she ever slept with him for real, she'd be a goner. Goodbye dreams of travel, goodbye independence. She'd be nothing more than a groupie, salivating after a pro athlete who didn't even like her that much.

"I actually have a date tonight," she continued, pulling out her phone and navigating to her dating app. She waited until a picture of tonight's date popped up and showed it to Andie. God, she hoped this one went well. Zac might think she hadn't noticed the little tally of her failed romantic endeavours he kept on the refrigerator whiteboard, but she couldn't help but see it - and the fact the 'win' column was depressingly empty.

"What do you think?"

"I think he looks like he'll chain you to a radiator and make you wear a nappy."

Izzy ignored that, because Andie was forty-two, happily married, and had met her husband the normal way before dating apps, by getting pissed together in the pub and then shagging on the back of a flatbed truck in the carpark. She thought all dating app dates were likely to result in Izzy being sold into sex slavery rather than a lacklustre fingering in the rideshare on the way home.

"Is that an eagle tattooed on his neck?" Andie asked now. "What the fuck is that? Is he American? Imagine what that'll look like when he's on top of you, pumping away. It'll look like it's flapping its wings when his veins pop."

"Stop," Izzy protested, laughter bubbling from her.

"Caw caw, caw caw," Andie flapped her arms and Izzy fell over on the couch, racked with giggles.

"I'm gonna cancel. I can't handle that imagery."

"No, you're not," Andie disagreed cheerfully. "But text me when you get home tonight, so I know you're not trapped under a writhing eagle."

"You're ridiculous." Izzy flashed the picture at the other two women. "What do you guys reckon?"

"Cute," Denise said. "Invite us to the nesting ceremony?"

"Hope your kids are a chirp off the old block," Clare offered.

Izzy sat back and locked her phone. "I hate you all."

The other women laughed uproariously, as the door to Cara's dressing room opened and she stepped out.

The room quietened instantly.

"Oh," Izzy managed, when she could find her voice. "You're stunning."

"That one," Denise said, Clare and Andie nodding their agreement.

Cara wore a simple, high-necked, ivory satin halter gown with a pleated column skirt. It was perfect - fuss free and elegant, the warmer shade giving her skin a golden glow and picking out copper highlights in her red hair.

She was ethereal. The perfect bride, ready to marry her Prince Charming. Izzy blinked quickly, dispersing the tears that threatened to overflow.

"You don't think it's too simple?" Cara stepped up onto the dais.

"No. It's flawless," Izzy said firmly, the other girls murmuring their assurances.

"Yeah." Her sister smiled. "I think so, too."

The sales assistant handed Cara a bouquet of fake flowers and pinned a veil to the top of her head, and there it was.

*Cara. A bride.*

Tears pricked at the back of Izzy's eyes. Her sister was beautiful. A storybook princess. Joy flooded Izzy. Finally, after all these years taking care of everyone, her sister was mere weeks away from her own happy ending. Not that it was an ending; more the start of a new adventure with her adoring husband. Izzy's favourite thing about Finn had always been his devotion to Cara, even when her sister couldn't see it. Now that her eyes were open, Cara fairly glowed with the security of being truly, openly loved. For the first time in almost a decade, the idea of leaving Aotearoa in the coming weeks didn't cause guilt to pinch at the base of Izzy's skull. Cara had been alright without her all these years, but only alright. Now? Now, she would flourish. Finn would ensure it. He would demand it. And she was privileged that they were making the effort to include her in the celebration of their happiness before she jumped on a ship and took off in search of her own.

The girls toasted to Cara, to Finn, to their upcoming nuptials. Cara didn't bother trying on the final dress, choosing instead to sit with them and finish her champagne while they discussed hair and accessory options.

As Cara paid for the dress, Izzy hugged her sister goodbye. Their mother had given Cara money for her wedding gown, and while it surprised Izzy that Cara had accepted it, she was pleased too.

It was good, she decided, as she walked along the quaint little strip of shops the bridal salon was in. Cara had been so resistant to any kind of help for so long, to see her opening herself up to people, accepting and asking for help, was a sign of her strength as much as her fierce independence had been.

Izzy paused, steps halting as she passed by one particular shop. Dozens of jars containing glittering beads sat in the window, strings of turquoise and jasper and cut glass hanging from above in a vibrant curtain. Before she could think twice, she pushed open the door.

"Hello." The woman behind the counter smiled. "Can I help you today?"

"Just browsing," Izzy murmured, eyes flickering over the shelves where row after row of jars sat, filled with tiny treasures.

"Sing out if you need anything. I'm Heather, by the way."

"Thanks, Heather, I will." Izzy was already moving, reaching out to touch jars, to pick them up and examine their contents. She started with the pearls. Little pink ones, chunky and unique baroque pearls, black pearls from the Cook Islands that shone purple and teal, like spilled petrol under the lights.

*Beautiful.*

She found a jar of small freshwater pearl beads and one of larger pieces, and took them up to the counter with a spool of jeweller's wire in rose gold and some earring hooks.

"Beautiful choice," Heather said, counting out her treasure into small paper bags. "What are you making?"

"Earrings," Izzy said. "For my sister."

"That's lovely," Heather smiled. She was either

schooled in customer service from a young age, the friendliest woman Izzy had ever met, or stoned. "Have you worked with pearls before?"

"I've never made jewellery before," Izzy admitted, and gratefully accepted a pair of jewellery pliers Heather recommended and a beading tray. The total cost of her supplies was still only ten percent of the gorgeous pearl earrings she'd seen in the store in Devonport, and she handed over her bank card gratefully.

"We hold jewellery making sessions on Tuesdays at noon," Heather informed her, handing over a bag containing her purchases. "If you're having any trouble or you'd like to come along and chat while you work, the ladies and gentlemen who attend have a ton of knowledge and are really friendly."

"Thanks," Izzy said, touched. "I'll think about it."

"Do," Heather encouraged. "Beading is a glorious hobby, but it can also be a bit of a lonely one without support."

Izzy grinned at the shop assistant's words as she made her way back to the car. She'd lived abroad since she was seventeen, never staying in one place for more than two years. She had friends of course, people she'd met at the school gates, or ski slopes, or in the case of her friend Nicky, on a church rooftop in Barcelona where they'd got plastered on a box of cheap sangria, but for the most part all her hobbies were lonely ones; she went to the movies by herself, to concerts and dinner and the theatre. She travelled alone, soaking in the experiences of new countries and cultures by herself.

She'd never thought of her life as lonely, though. Only as free. It always amused her when people equated doing things by oneself as lonely. If anything, she felt lonelier at the few family events she'd attended during the last decade. The ones where whispers about her nomadic lifestyle and speculation about her sexuality reached her from every corner of the room. The ones where Andie's mum asked her loudly in front of everyone when she would settle down and get married. The ones where she inevitably ended up at the kids table, all the parents in the family having shunted their children her way on seeing her, assuming that her career in childcare meant she wanted to watch over their children while they got Chardonnay-tipsy and she spent the night fetching Fanta for kids who barely remembered her.

It was the same every time. And it would be the same at Cara's wedding if she didn't do something about it. Determination fixed Izzy's jaw as she unlocked the door to Zac's Volvo. She had earrings to make and a date to prepare for.

"You look beautiful." His nephew sounded dazed.

"Thank you, Otis" Izzy said, and Zac looked up to see her standing by the stairs leading down to the garage, shoving her phone into a small black bag.

Holy shit. His mouth went dry. His nephew wasn't the only one who was impressed. Zac felt like he'd been hit with a two-by-four. Izzy wore a tight red sweater, black leather pants, and strappy black heels that made her long legs last forever, but it was above the neck that had him stirring in his jeans. Her blond hair was up in a tousled ponytail, dark makeup emphasising the whisky-brown of her eyes, her lips pink and almost sweet between the sultry eye makeup and siren-red top.

*Almost.*

As in, if he closed his eyes, he could almost pretend he hadn't noticed the sweet pillow of them, the way her bottom lip was a little fuller, giving her a natural pout. Could almost forget the number of times he'd replayed kissing them, the way they opened for him, the fantasy of what it might be like to have her trail them down his torso and wrap around his length.

Yeah, her lips looked almost innocent. But almost didn't count.

She looked like a woman either fresh from someone's bed or on her way there, and his gut tightened at the thought.

"Hot date?" Zac grunted, turning back to the freezer and shoving his head inside. He was supposed to be getting ice cream for the kids for dessert, but damn if he didn't need some cooling off himself.

"Something like that."

It was exactly like that. This afternoon in the locker room, Finn and Manu had chatted about Izzy's mission to find a date for her sister's wedding. Apparently, something had been said at Cara's wedding dress appointment, and there was talk of eagles lumped in with hearty guffaws. The instant Rangi Katu had offered to escort Cara to the wedding though, Finn had stopped laughing and his eyes got the flinty look that reminded the team his nickname of Prince Charming had been bequeathed because of his looks, not his conduct. Finn was a nice guy, no doubt about it – nicer than Zac by a country mile – but he was wildly protective of the people he loved, and that, apparently, extended to his soon-to-be sister-in-law.

Zac could relate. Not only had the urge to string Rangi up by his bootlaces in the showers caused him to grit his teeth hard enough to give him a jaw ache, but his frustration at not having a solid answer about his contract edged towards the surface every day. What was the point of having a career as a professional athlete if he couldn't protect the people he loved? His mother's house in Motueka was paid off, thank goodness, and he sent her money each month, praying she kept it for herself and didn't give it away to his piss-drunk father whenever he rolled by, so she was sorted. God only knew what was going on with Frances. His gut told him he didn't want to know. But Otis and Hazel? By God, he would protect them. His house was already willed to them, but their bank accounts weren't nearly where he wanted them to be by the time his playing career came to an end.

There wasn't a lot of money in being a washed-up league player. He didn't have the easy banter that made him a good fit for commentary or punter shows. He didn't model – the idea made him cringe. He'd never taken a sponsorship deal that wasn't directly related to the sport – boots or balls. All the cereal and toothpaste commercials were left to the other boys. Zac's instructions to his financial manager and agent had always been perfectly clear – the sport only. He wasn't a product to be wrapped up in pretty packaging with a bow for public consumption. He didn't need Otis and Hazel seeing posed pictures of him in his underwear like Finn Chalmers, or paparazzi shots of him stumbling out of clubs like Matt Hollis and Rangi Katu. It was the game, and only the game, that fuelled his finances. Yet with the uncertainty over his future as a Knight hanging over him, he was having second thoughts about that position.

*Does it really matter where the money comes from, as long as it comes?*

If he missed out on re-signing, his stock would drop, and so would his endorsement opportunities. Right now, he turned them down. But to not have them at all? Despite the chill of the freezer, Zac shivered.

"Well, have fun." He kept his voice light – no problems here! Totally normal – and grimaced at the ice tray when all he got in return was a cheery 'Thanks!'

"Uncle Zac, you're taking aaaages." Dessert waited for nobody, and certainly not Hazel, who was vocal about her desire for food at every opportunity.

"Sorry, mate." He yanked the container of wildberry ice cream out and shut the door, in time to see a flash of red as Izzy clattered down the stairs on her way out.

She was still out after the kids were in bed. Zac had watched three hours of various current events shows, and was depressed as shit by the time he heard the garage door slide up. He sat up straight on the couch, pulling the blanket across his legs and trying to look like he wasn't waiting up for her.

He wasn't, of course. He wasn't her father.

*You could be her Daddy...*

He banished that thought before he poked his own eye out with his erection and tried very hard to recall every instance of war, terror and famine he'd seen roll past on his screen.

Izzy crept up the stairs quietly, and stopped when she reached the top.

"Oh. You're up."

"Yeah, watching the news."

They both looked at the screen, where war, terror and famine had disintegrated into a story about a baby giraffe being born.

"Cute." Izzy moved into the kitchen, her high heels dangling from her fingers. "You want a cup of tea, or something?"

"Water would be good, please." He watched from his spot on the couch as she poured him a glass. Then, to his surprised horror, she picked up the pen attached to the refrigerator whiteboard and, next to the tiny record he'd been keeping, drew a table. On one side, the side where he'd marked her unsuccessful dates – four of them – she wrote a little 'Z' at the top, and an 'I' above the blank column. She glanced over her shoulder to where he sat with a stomach full of lead, smirked, and then made a mark in her own column.

Zac swallowed. Hard.

"What's that?" His tone was gravel because it was obvious she knew, but the voice inside his head shouted '*Deny! Deny! Deny!*' and that voice had kept him alive and well during some pretty rough times, so he did what it said.

"That's one for me," Izzy said, her voice heavy with satisfaction.

"One what?" *Deny!*

"One good date." He must have looked like he'd seen a ghost – shit, he *felt* like he had – because she burst out laughing when she took another look at his face.

"Zac, you're a nice enough guy, I guess –" and

wasn't *that* a ringing endorsement "– but you're not nearly as sneaky as you think you are." She wandered over and handed him the glass of water. "What I can't figure out is *why* you've been tracking my dates like a little social weirdo."

Zac slumped back on the couch and took a sip, hoping hydration would inspire a believable response. It didn't, though, so he had no choice but to be honest.

"It's nice to know I'm not the only one."

"The only what?" Izzy flopped on the other couch, red painted toes up on the brown leather armrest. If she was one of the kids he'd tell her to put her feet down, but she wasn't, and his normal rules didn't apply with Isabel Holt.

"The only one who's struck out with you. Whatever those other guys did, or didn't do, you've been pretty unimpressed each time you've come home. It's good to know I'm not alone, I guess."

"That's a very perverse viewpoint, Zachary."

He shrugged. "It is what it is." Another Fearon motto, along with *just act normal.*

She sat up suddenly, her brown eyes studying him like a science exhibit. He felt every place they touched like a brand, and the idea of someone looking at him so closely – seeing him – made him fidget.

"Why *did* you strike out?"

"Excuse me?"

"You and me, in the back room at Agatha's. Why did you leave?"

*Jesus.* A thousand fire ants crawled across his skin.

"Does it matter?"

"Probably not," Izzy shrugged. "But I'm a curious

kind of gal. You're not the kind of guy who hooks up often. At least you haven't since I got here, the lovely Michaela excluded, of course." He opened his mouth to remind her nothing had happened with Michaela this week, that he'd cancelled his future appointments, but she steamrolled on. "So even doing that seems out of character for you now I know you, but then you *left*? To take a *phone call*? With me half naked on a *desk*?" She must have seen the discomfort on his face. "I'm not trying to make things weird by bringing it up. I promise I'm not, but what *happened*?" Her voice dropped, became smaller. "Was it me?"

"No. God, no." Zac ran a hand through his hair. The idea of her blaming herself, thinking he'd found fault with her, was unacceptable.

"I was on edge that night," he confessed. "Like you said, I don't get out much. I was jumpy, irritable. Worried about Frances, my sister. I hadn't been able to get hold of her for a couple of days. I'd met my agent at Agatha's to talk about my contract finishing this year, and we'd wrapped it up when I saw you. You were beautiful – you *are* beautiful – and it robbed me of all common sense. One second I was approaching you at the bar and the next minute we were in the back room. I promise you," he swore, "nothing but Frances's ringtone could have stopped me. But I had the nagging feeling she was in trouble, and that meant trouble for the kids."

Understanding dawned on Izzy's face. "That was the night she left."

"Yeah." Zac ran his hand through his hair. "She told me I needed to come home immediately. When I got here, she was already sitting on the porch with the kids' bags. They were asleep in the car. She was a mess, and I just-" A lump formed in his throat "–I just couldn't let something happen to them. They need security. They need to know someone will always be there for them, damnit, and if it's not going to be Frances, it's definitely going to be me."

His forceful words echoed up to the high ceiling of the living room. He'd been louder than he thought.

Izzy stood up and crept across, curling her body into a ball next to his. She reached out and ran her fingers over the back of one of his clenched fists.

"Hey."

Her voice was like a balm. He let her turn his hand over, let the gentle stroke of her fingers loosen his taut muscles until she slipped her palm against his. Zac's breath hitched as he stared at their joined hands. It felt like his arm was on fire, his palm pressed against the source of the flame, almost painful.

"You're an amazing uncle," she said, softly. "Don't ever doubt that. Otis and Hazel are lucky to have you."

Zac's throat worked, and he swallowed before he spoke. "They deserve everything."

"And you give it to them. I don't have any doubts."

He finally managed to pull his gaze away from their hands to look at her. Her eyes were like chocolate, smooth and liquid in the low glow from the television. She smiled softly, encouragingly, and squeezed his hand again.

"I'm going to head to bed. You'll be okay out here?"

Zac nodded, his mouth dry.

"Good." One final squeeze, one final brand of

her skin against his, and she stood, collecting her shoes from the other couch, and padded her way towards the hallway door. She was almost there when it occurred to him.

"Izzy?"

"Yes, Zac?"

"The mark you made on the fridge. The successful date. You're seeing him again?"

"Yeah, I am."

"Oh." He swallowed, hard. "He was nice?"

"Nice enough. Besides, it's not like I've got a lot of options. Goodnight, Zac."

"Goodnight, Izzy."

Then she was gone, and he was alone in the dark once more.

# CHAPTER 7

*I*zzy was elbow deep in chicken marinade when the screaming started.

She washed her arms off –*quickly* – and followed the noise to Otis's room. The source was easy to find – he lay crumpled on the floor wailing his head off – and the cause even clearer. The large scale castle he'd been building before school for the last week was destroyed, blocks scattered everywhere like colourful shrapnel.

Hazel was nowhere to be seen.

"Otis?" Izzy plopped on the floor next to him, reaching out to place a hand on his back. He screamed again, no acknowledgement of her presence. "Otis, sweetie? Come here. Come on." She helped him into her lap and he curled into a ball, sobbing into her shoulder. "Can we practise our star breathing together? Can you breathe with me?" Gently she traced the edges of his fingers, breathing in as her finger travelled up each digit and out as it descended. On the third pass, Otis joined her, shuddering out each exhalation in jerky pants.

Izzy lost track of time sitting there, breathing in and out as she cradled Otis's dark head to her chest and ran her hand up and down his spine in slow, soothing strokes matching the tempo of his breaths. Eventually his pants became whimpers, and his whimpers faded into belly breathing.

"You okay, sweetie?"

His silky curls brushed her lips as he shook his head.

"Do you want to talk about it?"

"She broke it," Otis said sadly.

"Hazel?"

"Yes. Then she ran away and it was b...b... broken." His voice cracked on the last word and she took another deep breath, then another until he'd settled again.

"Was it an accident?" Izzy ventured. Chances were good that it was, but Hazel was a law unto herself. A lovely girl, incredibly kind and caring, but with a spine of steel that would hopefully aid her in running a government or Fortune 500 company one day, rather than a cult or cartel.

"Yes," Otis admitted, and Izzy's relief echoed through the room.

"Okay." She rocked Otis some more, back and forth while he played with the end of her ponytail. "She probably ran away because she was scared. Should we go look for her? You can tell her you know it was an accident and maybe she can help you rebuild it."

"No!" Otis was vehement in his response.

"Or you can rebuild it yourself," Izzy amended quickly. "And Hazel can help me make dinner while you work on it, so you'll have plenty of peace and quiet."

It didn't take long to find Hazel. The little girl was hiding in the wardrobe in her bedroom, dark eyes huge and shimmering with unshed tears when the sliver of light cut across her face and she saw Otis and Izzy standing before her.

"I'm sorry," she cried, throwing herself at her older brother and hugging him tightly. "I'm so sorry."

Izzy left the kids in Hazel's room playing with her stuffed animals, the Lego castle apparently forgotten, and checked her phone as she made her way back to the kitchen. Zac was due back soon from Australia and she wanted to make sure he'd landed. The Knights had won, thank goodness. Cara had come over, and they'd allowed Otis to stay up and watch the whole game, a point of pride for him. Hazel had been dark about being told she'd be sent to bed at half-time, but a small bowl of ice cream from Zac's secret stash had mollified her.

"Hey."

Izzy's heart leapt, and she dived away from the shadow in the doorframe. "Fuck me dead!"

Zac blinked at her dispassionately. "That's a revolting turn of phrase."

Izzy slapped a hand over her racing heart. "My apologies, good sir. Next time some random dude leaps out at me in the dark, I'll be sure to use a more dignified expression."

"It's five in the afternoon."

"It's always attack o'clock somewhere."

The left corner of his mouth bunched a little, the way it did when he thought she was being ridiculous, but he didn't say anything, moving out of the doorway to the kitchen so she could pass through.

"I thought you'd text when you landed."

"No point. It's always a crapshoot on how long it

takes to get here from the airport." Zac moved to the refrigerator and pulled out a jug of orange juice. "Want some?"

"No thanks." Izzy went back to rolling chicken thighs around in her Greek-inspired marinade of yogurt, lemon juice and oregano. It was a risk with the kids – well, with Otis. Hazel, it turned out, ate most things once she was given a chance, but Izzy was counting on the kids being so excited to see Zac they'd eat whatever she put in front of them tonight. Her quest to find items the kids would eat outside of the chicken-nuggets-and-fries oeuvre was a work in progress. Pumpkin soup had proven a winner already, as had bean and cheese quesadillas and shepherd's pie with lentils mixed in. The yellow chicken curry had been met with tears and revulsion but they were up to one stir fry a week. Her baking remained the most successful though - blondies made with cannellini beans and bran muffins were the biggest winners and she was almost confident enough to try brownie baked oatmeal slices in their lunchboxes next week.

"What's that?" Zac eyed the bowl of chicken hungrily.

"Greek chicken. We're having it with beans and mashed potatoes." Ideally, she'd roast the potatoes until they were the perfect balance of crisp on the outside and fluffy on the inside, drowning in a buttery sauce, but last week's attempt at such potatoes had been a dismal failure. Only mashed potatoes would do. Izzy was determined that she'd get Otis eating roast potatoes at some point, but she needed to bide her time. The chicken would be enough change tonight.

"Sounds great."

"You want some? There's plenty."

A whole bunch of prepacked, nutritionally balanced meals had arrived earlier in the day along with his usual Sunday delivery of groceries, but he was here and she had way more chicken than she needed to feed her, Otis and Hazel.

Zac looked a little surprised. "Yeah, that would be great, thanks."

Izzy shrugged and slid the chicken pieces onto a tray, then popped them in the oven to grill. Turning back to the kitchen counter, she washed her hands quickly at the sink and dried them on a towel.

"When's the next game?"

"Thursday." Zac grimaced. "Short turnaround."

"More time to recover before the next one."

"And then a bye. The week of Finn and Cara's wedding."

"Hmmm." Izzy murmured noncommittally.

"You don't sound excited." Damn his observant nature.

"I'm excited for them," Izzy admitted. "I'm less excited to be trapped in a room with my divorcing parents."

"They're not handling it well?"

"My mother is handling it like a fucking boss. My father is handling it like an arsehole, which is probably because he is one. He'll spend the whole event making it about him and trying to make sure my mum doesn't get a look in, and Cara will spend the whole event trying to make sure Mum's okay, and I'll spend the whole event drinking every time someone asks me why I'm not married yet like there's not a full floor show happening that highlights my good sense while they speak."

"Sounds rough."

"An understatement. Are your parents together?"

Zac pressed his lips together in a grim line. "Unfortunately."

"Want to talk about it?"

"Definitely not."

Izzy shrugged and grabbed a cloth to wipe the counter down. Zac had dumped several of his things on the counter in a pile – a tidy pile, naturally. His wallet, passport, keys and a pack of spearmint gum. She picked them up one by one and wiped under them, pausing on his passport.

"What are you doing with that?"

"Checking to see if you're human." She flipped it open. "Nope, still an android. Look at this picture. Look how good it is. This looks like a modelling headshot. My photo is so bad that the automated passport barriers don't recognise me as being the same person. I have to go through a manual immigration service each time. Truly, there is no justice in this world."

"It's a photo."

"It's a hot as fuck photo. If I had a photo where I looked this good I'd use it for everything. My driver's licence, my gym card. I'd get arrested so I could provide this photo to news outlets and have it beamed all over the country."

Zac's ears turned red. "Are you finished?"

"I guess." Izzy went to close the passport, pausing when she saw his full name.

Zachary Waitangi Fearon

"You're Māori?" She looked up from his passport and he grunted at her.

"Part. On my mum's side."

"What's your whakapapa?"

"She's from Motueka. Upper Moutere. That's where I was born."

She considered him further and he ran a hand through his hair, a sure sign he was uncomfortable. "What, you want my pepeha? Ko Zac toku ingoa."

"Don't be silly." She snapped his passport shut and slid it across the counter to him. "I'm just curious."

"Why?" God, the suspicion!

She shrugged. "I like people. I like learning about their cultures and where they come from and what makes their homes unique. I enjoy travelling to places I've heard about from locals and seeing why they love it."

"Oh." His shoulders sank a little, some of his defensiveness evaporating.

"Why are you so weird about it?"

He grimaced. "I don't feel like I truly belong there," he admitted. "I don't feel... Māori enough, I guess. The iwi gave me all these scholarships so I could move away and pursue league, but I don't really feel like I earned them. I hardly go back, maybe once a year to see Mum. My reo is for shit. I haven't set foot on a marae since my twenty-first."

"You don't earn your identity," Izzy said softly, blown away by his speech. She'd never heard him string so many words together, let alone the personal nature of them. "What do you love about Motueka?"

He sighed, as though being asked to describe his hometown was a task worthy of great suffering. "The beaches. It's a fifteen minute drive to Kaiteriteri beach, and it's so beautiful. Have you been?"

She shook her head, and he continued. "You

should. It's got perfect golden sand and the bush comes down to the ocean, but the actual beach in Motueka is all rocks and the wind whips the surf up. It's a little rougher, wilder. There's a track you can take and I used to run it every morning growing up. The people are friendly, kind. There are some unexpectedly amazing cafes popping up all the time and you've got millionaires coming in from their mansions and sitting there having their flat whites next to hippies who are living in vans. It's positioned in the middle of three national parks, so there's always something to explore, a new place to visit. It's peaceful, I guess."

"You feel peaceful there?"

"Yeah."

"Then that's your place."

Zac shook his head. "That's not my place."

"Where's your place then?"

His eyes tightened at the corners, determination pulling his mouth into a firm line. "Wherever Otis and Hazel are. That's where I belong."

Izzy's heart softened. It wasn't a healthy answer, not when they had a parent of their own, but the depth and breadth of his love for them was admirable, nonetheless. "You feel responsible for them, don't you?"

"I *am* responsible for them," Zac corrected her. "As long as I'm alive, my responsibility will be to my family. There's nothing more important than that."

Izzy smiled, but it felt odd. Too tight, too pantomime. "You'd better go see them, then," she said. "I believe Otis has some feedback about your defence last night."

Zac gave her a quick grin – the briefest flash of white teeth in dark stubble that just about knocked Izzy off her feet – and stood. Before he turned to go though, he looked her directly in the eyes. Still unsteady from the power of his grin – Jesus, thank goodness he didn't go round smiling at people all the time. There wasn't enough deodorant in the world to cope with the impact of that heat – Izzy was trapped, caught in his silver gaze.

"Thanks, Izzy," Zac said, voice deep with sincerity. "I appreciate the talk."

"No problem," Izzy squeaked. She watched him wander out to the hallway, heard the excited squeals of the kids as they greeted him, and leant against the counter to catch her breath.

*Oh, no. This is definitely going to be a problem.*

Zac was in his usual spot on the porch swing when Izzy edged through the gate the next morning, fresh from her run.

"Hey," he greeted her softly, holding out the latte he'd made for her.

"Hey." She accepted the coffee with a grateful look and sat down next to him, pulling the spare blanket he'd brought out with him across her legs as she took her first sip.

"Mm!" Her surprised little hum drew his attention and when he looked at her, she was watching him from the corner of her eye.

"Hazelnut?" she inquired.

Zac shrugged. "It's what you ordered when we first met in that cafe to talk about the job. I figured it was your usual."

"It is." She sipped again, eyes closing.

*He remembers what you ordered a month ago?* "It's delicious, thank you."

He didn't reply but watched her as she sat there, cast rose gold by the dawning light of the sun. It played across her features, the tiny upward slant of her nose, dusted with barely-there freckles, the delicate skin of her eyelids, the tips of her eyelashes. Her perfect, lush lips, the curve and dips of them painted in shadows and light, spotlit by nature. Zac could no more look away than he could slow the sun's progress, and he gave a quick moment of thanks to Maui for having done just that so he could sit here each morning and soak in these peaceful golden moments with Isabel Holt for the short time he had her in his life.

He knew better than to let his imaginings wander beyond the bounds of her short-term employment. His childhood had taught him that people were flighty, fickle. Izzy had been open, eager even, to talk about the cruise ship she was leaving on in July and even if she hadn't been... well, people never stuck around anyway. Even Frances, the one person in Zac's life he'd thought was solid, was gone, disappeared into the ether without a flicker, but she'd be back. He knew it in his bones. Whatever was happening with her wouldn't be enough for her to abandon her kids forever. But he couldn't help the tinge of resentment that crept along the base of his skull when his sister crossed his mind.

No, he reasoned, better to be realistic and focus on what was real, not some smudge of an imagined future that twirled in front of him like smoke, faint and intangible but as capable of doing damage as the pyre that set it free.

Izzy was here, on his porch swing, watching the sun rise above the water, cradling the coffee he'd made her against her chest.

Imagining more was deluding himself, and doing her, with all her lofty goals and dreams, a disservice.

They remained like that, Zac watching Izzy, Izzy watching the ocean. He used his foot to gently sway the porch swing back and forth as the sky faded from indigo to lilac, pink-tipped clouds heralding the coming day above the row of pohutukawa trees lining the reserve across the road like green-clad soldiers.

"I suppose I should get the kids up," Izzy sighed reluctantly, breaking their peaceful bubble of silence.

Zac murmured his assent. He couldn't bring himself to stand first, to bring this moment that seemed to stretch between them like a fine gold thread to an end. Intellectually he knew he was pushing it for time. He would need to ferry into the city and catch a car to Knights Stadium, because by the time he got ready he'd have missed his window to make it across the traffic-packed Harbour Bridge in time, but he didn't care.

It felt good not to worry. Not to have the weight and expectations of others pressed against him like a visceral force, squeezing his innards as he struggled to contain every aspect of his life. The porch at daybreak felt like a lifeline some days – a singular moment in time that gave him repose and strengthened him for the day ahead. The first time Izzy had joined him post-run he'd worried that all that irrepressible energy packed into athletic attire would throw off his entire routine, leave him backfooted to stumble through the day without his centre. Instead, the opposite had happened. She'd assimilated, making herself a part of these early morning moments as if she'd been there from the start.

Beside him she stood and stretched, and he made a concerted effort not to stare at the exposed segment of her stomach that peeked out from between the waistband of her leggings and the hem of her workout top. It teased him, flashing in the corner of his eye, but he didn't look.

He. Would. Not. Look.

Funnily enough though, when Izzy lowered her arms and headed for the front door, he didn't feel noble for his sacrifice, merely disappointed that the opportunity was gone.

That edge of disappointment rode him all the way into the city and stayed with him in the locker room while he changed and made his way onto the field. Out there it was even worse, turning inward in a dark twist when he made a couple of basic errors.

"You okay, Fearon?" Chalmers kept his voice low as he bent to pick up the ball that had slipped through Zac's hands.

"Yup," Zac replied tightly, shoulders bunching with tension as he watched the backs' coach whisper something to Harro on the sidelines. Harro shook his head, eyes firmly fixed on Zac. His fists tightened by his sides.

*Fucking rookie errors. You're better than this.*

The whistle sounded. "Take five," Harro yelled, and accepted a tablet from the backs' coach.

*Probably looking at footage of another winger for next year.*

He needed to be better than this. His entire

career was on the line with the looming deadline. If he couldn't convince the Knights he was worth another contract... Well, he didn't even want to think about that. That shit was what he paid his agent to be concerned about.

"Don't worry about it," Chalmers slapped the ball into Zac's stomach. "We all have off days, right?"

Zac grunted. Chalmers was a nice bloke, but he was an eternal optimist, and he'd given Mary fuckin' Sunshine a run for her money since Cara had agreed to marry him. Chalmers didn't need to worry about contract extensions. He was their captain, for Christ's sake. His position was as solid as a player's could get, barring injury. As far as Zac was aware, Finn's biggest financial output was his upcoming wedding, a few charities and custom outfits for his ratty little dog. Although Dom McQueen contributed pretty regularly to the mutt's wardrobe as well. Probably the rates on Chalmers' big fuck-off-sized mansion in a gated community ran steep, but Finn was from money even before he signed with the Knights.

"You sure you're okay?" Finn peered at Zac closely – too close – and Zac stepped back, dropping his eyes to the grass. "Everything alright at home? Izzy working out?"

"She's good," Zac muttered. He cleared his throat and tried again. "Great with the kids. She's got them to eat all kinds of shit. Flaxseed and stuff. It's a goddamn miracle because Otis reacted like I was trying to poison him when I gave him a carrot to eat in the first week."

Finn smiled, his face lightening as the last vestiges of worry swept away. "She's great, isn't she? Nothing fazes her. I remember the first time I met her. It was the Christmas holidays and she'd come home from her first big au pair job from some Swiss family. She looked me up and down right there in her parents' kitchen and immediately hit me up to help at a coaching clinic for some kids from the local school that her mate was running."

"What did you do?"

Finn chuckled. "I was trying to impress Cara. What do you think I did? I was down at the field every day that week, but that's Izzy for you. She pops into people's lives, makes them better, then disappears again. Cara wishes she was around more, but she says that nothing will tie Izzy down until Izzy's good and ready to be tied."

Visions of Izzy wound in rope and ribbon crowded into Zac's head, detonating his equilibrium. He worked to keep his face impassive as his imagination ran wild.

Izzy, scarlet satin covering her eyes.

Izzy, hands secured behind her back with thin leather cords.

Izzy, hair spread out across his pillow as she gripped the headboard.

Fuck, he'd never shown any interest in bondage before, not past a couple of sessions with an old fling and a flimsy pair of cheap sex-shop handcuffs during his early days in Auckland, before Frances moved and he stopped going out, stopped meeting anyone or indulging in random hookups.

The idea of experimenting with Izzy though? That got his attention, and his dick twitched in his pants. She was exactly the kind of woman who could tempt him into trying something new. Hell, with her adventurous spirit, she probably had a mental artillery of ways to twist him inside out sexually. God knew, she'd already done it to the rest of his life. Why not let her ruin him on every level?

The whistle blew, long and sharp. "Fearon! Go again!"

Zac nodded in Harro's direction and chucked the ball back to Rangi Katu so they could reset the play he'd mangled.

Ah. That's why.

Because Izzy Holt was a fantasy. Finn had said so himself. She came, she dazzled, she left. Zac had been left too often for that kind of relationship to hold any appeal for him, no matter how smooth Izzy's skin was or how well she slotted into place with the kids. Otis and Hazel needed stability and structure as much as he did. There was no place in their lives long-term for a globetrotting chaos fairy like Izzy Holt, and Zac damn sure wouldn't let the kids fall in love with someone who'd be leaving them in the rearview mirror in a few weeks' time. He'd been there, and he'd never let them go through that.

No, he decided, catching the ball as it spun his way out of the ruck, his feet pounding the sun-baked grass as he ran it straight down the sidelines. He needed to focus on the team and let the idea of Izzy go.

Nothing good came from wanting what you couldn't have.

# CHAPTER 8

*T*hread and twist, thread and twist.

Izzy repeated the mantra to herself as she bent the jewellery wire to her will and held up the resulting piece. Not bad. She'd decided it would be worthwhile practising before giving Cara's earrings a shot, so she'd returned to the bead shop and Heather had loaded her up with a few cheaper packets to practise with. Armed with her colourful array and several designs she'd bought from some beadmakers online, she'd carved out a nice little chunk of time each day to bead and it was paying off. Her latest effort was certainly better than those she'd attempted earlier in the week. Normally she practised when the kids were at school, but she'd been so close to finishing this pair she'd slipped away to her room to complete them after Otis finished his spelling words. Dinner could wait twenty minutes, but her muse had itchy palms.

A violent knock rattled her door.

"Izzy?"

"Yes, Hazel?"

"Somebody put a box on the porch. Can I get it?"

Izzy poked her threading needle into her tray

and stood, stretching her arms above her head. She felt her spine pop like bubble wrap as she reached high.

"Hang on, I'll come with you."

"But you'll take ages!"

Izzy grinned as she crossed the room and opened the door. "Ages?"

"Oh good, that was very quick." Hazel nodded approvingly. She was such a trip.

Hand-in-hand they moved to the door and opened it. Autumn light spilled across the kauri floorboards, and as established by Hazel, a medium sized box covered in 'Fragile' stickers sat on the doorstep.

"Can I open it?" Hazel asked in hushed reverence.

Izzy shot her an amused look. "Let's see who it's for first. It's probably for Uncle Zac, so we'll have to wait for him to get home."

"That's not fair–" Hazel started, but Izzy gave her a stern look, so she settled for pouting instead.

Izzy picked up the box, careful to hold it upright, and moved inside with it.

"Can you get the kitchen door for me please, sweetie?"

Hazel's bare feet slap-slapped on the floor as she scampered ahead, opening the door that led to the kitchen and living area, where Otis sprawled on the couch watching Lego creation videos on Zac's massive TV.

"Who's that for?" he asked, jumping to his feet and joining them in the kitchen area as Izzy placed the box on the counter and checked the address sticker.

"It's for me," she replied, puzzled. Maybe Nicky,

her best friend in London, had sent her a care package.

But when she sliced the box open using a steak knife – kids safely out of the way – it wasn't stuffed full of Minstrels and toffee popcorn. Instead, packed in acres of shredded tissue were six perfect, full-sized jars of dulce de leche, all the perfect shade of golden brown.

"Oh my gosh," she murmured, hefting one out of its packaging. It was larger than the jars she'd made room for in her single suitcase. She checked the sender details, her breath stuttering from her when she clocked the name of the small village in Uruguay where she'd bought her original jars.

"What is it?" Hazel demanded, sifting through the shredded tissue." Is it gold?"

"It's better than gold," Izzy assured her. Worth more too, if her memory of the farm's international shipping rates was correct.

"Nothing is better than gold," the little dark-haired mercenary at her elbow declared.

"Well, we can eat this," Izzy told her. "We can't do that with gold. Have you ever had breakfast for dinner?"

Hazel remained suspicious, eyeing the jar with scepticism as Izzy whipped up a batch of French toast. She didn't hesitate cracking open the lid of a jar to drizzle sweet caramelly satisfaction over the warm bread, not when she had five –*five!*– more to use. Heaven was a well-stocked dulce de leche supply.

And French Toast. Otis and Hazel's eyes widened in pleasure as they scarfed down the first batch of toast and Izzy was prepping another batch when Zac stomped up the stairs from the garage.

Their eyes met amid the kids' chorus of greetings, holding for a long moment before Zac's gaze dropped to the jar in her hands. Something passed over his face, a flicker of satisfaction or guilt, perhaps a combination of the two, before he raised his eyes to hers again.

Izzy turned down the burner and plopped the jar on the counter as she moved towards him. He hadn't taken the last stair yet, and the height difference put them eye-to-eye. This close, she could see him swallow, his Adam's apple bobbing under the delicate skin of his throat.

"It's from you?"

It was a ridiculous question, there was nobody else the package could be from, but she asked it anyway, needing the confirmation. Needing to know her heart wasn't thrashing against her ribcage for no good reason.

Zac jerked his head once, a stiff nod.

"Thank you."

He swallowed again, with a shrug. "I ate yours."

"It was fine. I overreacted. I–" she motioned behind her to where the box still sat on the counter, "–I didn't expect you to replace it. It means a lot."

Zac's grey eyes slid away. "You should have everything you want," he told the wall next to her.

And Izzy, who'd left home at seventeen because the things she wanted couldn't be heard above the noise of everyone telling her what she needed, felt a little piece of herself crack open. Silver light streamed in to warm the dark spot in her chest she'd papier-mâché'd over with frequent flyer miles and magazine worthy photos to block out the hurt of never being seen, never being wanted, never being known for herself, merely as an extension of another Holt.

*Steve's daughter. Linda's youngest. Cara's sister.* And all the messy, sour things that came with those labels, buried under a fine layer of good manners and country geniality that wasn't quite enough to hide the vitriol in her sister's eyes when she looked at their father, or the way her mother retired to bed too early some nights and how nobody ever, ever actually *told* Izzy anything but somehow had her life marked out like a stage role. Hit this spot and turn right for university. Pause here for kids and marriage. Don't drop the smile until you're in the wings. And the lingering sense of disappointment when she hadn't played her part, when she'd smeared off the facade of perfection they'd painted her with and exited stage left on a 747 bound for the other side of the world, returning only for brief guest appearances since.

"Well," she managed after a second. "Come get some on French toast. It'll change your life."

He shook his head. "It's for you."

The silver light pulsed again, darker, the colour of Zac's eyes and Izzy pushed that thought down until she could take it out and examine it later in private.

"I'm sharing," she insisted. She reached for his hand but he moved, her hand passing across empty air instead, the silver light fading to a dull grey shadow as Zac took the final stair and moved past her.

"I need a shower," he mumbled. "Maybe after." He disappeared through the door to the hallway, leaving Izzy in a kitchen that smelled like caramel, butter, and an overwhelming sweetness that had nothing to do with dinner.

~

HE'D FORGOTTEN about the dulce.

He didn't regret buying it. It obviously meant a lot to Izzy and he certainly had enough money to replace the jar he and the kids had eaten, but he hadn't been prepared for her reaction. For the gratitude in her brown eyes or the way they shined at him like he'd hung the moon instead of tapping his credit card details into his phone after a night stalking her socials. And honestly, what he'd done in the shower after an hour of watching Izzy's life scroll past in little square pictures and videos made him pretty ashamed of the whole scenario.

But he'd spent half the day talking himself firmly out of the inconvenient lust riding his nerve edge, listing off the ways that letting his attraction to his nanny could go wrong – *spoiler alert, all of them* – so coming in and being hit with the full force of Izzy's sunshine charm had knocked his defences sideways. He tossed his gym bag on the floor of his room and flopped on his bed. He didn't need a shower – not a hot one anyway – he'd had one at the stadium before he came home. For the remainder of practice he'd managed to pull his head out of his arse, thank God, and had been focused during their Wednesday weights session and game tape viewing. Enough that Harro had stopped side eyeing him, at least, but not enough for him to relax. He'd relaxed exactly twice since he was fourteen. The first time was when he moved to Auckland on a contract with the Knights after years of coming up through the

South Island development squads. He'd gone out, partied as much as a man who didn't drink could, met girls, fucked a few of them, stayed up late and spent off-training days lazing around the city, exploring the hidden gems it had to offer, his shoulders free of the tension that had ridden him for years knowing he was merely a phone call, and a few hours drive, from the shitshow that was his father's life if something went wrong.

Then it had all gone wrong. Frances had called him, sobbing, and told him she was pregnant. All the lightness that had buoyed him since setting foot off the plane in Auckland disappeared in an instant, buried under the rockfall of that revelation. Everything became about Frances, about getting her to the city, sorting a place for her to live, and then about Otis a few months later. There had been a nice little window after she got married and Hazel arrived, but then her husband had died and it was back into the trenches for them both.

The second time... the second time had been merely a blip, a few stolen minutes that sang of escape and release. He was wiser when the second time rolled around; he knew it wouldn't last, knew by then he'd never truly be free from his responsibilities, but for a tiny stretch of the night he'd fallen into a woman with golden hair and whisky brown eyes and the reprieve had been glorious.

Until he fucked it up. Until he'd kept fucking it up, because now that same woman lived across the hallway from him and looked at him in a way that made his stomach hurt for ordering dairy products from Central America, and he couldn't do a damn thing about it. Her life was overseas. His life was here. And even if some miracle occurred and she decided to stay, his career was up in the air and so was any sense of stability he could offer. Hell, he could barely keep his head above water with his family, and he'd been trying to navigate that for decades. A relationship with a woman, with Izzy, was out of the question.

Not to mention, Izzy was actively dating other people like it was a competitive sport. That slimy bastard – he was assuming – had secured a second date. Meanwhile, Zac could barely make eye contact with her for more than three seconds without his vision blurring at the edges.

He lay like that for a while, staring at the ceiling, letting the maelstrom of feelings whirl inside him. He tried reading, scrolled his phone, but Izzy niggled in the back of his mind, a constant presence.

"Zac?"

There was a soft knock at his door.

"Come in."

The door swung open, and she was there, bathed in the light from the hallway.

"Are you – woah!" Izzy stopped suddenly inside his doorframe and stared at him.

"What's wrong?"

She didn't answer and Zac's chest clutched. He sat up. "Izzy?"

She shook her head as if coming out of a trance. "Sorry. Sorry. You wear glasses?"

"What?" Zac reached up and pushed the frames of his reading glasses further up his nose. "I have them for reading, yeah."

"Interesting," she said faintly.

"I'm okay to drive without them," he hurried to assure her. Maybe she was worried about the fact that she'd been in a car with him and his presbyopia. "I don't need them for day-to-day stuff, only for reading."

"Sure," Izzy said. "That makes sense."

Zac frowned. "Are you okay? Is everything okay with the kids?"

"What? Oh. Yeah. The kids wanted to say goodnight to you. They've had their baths."

"Sweet as." Zac heaved himself off the bed, barely noticing the sway of Izzy's hips in skin-tight leggings as he trailed her along the hall.

Fine. He noticed. Her arse was perfection, but he wouldn't do anything about it.

The kids were in their bedrooms, and he swerved into Otis's first as Izzy continued to Hazel's.

"What's up, mate? All ready for bed?"

"Yes, but Uncle Zac, look at this!"

Zac endured a ten minute reenactment of Lego Mario beating Lego Bowser on an obstacle course Otis had constructed on his bedside table, before he could escape.

He made his way across to Hazel's room, where Izzy was finishing up an illustrated children's biography of Rosa Parks. Dolly Parton, David Attenborough and Muhammad Ali's books were spread across her unicorn comforter too.

"I love these books." Izzy smiled up at him from the floor by Hazel's bed. "My last family in London had them too. They're the best for kids."

Zac nodded. "I bought the set when Hazel was born, but they keep coming out with new ones. Did you like that one?" he asked Hazel, who nodded enthusiastically.

"Yes! Brown people are not allowed on buses!"

Zac burst out laughing.

"What? No!" Izzy looked horrified. "That's the way things used to be in some parts of the United States, but thanks to the important work of people like Rosa Parks, now everyone can use the buses."

"Ohhhh," Hazel said. "That's fair."

"Yes, yes, it is." His nanny shot him a dark look and Zac kept his gaze firmly on the ceiling. He couldn't stop the grin tugging at the corners of his mouth though. *Jesus.*

He waited while Izzy wished Hazel goodnight, watching as his niece wrapped her arms around Izzy's neck and squeezed. Then as Izzy bade goodnight to Turtle and Puppy and Snow Leopard, Hazel's very imaginatively named stuffed animals. Then Izzy slipped past him, and Hazel reached her little arms up sleepily.

"Hug?"

"High five, sweetheart." Zac tapped each of her palms lightly with his own, then repeated the process on two plush paws and a flipper.

He promised to return in five minutes to check on her, turned to go and saw Izzy watching him from the doorway.

"What?" he asked softly as he approached.

"I'm starting to work you out," she murmured as she moved towards the kitchen.

Zac pulled Hazel's door closed and followed, trepidation in his gut.

"What do you mean, work me out?"

"You're an interesting man, Zac Fearon."

"No, I'm not."

"A riddle, shrouded in an enigma, wrapped inside a grumpy bastard," she continued as if he hadn't spoken. "But I think I've got it now."

"Got what?"

He didn't want to know what she thought, but he couldn't stop the words.

Izzy reached out towards his face and he flinched away from her hand.

"There it is," she said. "How long has it been?"

"Since what?"

"Since you let someone touch you."

Goosebumps broke out on Zac's skin.

"I touch people," he croaked.

"You do." Izzy looked him dead in the eye and he got that fuzzy sensation at the edges again, except this time it was laced with panic. "But you don't let them touch *you*."

He pushed the panic aside. "I play a full contact sport for a living. People touch me all the time. I've had more grown men on top of me than you have." The bluster in his words made them aggressive.

"Debatable," Izzy said lightly, her dark eyes searching his. "But that's a violent touch, or a celebratory touch if you score. Not a kind touch. Not a touch from someone who cares about you."

"I don't–" Zac cleared his throat. "You don't know what you're talking about."

"I know that when I reached for you, you moved your hand. I thought it was me, that you didn't want to touch me, but then Hazel asked for a hug and you didn't give it to her. You love Hazel. Anyone with eyes can see it. She's part of the fabric of your world, and you'd do anything for her. But you didn't do that."

In the soft light of his own living room, Zac felt as if he was drowning. He swallowed rapidly, clamouring for air while rocks settled in his stomach, hard and heavy. The thrum of his pulse filled his ears and he breathed through his nose.

"Hey, hey, hey." Izzy was beside him in an instant. Not touching him, though her hand hovered in the air above his arm. "It's okay, Zac. You don't have to let anyone touch you. Not if you don't want to. I won't force you into some kind of weird hugging party if that's what you're worried about."

"It's not," he croaked out. "I hadn't realised."

"You hadn't realised you don't let people touch you?"

"Yeah." Thousands of images flashed through his mind, tiny snapshots of moments in his life. There were some that stood out – Frances hugging him on her wedding day, baby Otis grasping his thumb, but mostly he could filter through them and see she was right. He touched people, but usually only when he had to. The instances with Frances and the kids touching him were few.

"Even Michaela," he said wonderingly, as their encounters made their way through the reel in his mind.

"Michaela doesn't touch you?"

"Kind of. A little, but more as a response to me touching her. She doesn't initiate it."

It should have felt strange, talking about his experiences with a sex worker to this gorgeous woman who had him fucked up mind and body over her, but it didn't. Izzy had been nothing but respectful of Michaela when they'd met and when he'd mentioned her later that day, and now that he'd brought up that dynamic between them, she only looked curious.

"Maybe one of the benefits of that arrangement was that you could negotiate touch as part of sex without having to make yourself vulnerable," Izzy suggested and Zac was fucking near winded.

"Jesus, Isabel," he grumbled, running a hand through his hair. His chest felt like a goddamned Tilt-o-Whirl and she thought it was the time for a psychoanalytical breakthrough? "Or maybe I just enjoyed fucking her."

He was being a dick, red flags flying through his mind screaming *Danger! Danger!* but she ignored the jab, carrying on as if she hadn't decimated his psyche and left the pieces scattered across his living room like cookie crumbs.

"Maybe," she agreed cheerily. Then, "Do you want to try with me?"

"Fucking?"

Izzy gave him a long suffering look. "Touching. You don't have to, of course, but I'm more than happy to try if you want to give it a go."

He didn't want to give it a go, but more than that, he didn't want to be a broken man who couldn't let his niece and nephew touch him, so he shrugged and tipped his chin in reluctant agreement.

Izzy sat down on the couch and patted the cushion next to her. Zac sat awkwardly, one knee jiggling hard enough to vibrate the couch.

"Is there anywhere you're uncomfortable with me touching you?"

*Everywhere.* "No."

"Okay. How about your arm?"

"Arm's fine."

Izzy's touch to Zac's forearm was feather-light, but it felt like fire, a hot pulsing brand that took all his focus even as he tried not to think about it.

"How's that?"

"S'okay."

"You're doing great." She spread her fingers a little wider, dragging the pads of her fingertips further across the surface of his skin and Zac grit his teeth.

"When was the last time an adult touched you when it wasn't sex or sports?"

"Frances' wedding. She hugged me. So did my mum."

"Was it a nice wedding?"

"Yeah. It was pretty small."

"Oh?"

"Ben was an only child, so it was his parents, our mum, Otis and a couple of friends each. They had it at the Botanic Gardens and we went for lunch afterwards."

He'd paid for the whole thing, including the pretty white sundress Frances had picked out to wear, and it hadn't even taken a week's salary.

"That sounds really lovely."

Zac grunted. "They were happy with it. Frances was already pregnant with Hazel and she was exhausted so they wanted to keep it easy."

"Your dad wasn't there?"

Rage burned through Zac's veins the way it did whenever his father came up. "Frances wanted to invite him, but nobody could find him."

"What do you mean 'find'?"

"He's an alcoholic. Goes on benders for weeks, months sometimes. In and out of rehab and court for the dumb shit he does when he's pissed. Shows up at Mum's now and again, full of sob stories and promises, and she falls for it every time. The longest he's stayed sober my whole life is a year and a half. Then he took off with my piggy bank one Anzac Day and we didn't see him again until Christmas. "

"How old were you when that happened?"

"Eight."

Izzy exhaled heavily beside him. "Wow."

"Yeah."

A pause. Then...

"Was he ever violent?"

Zac let out a shuddering breath. "Sometimes. Only to me though, thank God. He left Mum and Frances alone."

"Oh, honey." Izzy's voice dripped with sadness. "You poor thing."

She rubbed his shoulder, and it was then he noticed her hand had moved slowly up his arm while he spoke. It didn't feel heavy now, not when he'd spilled all his ugly past in front of them. It felt like her touch held him together, as if he was drawing strength from the gentle press of her skin to his.

He pressed his hand to hers, holding it against his shoulder, keeping him grounded.

"I'm okay. I got out. I got Frances out, too. My mum, she's still there. She's got a good job. I paid off the house, but she won't leave Motueka, won't leave *him*. And it makes me sick. I love my mother, but I don't respect her. For not choosing us over him. For not choosing herself. I haven't told her Frances is gone, because there's a good chance she'd say she can't come, that she needs to be there for Dad through his latest fuckup instead of being here for these incredible kids she barely even knows."

By the time he finished, he was breathing heavily, the heat of Izzy's gaze on him prickling like a rash, all of him exposed and vulnerable under the weight of her stare.

"You," she said slowly, "are so much more than I imagined. You're incredible."

He shook her words off. "That's nothing. Kids all over this country have it worse than I did every day."

"I'm not talking about kids all over this country. I'm talking about you. You, Zac Fearon." She ran her other hand across the back of his neck and Zac suppressed a shiver. It felt way too good while they talked about his shitty childhood and even shittier father. "You are kind, generous, and caring. And it's a damn shame you had it so rough growing up, but what you've done since you left? Taking care of your sister, Otis and Hazel? You're a role model, and it's got nothing to do with how you play sport."

He turned to look at her, to gauge her honesty. There was no trace of artifice in the way she looked at him, no wry twist of her mouth. She stared straight at him, honest and kind, and in that moment with her arms around him Zac felt a groundswell of tangled emotions. Gratitude and grief and sexual attraction warred within him, wrapping a tight band around his chest that caused his breath to come in jagged jerks and his fingers to tighten on Izzy's.

"You're touching me," he managed eventually. "Both hands."

She nodded slowly, brown eyes warm. "I am."

"Feels nice."

"Yeah?" She smiled when he nodded. "I'm glad. It feels good to help you feel good."

That was Izzy in a nutshell, wasn't it? Chalmers had told him as much. She was a fixer, a helper. Her hands on him were nothing more than her trying to Band-Aid the touch aversion he'd inadvertently developed as some kind of response to childhood trauma. Zac had done enough research into armchair psychology back when he'd thought there might be a chance he could help his father recover from his addiction to recognise that.

Still... It didn't hurt to ask.

"Can I touch you?"

Izzy swallowed. "Sure."

Slowly, he lifted one hand and tucked a few wispy strands of hair that had fallen free of her ponytail behind her ear. They felt like silk and he let his fingers travel further, tracing the baby-soft lobe of her ear, the vein that ran down her neck. He ran his thumb over the delicate swell of her collarbone and followed it towards her shoulder.

"You feel nice, too."

Izzy's eyes drifted shut. "I do?"

"Uh huh. Really nice." Zac dipped his head and brushed his lips against her cheek.

Her eyes fluttered open, heavy with lust, and Zac's pulse pounded in response. Her gaze stoked the desire in his veins, turning it thick and hot, and he stiffened in his shorts.

"God, you're beautiful." He breathed the thought aloud and the smile she gave him in return was a gift, soft and sweet, and he'd give his left nut to see her smile like that at him every day of his life.

"Uncle Zac?"

*Fuck.*

"Yeah, mate?" He dropped his hands from Izzy and moved around to look over the back of the couch. Hazel stood there, sleepy-eyed, in her purple dinosaur pyjamas.

"Has it been five minutes yet?"

Shit, he'd told her he'd check on her.

"It has. Do you want me to tuck you in?"

She nodded, dark hair all mussed, then turned and stumbled back towards the bedrooms.

Zac put his hands on his hips and exhaled heavily. "That can't happen again," he told the carpet.

Izzy didn't say anything.

"I told her I'd come back and I didn't. These kids need to rely on me. They need that stability. You're leaving soon. We can't do this to them."

"They don't have to know, Zac. We're hardly going to be boning on the hallway floor."

Frustration gnawed at Zac. "What do you think Hazel would have seen if she'd come in here five minutes from now, Izzy? You think it would have been PG-rated cheek kisses then? No." He shook his head. "The things I want to do to you... I can't think about them while the kids are here. They are my priority."

"Sure." He closed his eyes against the ice of Izzy's clipped voice. How many ways could he fuck up with this woman? "That makes sense. I'm going to turn in. I'll see you in the morning."

Zac steeled himself for another touch as she walked towards him, but she gave him a wide berth, and when she disappeared down the hall, every beat of his heart tempted him to follow her to her bedroom and wrap her in his arms until she could see his point of view. But she was leaving anyway, so he made his way to Hazel's room and when she asked for a hug this time he let her pull him down and squash his face against her soft, round cheek, because he'd be damned if these kids would grow up to be a total emotional fuck up like he had.

## CHAPTER 9

There were some things a man could not avoid. The crack of his adolescent voice in class. His first grey hair. And in the case of professional athletes, the stag do of his teammate.

A code of honour deeper than his dislike of crowds had spurred Zac to shower, shave, pull on a clean black Henley and pressed grey trousers and thank Mrs Purdy a third time for offering to watch Otis and Hazel for the night. Cara was holding her hens party on the same day and Izzy had disappeared that morning with three bottles of champagne and a feather boa sticking out of her backpack. He shuddered to think of the shenanigans likely to occur with both Holt girls loose on the town, and armed with penis straws.

He'd managed to skip the golfing and go-karts portion of the event, claiming familial duties, but there was no way he could get out of dinner and drinks with the team while they celebrated their captain's upcoming nuptials.

Dinner was sure to be decent. Manu had organised it and the man took his food seriously. He'd booked a private room at a downtown restaurant that specialised in farm-to-table dining and had won numerous awards for its steak and lamb dishes.

Zac turned his coat collar up and tucked his chin down as he stepped off the Devonport ferry at the downtown Auckland ferry dock, weaving his way through the people sitting outdoors at the harbourside bars and shops soaking in the early evening sun. The restaurant was easily within walking distance and the last thing he needed was to be accosted by fans with a few drinks in them, offering tips and constructive commentary on the Knights' game plan. He needn't have worried. Everyone was too busy making the most of the last few weekends before Daylight Savings ended and plunged them all into months of darkness to pay attention to him, and he reached the restaurant precisely on time.

Only to discover he was extremely, laughably late to the party.

Finn and Cara's decision to hold their wedding during the league season had obviously required some delicate scheduling, not least the fact that their hen and stag dos were held on a Monday night, a mere three days before the ceremony itself. The team, it seemed, had taken to the short reprieve of their unofficial, unspoken season-long ban on heavy partying with a vengeance. Even Manu, who never so much as looked at a second beer or a dessert plate from New Year's to their final game, was three sheets to the wind, tie looped around his head like Rambo, holding an entire chocolate cheesecake in one hand and a fork in the other as he balanced upright on a chair and declared a toast to Finn.

The other men, in similarly fashionable states, roared their agreement, beer bottles and whisky glasses clinking as they were enthusiastically shunted together in the middle of the long table.

*Jesus.*

"Can I grab a Sprite, please?" Zac snagged a passing waiter. "And a menu?"

"Set menu," the other man replied. "I'll be back with your drink in a minute," he called over his shoulder as he zipped away. Zac didn't blame him. Rangi and Matt had reputations as big partiers that they'd certainly earned, but the rest of the team were more likely to cut loose at someone's house, if at all. With the exception of their Grand Final win two years ago, where the celebration had lasted three days, it was incredibly rare for Auckland service workers to be faced with tables of huge league players demanding drinks and food en masse.

"Zac!" Finn called. "Over here!" He waved enthusiastically, loose and gangly, like a baby octopus.

His proclamation garnered the attention of the other players, and Zac made his way to the table to a chorus of cheers and greetings.

"Hey, man." He shook Finn's hand and the other man grinned loopily up at him from under a blonde Marilyn Monroe wig. "Congratulations."

"Thanks." Finn beamed. "I can't wait. You want a drink? I got some juice for you." He gestured to a pitcher of orange juice sitting untouched in the middle of the long table, surrounded by empty beer bottles and wine glasses.

Zac was surprised, and a little touched. He didn't make a big deal about the fact that he didn't drink and neither did the team, but he certainly wasn't used to having someone preorder beverages to make sure his needs were accommodated.

He took a seat next to Finn and poured himself a glass as the bread baskets arrived. With the exception of Manu, who'd seemingly magicked his cheesecake out of thin air, the team fell on them with fervour.

"Oh my heavens," Zac heard behind him. It was the waiter from when he'd walked in, talking to a waitress while he watched the team devour dinner rolls. "Run to the kitchen and bring out every bread roll we've got. And tell the chef to start cooking the mains immediately. Pasta. Lots of pasta."

Zac bit back a smile as he turned his attention to his own dinner roll. He could appreciate the concern in the other man's eyes, but as much as the stench of whisky stung his nostrils, as glassy-eyed as legendarily stoic loose forward Victor Hewitt looked as he ripped apart a roll with his teeth, he wasn't worried. Usually, being with drunk people wound him up, tension prickling across his shoulders and coiling in his muscles as he waited for the other shoe to drop. For the smiles to fade to scowls, slurred declarations of love and friendship to sink into personal attacks that scarred the recipient's psyche. For the celebratory clink of glassware to turn to crashes against concrete floors, calls for taxis and visibly upset bar staff. The Knights might be messy tonight, but there was an undercurrent of camaraderie to it all. Nobody brought any shit to the table that would ruin this night for Finn.

"We're meeting up with the girls later," Finn yelled in his ear as platters of steaming pasta appeared in front of them. "Cara messaged me and told me where they are."

Zac paused. The idea of seeing Izzy in all her extroverted glory while he hid in the corner with a soft drink was not an appealing one.

"I might not be able to make that."

"Fearon." Chalmers slapped a hand on his shoulder and stared into his eyes intensely. "It's my stag do. You're making it."

That was that then.

Zac was still apprehensive an hour later when the team arrived at a nondescript door off Queen Street and were nodded through by an unsmiling bouncer.

They made their way up the stairs, following the sounds of music. The karaoke bar was small but luxurious, hanging ferns and potted palms dotted the space and large squashy velvet chairs clustered around tables where candles flickered, creating low, intimate light. The stage was lit better, a canopy of fairy lights creating the illusion of stars in front of a glitter backdrop. A classy location to undertake what Zac had always sort of considered a gauche act.

He hadn't seen Izzy do it, though.

When they walked in, she was on the stage directly to his left, her and Cara belting out a song with a distinctly country twang to it, looking hotter than hell in a black tank top and sequin miniskirt, red cowboy boots on her feet. Her hair was down and wild, eyes shining as she held up a glass in one hand and declared that someone named Earl had to... was that *die*?

"Finnegan!" Cara's voice echoed in the room as she spotted them and she flung herself off the stage into her fiancé's waiting arms, wrapping her legs around his waist and proceeding to pash him into the beginning of next week. Finn turned and put her against the wall as they made out like horny teens, the rest of the team carefully averting their eyes as they filed in and made their way to the bar or took seats with Cara's friends.

"Zac!"

He turned.

Izzy was off the stage, making her way towards him. She threw her arms around him as she approached and he let her, let her pull him in against the warm press of her body. Whatever emotional barriers he had to touch were decimated in the face of her open smile, her genuine happiness at seeing him. He was so glad she'd insisted they practise touching, because without it he might never have had this moment, this perfect instant where her arms wrapped around him, her cheek against his shoulder, surrounded by the scent of... was that his shower gel? On her?

"I'm so glad you came," she said, pulling back. This close, he could see the smattering of freckles on her nose, the smudge of makeup under her shining eyes. She looked like heaven.

"Couldn't not," he shrugged. "Finn deserves it."

"He does." She glanced warmly at her future brother-in-law and promptly groaned. "Get a room, you losers," she hollered towards the entwined pair. Without pausing, Cara gave her the middle finger above Finn's head.

"Young love, huh?" Izzy grinned and tugged him towards the bar. "You want a drink?"

"Just Sprite thanks." The sugar crash would kill him later, but it might be worth it.

He waited while Izzy ordered their drinks, surprised when she got the same as him.

"You're not drinking?"

She shrugged. "I finished with the wines a couple of hours ago. The last thing I need is a hangover when I'm trying to hustle the kids out the door for school tomorrow."

"I already asked Mrs Purdy if she could do that in the morning."

"You did?" Surprise passed over her face. "But it's my job."

Zac shrugged. "You deserve a sleep-in the day after your sister's hens do." Honestly, it hadn't occurred to him that she'd be in any state to get the kids ready. God knows, his dad never had been the morning after a night out, and with his mum working around the clock it had usually fallen to Zac to get himself and Frances out the door. He'd been doing it regularly by the time he was seven. There were benefits to small-town living with their school only a block away. When he'd gone to boarding school he'd messaged Frances every morning to make sure she was awake in time. Their parents' inaction was no reason to miss out on her education. He had sports, but he was convinced it was Frances's brain that would get her out of Motueka. It hadn't been, though. It had been him, organising flights and a place for her to stay and a midwife when some fuckwit had knocked her up, right before her final school exams but she'd somehow still passed with distinction even while spewing her ring out three times a day.

The mantle of responsibility hung like an anvil around his neck and he frowned into his soda. He'd failed her. Failed them.

"Hey." A soft hand touched his. "Where did you go?"

"Just thinking."

"Well, your thoughts made you all frowny. I don't like it."

Despite himself, a glimmer of amusement crept through him. "You don't?"

"No. And there's only one way to turn that frown upside down, mister."

*Let me look down your shirt?*

"You need to sing."

Zac recoiled like she'd electrocuted him. "The fuck I do."

"The fuck you *do*," Izzy nodded solemnly. "It'll produce oxytocin. No offence, Zac, but I've never met anyone in more need of oxytocin than you."

He ignored that. "I can't sing."

"You're lying." Izzy sat back, and smugly took a sip of her drink. She tried to, anyway, but she missed her mouth with the straw. Zac watched her try to recover, his blood stirring when she used her tongue to guide the straw back towards her lush pink lips. "I heard you in the shower once. And–" she lifted a finger, like a TV lawyer in closing arguments, if they wore sequins and were adorable when tipsy "–you have a guitar."

"Everyone has a guitar."

"Nooo. Only people who play guitars have guitars. Everyone else sells theirs on TradeMe by the time they finish uni. Ergo, you play the guitar. Ergo, you sing."

"I'm not singing."

"Au contraire, mon frère."

Zac sighed. He did play guitar. He could probably even sing, but had no desire to do so in front of his workmates and Cara's friends, not even for the prettiest woman he'd ever known. He needed to distract her, because another two minutes of her looking at him with those liquid chocolate eyes and he'd be performing arias in his underwear if she asked.

"What else?"

"Hmm?"

"What else do you want? What will it take for you to drop the idea of me singing?"

Izzy's eyes lit up like a kid on Christmas morning. "Anything?"

Zac grimaced. "Almost." He was pretty fucking desperate to avoid any video footage of him mangling 'Bad Medicine', but he wasn't a fool. Eighties rock might end up being the lesser of two evils.

"Will you take photos with me in the photo booth?"

Zac scanned the room and saw it, an old fashioned booth with a red velvet curtain in the corner.

"That's it?"

"No, that's not it. You need to wear a costume and you need to smile. Like you mean it."

It was better than Bon Jovi.

"Fine."

"Yay!" She claimed his spare hand and used it to tug him across to the booth. They set their sodas on a small props table and Izzy riffled through the selection, coming up with an eyepatch and a pirate hat, which she gleefully jammed on his head.

"Is the hat not enough?" Zac asked it more out of habit than a genuine desire to avoid costuming. If Izzy asked him, he'd do it. He knew enough about himself to recognise that. He could only pray she never realised the power she held over him.

"Zac." She was looking up at him, eyes solemn in her heart-shaped face. "You were *born* to be a pirate. The first time I saw you, I thought, 'Holy shit, I want that man to ravish me.' That's what pirates *do*. You're a ravisher and ravishing pirates wear eye patches. Everyone knows that. It's lore. Sexy, sexy pirate lore."

His brain had stuttered on the ravishing part, but his body responded, plucking the costume eye patch from her hand and putting it on, even as blood tunnelled south, his dick thickening at the memory of Izzy glowing gold under the lights at Agatha's, at Izzy now, hot and sweet, the soft skin of her upper arm brushing against him as she settled a crown on her head. He followed her into the booth without a word, waiting as she pulled the curtain behind them.

"You promised to smile," she reminded him, as she wrapped an arm around his waist and he bit back a feral groan as her hair brushed his chin. He settled his hands on her waist, facing her as she twinkled towards the camera. He didn't move when the flash went off and she turned, the cotton of her tank catching on his thumb, riding up, bare skin pressing against his palm. It was the single most erotic experience of his life.

"You'd better have smi–" her voice trailed off as she looked at him. Brown eyes widened. "Zac?"

He swallowed hard, wrestling his lust down, down, down. "Smile, Isabel." The rasp of his voice sounded almost animalistic. "You wanted to take pictures. Let's take some pictures."

She blinked up at him, and he rubbed his thumb along the dip of her waist, the hem of her tank top at his wrist as he filled his hand with the warm curve of her. Back and forth with his thumb, a slow descent into madness. But if this was how he went, damn what a way to go. If his last lucid memory was of Isabel Holt's warm skin in his grip, her gaze caught in his, the hitch of her breath echoing in the space between them, he'd die a happy man.

The flash went off again.

"Zac?" Izzy's voice was unsteady.

"Yeah, baby?"

"What are we doing?"

He pressed his forehead to hers. This close he could see the ring of amber around the chocolate brown of her irises, could feel the brush of her breasts against his chest when she breathed.

"We're not doing anything. Not if you don't want to." Her eyes drifted closed as he rubbed his nose against hers. "It's your choice, Isabel. It's always been your choice."

*Flash.*

Her breath fanned his lips, sugary sweet from her drink, and he inhaled, sucking it into his lungs like it could ever be enough. Like the ghost of her air could sustain him if she said no and tore herself away, leaving his hands empty and useless when they were made to hold her.

She didn't say no.

Instead, she lifted herself onto her toes, her chest pressing more insistently against his, and he bit back a groan. Without opening her eyes, she tilted her head, her lips brushing his, one, twice, light as butterfly wings. A gossamer glance of what could be.

Zac froze. Waited.

Then, she kissed him again. Harder this time,

her tongue flicking out to trace the seam of his lips, and he was gone.

Desire roared through his blood like an inferno, uncontrolled heat in his veins as he gripped Izzy's hips and pulled her flush against him. Her other arm swung over his shoulder, fingers tunnelling through his hair as their tongues tangled. She tasted like sugar syrup, hot and sweet, familiar too, their mouths finding that perfect rhythm they'd had at Agatha's. The best kiss of his life until now, the one that had haunted him every time he'd caught a flash of blonde hair or a peek of collarbone in the last month. It was gone, wiped from his memory by this; the plush curve of Izzy's lips, the sweep of her tongue against his, the way her hand roamed over his arm and across his chest, stroking him through the soft cotton of his shirt. She scraped a nail over his nipple and sensation shot through him, wrenching his balls tight behind the iron bar of his cock.

*Flash.*

"Fuck," he gasped as he pulled his lips from hers. "I can't think for wanting you."

"Good," Izzy panted, eyes open now, and the heat he saw reflected at him in her gaze almost took him to his knees. "I don't want to think. I only want you."

He licked up the salty curve of her neck, loving the way she shivered in his arms, the way she ground the tight points of her nipples against his chest.

"You can have me." He pressed the words into the skin of her shoulder and groaned at the bite of her nails as she curled the fingers of her left hand into the back of his neck.

She moaned, the heady sound making his dick weep.

*Would she make those sounds with me inside her?*

Then her hand was on him, stroking him through the thin material of his dress pants. Heat clawed at his skin, ripping at his insides as he pressed into her touch, the ragged, uneven saw of his breath surrounding them like a living thing, powered by the electricity crackling between them.

"Want this," Izzy murmured, her eyes locked on her hand, the way it moved, tracing the shape of him, moulding her touch to his thickness. "Wanted it since Agatha's."

"It's yours," Zac vowed, bucking into her touch. "Stroke it, sit on it, lead me around by it. I'll write your fucking name on it if you want. Anything."

A wicked smile tugged at the corner of her mouth. "Anything?"

"Anything," he vowed. "You want it, I'll get it for you. Caramel from Uruguay, sushi from Tokyo, a date for your sister's wedding. If you want it, I'll make it happen."

Brown eyes met his. "You'd find me a date?"

"Fuck no," he bit out. "I'll be your fucking date. You want someone by your side at that thing? You'd better believe it's going to be me."

She looked at him for a long moment, then leaned forward and... sniffed?

She was smelling him?

"God, you smell good," she sighed, and then, as her hand continued to riff him up and down like her own personal joystick, she sank her teeth into the meat of his pec. Not a full bite. A tease. A promise.

And Zac lost all control.

He held his weight on one arm, palm flat against

the solid wall the photo booth was set up against, his other hand rucking up Izzy's tank top to reveal her gorgeous tits, propped up in a black lace bra like a sumptuous dinner buffet. His mouth watered with hunger and he yanked one of the cups down, almost weeping at the sight of her breast, small and high, topped with a light pink nipple. He dipped his head and sucked the bud into his mouth – no finesse, he was too far gone for that. He laved and sucked, working it with his tongue as Izzy cried out above him, one leg coming up to wrap around his hip as he ground his pelvis into hers.

Fuck, she was perfect, so good and tight and right against him. He bucked against her, catching her gasp in his mouth, reaching around to palm her arse, and she twitched with pleasure as he rubbed his cock against her.

"There," she gasped against his mouth, and satisfaction swelled inside him, hot and thick. He could get her there.

*A few more pumps.* He bent his knees, rock rock rocking his hips and she grabbed his hair, her fingers tight against his scalp, hot little moans leaving her body as he pulsed and ground against her through their clothes.

*She's almost there.*

He slid one hand up her thigh, under the hem of her skirt to grab her arse, dizzy when his hand only encountered bare skin. Venturing further, he found a thin scrap of lace between her cheeks and he tugged it tighter as he moved; revelling in the noise she made, a god among men with his mouth on hers and her thong in his fist.

*So close, so close, so close.*

"Well, what have we here?"

Izzy's surprised squeak was like cold water into his veins, dulling the heat. He pulled back, taking a second to adjust her top and bra to cover her exposed breast before he turned to snarl at the intruder.

"The fuck do you want?"

Matt Hollis grinned at him like he didn't have a care in the world. "I wanted a photo, but now I'm here, I'm in the mood for something else." His lascivious glance slid past Zac to Izzy. "What's up, Baby Holt?"

"You can call me Isabel." Izzy replied crisply from behind Zac.

"First name basis, huh? I like that." Hollis looked back at Zac. "Remember that time we shared a girl in the Under 20's?"

Shame flooded Zac, heating his neck.

"Jesus, you're a dick Hollis. Get out of here."

Zac shoved the other man out of the booth and turned back to Izzy, leaning against the solid wall of the photo booth, her skirt rucked up around the top of her lithe thigh, lazy posture at odds with the assessing gleam in her eyes. "I'm so sorry."

"Don't be." She grinned as she stood up, not even wobbling on the heels of her cowgirl boots.

"We were young and stupid, I don't really remember it..." He trailed off as she laughed, low and wicked.

"Are you embarrassed, Zachary? Why? Because you did it, or because he told me?" Her brown eyes twinkled with delight as she adjusted her crooked crown. "Oh my sweet, summer child. You're not the only person in this photo booth who's had a threesome."

He paused, stunned, and she gave him a pat on

the cheek as she moved past him and through the curtain, leaving him agonisingly hard and painfully alone.

He waited until his erection had subsided – the sound of someone butchering Lady Gaga on stage helped – and then made his way to the bar, snagging the pictures out of the booth and tucking them in his pocket without looking at them. Matt leaned against the polished wood, backlit by rainbow coloured bottles. Zac's former captain raised his glass in a toast to him, and anger kicked through Zac's blood. He stalked over to the other man.

"What the fuck was that?"

Matt's cocky smirk stayed in place, but his gaze flickered over Zac's face and Zac caught a glimpse of the boy he'd once known.

"What was what?"

"Come on, man," Zac ground out. "I know you're going through it, but that was a dick move."

Hollis's smile slipped a millimetre. "Hey, if you didn't want to get busted, you should have chosen a more private location."

Zac stared at him, letting Hollis see the full extent of his distaste until the other man shuffled his feet.

"Yeah, okay," Hollis muttered. "I'll find Izzy and apologise."

"You do that." Zac's voice was firm enough that he caught the bartender watching them warily out of the corner of his eye. "I don't get it, Hollis. We grew up together. I've known you since Under 16's. When I got this contract, I was actually excited to play with you again. I'm sorry about Lauren, I really am." Matt's face fell, devastation painting his handsome features, and Zac paused, glancing towards the bar, giving him some privacy. When he looked back, Matt's cocky mask was back in place, the only trace of his hurt in the weary lines of his eyes "But this shit is beneath you. The drinking, the clubs. You're a good man under all that bullshit. Get your head out of your arse before there's nobody else who sees it except me, because after that stunt, I'm losing patience with you myself."

Zac turned to go, and Hollis stopped him with a hand on his arm.

"I'm sorry," Zac's former captain said tightly. "I mean it."

"I know you do," Zac said. "But now you have to show me." He shook the other man's hand off, and headed into the crowd to find his nanny.

"I LOVE HER SO MUCH," Finn was saying, a goofy grin plastered all over his Prince Charming face. A face that was covered in eighty dollar lipstick. A fact Izzy was sharply aware of, because it was her eighty dollar lipstick that Cara had borrowed and now Izzy was going to have to tell her to keep it because she'd never be able to wear it again without remembering her sister being dry humped against a wall in a karaoke bar.

Not that Izzy was one to be casting aspersions about what went on against the walls of this karaoke bar. She only hoped she hadn't left a watermark on the drywall behind the photo booth.

Fuck, Zac Fearon could pseudo-fuck. It didn't seem fair. He had that face, and secret Hot Guy Glasses, and he was nice to kids and old people, and now she knew for sure he could get her off without removing her knickers. The facets of the man were endless and superhuman.

It was like finding out Clark Kent was a porn star.

"Of course you do, sweetie," she assured Finn. "She loves you too."

"Yeah," her future brother-in-law sighed happily, slumping against the bar and sloshing water all over himself. "I'm so lucky."

Luck didn't have much to do with it, in Izzy's opinion. Finn was gorgeous, kind, and had been arse-over-tit in love with Cara since day one, a fact everyone except her sister had been painfully aware of. Perseverance had more of a stake in their relationship than fairy dust and four leaf clovers, but hey, if it made Finn happy to think so...

"There you are," a voice growled beside her and she turned to see her own partner in wall-crimes glowering down at her.

"Here I am," she replied lightly, toasting him with her soda.

"It's Zac! Hey Zac!" Finn threw an arm around the taller man's shoulders, and Zac froze, panic flickering across his features.

Energy zipped through Izzy. "Are you okay?" She asked in a low voice, moving to slip under Finn's other tree-trunk arm, gently trying to pull the Knights captain's weight onto herself.

"Fine," Zac gritted through his teeth, obviously lying. Tension bracketed his lips, which pressed together in a thin line. His dark eyes were hard as he stared past Finn's sandy blond curls, emotionally as removed as he could be from the drape of his teammate across him.

"Come here, Finn," Izzy pulled him harder, relief

sweeping over her as he turned, his body separating from Zac's. "I'll take you to find Cara."

"Cara?"

"That's right, buddy. Let's go find her and you can flop all over her like a hundred kilo fish instead. Zac doesn't need that shit."

"Okay," Finn nodded placidly. "I like laying all over Cara."

"Sweet Jesus, my brain," Izzy muttered. Somehow Finn's near-obsession with her sister had seemed sweeter from the other side of the globe, free from his drunken declarations and the bereavement of losing her favourite Lisa Elridge lippy to their love. "Did you drive here?" she asked Zac, who blinked at her like he was coming out of a coma and gave a short shake of his head.

"Ferried."

"Go outside and order a car, yeah? I'll be there in a sec."

He seemed to hesitate, and she wished he wouldn't, because Chalmers weighed a fucking ton.

"You want to leave?"

"God yeah. Let me drop this lug off with his fiancée and I'll be right out." She clocked his furrowed brow and raised her own. "My treat. You wouldn't believe how much my boss overpays me."

"No. That's okay." He didn't smile, but why should he? Not as if he'd done anything nice this evening, like hump her halfway to heaven behind a thinly veiled partition. What was wrong with this guy? She'd let him off the hook for singing, she'd let him into her pants, she was physically dragging his trauma-ghost of Physical Touch Past across a crowded room and he couldn't even give her a token grin.

This was why women stayed single.

Izzy dropped Finn off with Cara, who looked delighted to see him and promptly went about wasting more of Izzy's lipstick.

"I'm gonna take off," Izzy had to shout in their general direction in order to be heard because a giant of a man with long blond hair was performing 'You Shook Me All Night Long' with all the fervour of Brian Johnson himself.

"'Kay," Cara yelled back when she came up for air. "Love you! Call me tomorrow!" She threw herself, lips-first, towards Finn, the blond guy slid across the stage on his knees to raucous applause, and Izzy hit the stairs.

Zac stood on the footpath outside, his breath hanging in tiny puffs around him. Light from the streetlight overhead shone gold in his hair as he stared at the dark buildings across the street, hands in his pockets.

He turned as she approached.

"Hey."

"Hi. Did you order a car?" Izzy glanced up the street behind them but it was dark.

He nodded. "It'll be here in five minutes. I needed a moment."

"From when Finn hugged you?"

"From everything." His dark brows drew together and he looked down, scuffing one booted foot against the concrete. "It's the smell more than anything, you know? The touching, I freeze with that sometimes, but I can make it through. The smell of rum about takes me out at the knees. He came at me and I just wasn't expecting it. Finn normally drinks beer. I can cope with beer. I don't love it, but it doesn't make me feel like I'm going to toss my cookies all over the floor."

He pulled a hand out of his pocket and ran it through his hair impatiently.

"I hate this. I hate that I can't do something simple like go out with my team without my fucking father in my head ruining it."

Izzy reached out instinctively and grabbed his hand, linking their fingers together. "I'm sorry you see it like that," she said softly. "For what it's worth, I think you're incredibly brave."

He shot her an incredulous look and her heart squeezed in her chest. "I do," she insisted. "It must be so difficult to navigate your job and the culture around it when it comes to your history with alcohol. You could have stayed home tonight, but you didn't. You put yourself in a situation that was difficult for you to make someone else happy. That's bravery, Zac."

He blew out a stunted breath. "I don't feel brave. I feel weak."

"You're the strongest man I know." Her words left her on a whisper, twirling into the pocket of darkness between them and disappearing. She wouldn't have thought he heard them if not for the way his hand tightened around hers.

"Izzy..." he said, stepping closer. Her breath caught in her throat. She couldn't see his eyes with the way the shadows cut across the sharp lines of his face, but their proximity prickled awareness across her skin, goosebumps racing up her arms that had nothing to do with the cool night air.

He reached up and tucked a strand of her hair behind her ear. His fingertips were rough, and she turned her cheek so that they drifted down the line of her jaw, light as butterfly wings, an endless study in contrast. She wanted to kiss each fingertip, show them appreciation for the hard work they went through. Week after week, day after day, working to make money for his family, then coming home and taking care of them, building Legos with Otis, hunting for cool rocks in the backyard with Hazel, stacking wood for the Purdys. For a man who had a reputation as a grumpy bastard, he was marshmallow inside – achingly sweet - and she was suddenly struck with the urge to tell him.

*I see you.*

*I see you and I like you.*

Not for what he could do with a ball, not for what he could do for anyone else. For himself.

"Zac," she whispered the word against his palm. "I want–"

His phone beeped as car headlights swept across them and a tidy sedan pulled up nearby.

Zac dropped his hands like he was on fire. "That's our ride."

Izzy stumbled a couple of steps, dizzy from hormones and the sudden loss of heat. She caught herself – the cowboy boots had definitely been a better idea than heels – but Zac was already striding away, his long, lean back rigid as he stalked towards the car idling at the curb.

Izzy followed, disquiet mixing with vodka and Sprite in her stomach. She slipped in beside Zac in the backseat, sliding a glance towards him as she fastened her seatbelt but he was staring out his window. The car slid down towards the Queen Street intersection and turned to take them towards Devonport. Nobody spoke. Apparently, their driver was as adept at reading a mood as he was at reading maps.

Izzy had never been great at silence, and growing up in a house where nobody talked about their problems had given her even less interest in living that way, so as they glided across the Harbour Bridge she spoke.

"Are you regretting telling me that?"

"Telling you what?" Zac kept staring out the window.

Izzy rolled her eyes. "The stuff about how the smell affects you."

"No."

*Great.*

"Are you regretting the other bit then?"

"What other bit?"

"The bit where you got me off in a photobooth."

He looked at her then, with a long-suffering exasperation. Never had a man endured so much. In the front seat, the driver turned the radio up.

"No," Zac replied, stone faced. "I don't regret that at all."

Izzy shrugged. "I won't hold you to anything if you do. You don't need to be my date for the wedding. I can find someone else."

"Stop," Zac growled. His eyes flashed as they passed under streetlights. "I said I'm taking you."

"You don't seem very happy about it." She was needling him, but she couldn't help it. The only thing worse than no date would be a pity-date from her employer.

He let out a sound that was part-laugh, part-groan. "I don't do things I don't want to do, Isabel. That's true of your sister's wedding and it's true of the photobooth."

"Just checking."

"Well, stop. I don't want you following me around with puppy dog eyes for the next three days worried I'm going to change my mind."

"Okay." Her stomach still roiled in a way that had very little to do with the amount she'd drunk. People had a habit of changing their minds when she was involved, and Zac was hardly Mr Sociable. If he thought he could get away with faking a stomach virus the morning of the wedding and not having Chalmers hold it against him for life she had no doubt he'd do so.

"I mean it." Zac's low rumble reached across the backseat of the car to her. "I don't break my promises."

A shiver skated up her arms. "You haven't promised me anything, though."

"Haven't I?" His voice was still low, but silkier now. In the recesses of her mind she understood that this tenuous sense of false intimacy was simply a result of the darkness that surrounded them, a grown up version of the safe shroud that children whispered their secrets to one another in, across sleeping bags and candy wrappers. Vodka and dark backseats to soften the sharp edges of trust instead of mattresses dragged into living rooms and blanket forts. It didn't help her though when he continued. "Well, I am now. You're part of our family. I promise you, Izzy, you can count on me. I won't let you down."

eddings, Izzy decided, were one of life's greatest charades.

Oh, she was happy for Cara and Finn. Thrilled, even. But as much as they loved each other, surely even they were reconsidering the way they'd gone about things.

The champagne breakfast had been delicious, though Izzy had never met a champagne breakfast she didn't feel a strong connection with. She'd downed her weight in croissants and fresh fruit. She'd even made a concession to the length and ordeal of the day by eating a yogurt and granola pot as well - weddings were a marathon, not a sprint and the protein would come in handy if she didn't want to pass out before the processional. Cara, bless her heart, had ordered a platter of sandwiches from the winery kitchen to be delivered to the winery lodge she was getting ready in, and Izzy had wrapped a couple in napkins and shoved them into her purse to take back to the little cottage on the property she'd been assigned. The setting was gorgeous; a large mudbrick winery on Waiheke Island with wooden accents that sat upon a hill overlooking rolling acres of vines that stretched towards the Hauraki Gulf, shining blue in the autumn sun. The larger house Cara and Finn had claimed sat slightly up on a rise behind the winery, the master bedroom facing a steep hill so it looked as if the land dropped into the sea. They'd be able to spend their first morning as husband and wife watching the sun rise over the water.

A little to the east, connected by winding lavender-lined paths of golden pea gravel and hidden behind tall hedges were three tiny cottages, popping up out of nowhere like something from a fairytale. They were covered in ivy, with each front door painted a different colour. Izzy's door was a soft sage green, and she'd been delighted when she walked in to find the French provincial theme carried on throughout the house, from the fancy linen armchairs and chaise lounge, to the whisper-soft velvet quilt on the king sized bed in the same shade as the front door. Heavy drapes, polished floorboards, a small fire in one corner of the living room, and a kitchen nook and bathroom tiled in creamy-gold marble completed the luxurious interior and Izzy was quietly positive that if she ever decided to settle down and build her own dream home, it would look a lot like her accommodation for the night. If she could stay there the entire time, snuggled up next to the fire, watching the lights of the boats sailing across the harbour, it would be perfection.

But, this wedding.

Despite Cara and Finn both having issues with their parents, everyone had been invited. Isabel's own parents had arrived from Taranaki the day before and were in the other two cottages on the property – Steve with the blue door and Linda with the red – and when Izzy had enquired whether Finn's parents would stay on-site as well, despite living in Auckland, Cara had shrugged and said, "Fuck them," about as sharply as Izzy had ever heard her speak. Finn had pressed his lips together like he was trying not to laugh, and when Cara saw it and repeated, "Seriously, Finnegan, fuck your family," he'd merely grinned at her and kissed the back of their joined hands, his lips lingering on Cara's diamond engagement ring.

So there was that.

Their mother, Linda, was in a right old tizzy. Having had her hair and makeup done first, she flittered between Cara, who was surrounded by a bevy of professionals, and Izzy, who was leaning over the bathroom sink, mouth open, trying not to fuck up her liquid liner, fussing that they had everything they needed.

"I'm fine, Mum," Izzy said for the third time, and promptly stabbed herself in the eye with her mascara wand. Cara had offered to pay for her to have her hair and makeup professionally done but the beauty of not being a bridesmaid was that nobody would look at Izzy and she had enough practice and skill to ensure she could pull off wedding guest makeup, even if she had needed to stop and buy a new lipstick on her way to the ferry when she realised she'd sacrificed her favourite pink to Cara and Finn's ardour on Monday night.

"If you're sure," Linda said, as Izzy swore and tried to rub the offending black blob away. "I want everything to be perfect for Finn and Cara."

Hence, the charade. Linda and Steve weren't speaking, but after thirty years of marriage they were more than capable of sending loud 'fuck yous' across a room with their eyes alone and had been doing so since they arrived. Finn's parents, who after a quick recap from Cara, Izzy wholeheartedly agreed should fuck off to the moon, arrived last night in time for the rehearsal dinner, and icicles could have formed on the smile Finn's dad sent the happy couple. Finn's mother, Helena, seemed far warmer and genuinely pleased for them, but after the initial greeting she sat by her husband's elbow all evening and whispered to him as he glared into his whisky glass. The Knights' former captain, Matt Hollis, was obviously invited, but so was his estranged wife, Lauren, whom Cara had informed Izzy was the only one of the couple she was actually interested in having at her wedding. Between the interpersonal issues and the rest of the wedding minutiae being handled, albeit excellently, by Star and Steel, the event planning company owned by Clare's sister-in-law, Izzy could well understand the article she'd read in the bridal salon while Cara picked up her dress the day before claiming elopements were on the rise.

As for Izzy, she struggled to contain her nerves. Mrs Purdy was looking after the kids for the night and Zac had messaged her and said he'd meet her at the ceremony site ten minutes before the wedding was due to start but a small voice inside her whispered that he wouldn't. Not to mention, the earrings she'd spent a week working on for Cara were burning a hole in the pocket of her gown.

"Iz?" Cara popped her head into the bathroom Izzy had claimed for her own. "You good?"

"Almost." Izzy gave her lashes a final sweep and checked to make sure all evidence of her blunder with the wand was gone. It was, save for a little redness around her right eye that she could pass off as wedding day emotions if anyone was uncouth enough to ask. She turned to face the bride. "This okay?" She was wearing her one designer dress, bought at a huge discount on Oxford Street several years earlier, and never had the chance to wear. It was black and long, the neckline cut in a deep V that made the most of her meagre cleavage without being tacky. Small lace cap sleeves added detail and followed the deeper V of the dress's back like tiny black gossamer fairy wings, and a split above her knee in the centre meant she could walk and dance easily in it. She'd paired it with silver sandals and wore only her raw amethyst pendant on its silver chain around her neck. Her hair was out and wavy, and she looked the complete antithesis to Cara with her high bun and the sleek, polished lines of her creamy silk dress.

"You look perfect," Cara smiled widely and Izzy had seen her lie enough growing up to recognise the truth in her eyes. Her sister reached out and squeezed her hand. "I'm so glad you could be here for this."

A little bolt of surprise shot through Izzy. "I wouldn't have missed it."

Cara's smile tightened a little at the corners, and Izzy repeated herself. "Cara, I wouldn't have missed your wedding. If you'd chosen a different date, I would have come back for it."

"Well, now you don't have to," Cara said lightly, doing nothing to dispel Izzy's uncertainty.

*She knows I'd be here for her on her wedding day, no matter what, right?*

"I made you something," she said quickly,

pushing the thought away. Of course Cara knew. "Here."

She thrust the small paper wrapped package at her sister. Thank goodness for dresses with pockets.

"You don't have to wear them," Izzy managed, her nerves at boiling point as Cara unwrapped the parcel. "I thought you might like them, but if you already have something else planned..." She trailed off as Cara held up one of the earrings.

Lustrous pearls wove together in a vine pattern that the jeweller's wire peeked through, sparkling enough to elevate the item from everyday to extraordinary in a luscious approximation of the way the halcyon light danced through the vines outside.

Izzy held her breath. They looked perfect. She'd worked on them every moment she had for over a week. What if Cara didn't like them?

It's okay if she doesn't, she reminded herself firmly. It's a gift. Not every gift suits every person. It's not going to be a rejection of you if they're not to her taste.

She'd tried so hard to make sure they were, though. Cara's country-girl style of sundresses and ankle boots was miles from Izzy's running gear, easy-rolled travel pieces and skintight dating clothes, but she'd toyed with them night after night, trying to get the right balance of easy glamour and originality that her sister personified.

"Izzy." Cara looked from the earring to her, and back again. "You made these?"

A spiked ball of nerves rotated in Izzy's chest. "Yeah, but you don't have to wear them," she repeated quickly. "I saw some like them in a shop and they reminded me of you. Of something you might like."

"They're perfect." Cara's eyes, the same brown as Izzy's, filled with tears. "Of course I'm wearing them." She placed the paper wrapping gently on the vanity and nudged Izzy aside with her hip, taking up the space in front of the mirror so she could thread them through the holes in her lobes.

"You really like them?"

"I love them," Cara said firmly, moving her head side to side and watching the gentle dance of the pearls above her bare shoulders. "I can't believe you made them. You're so talented."

"I had a lot of help. I joined a beading group in town," Izzy admitted. "They meet every week and they're so generous with their knowledge."

Cara met her eyes in the mirror. "That's awesome. I'm a fan of anything here that makes you happy." She wrapped an arm around Izzy's shoulders and pulled her in for a quick hug. Izzy held her face carefully away from Cara's dress. "Anything that means you might be happy coming home more often is A-OK with me."

Izzy's eyes prickled, and she opened her mouth, but before she could say anything, a petite redhead with a headset appeared in the doorway.

"Cara?" The event planner, who'd introduced herself as Jessie when Izzy arrived, tapped her watch. "We've got fifteen minutes." She looked at Izzy. "Guests should all be gathering at the site."

"Yup, yup." Izzy pulled back from the hug and turned towards the mirror to ensure her watery-eyed moment hadn't done any more damage to her face, but she looked fine. Great, even. She faced

Cara again and squeezed her hand. "See you on the other side."

"I'll be the one looking gloriously happy," her sister replied, with a satisfied grin.

Izzy grabbed the small duffel bag that had her street clothes and makeup in it, and hightailed it down to the cottage. She dropped her bag inside the green door, then locked it again, pocketing the key – yay, pockets! – and hightailing it once again towards the winery building itself. The parking lot was littered with luxury vehicles, but as Izzy made her way past olive trees and neatly trimmed topiary bushes there was nobody to be seen. Ivy crept up one wall of the mudbrick building, weaving its way up to the wooden shingles and along the wrought iron fence that led the way to the rooftop patio, a discreet 'ceremony' sign planted at its base. Through the open oak double doors, Izzy caught a glimpse of parquet flooring, and the winery's giant vintage chandelier that was used as part of its branding. She'd never visited this particular winery before, but knew it was one of Cara and Finn's favourites and nobody in Auckland was unaware of its sterling reputation for food and wine. That her sister had managed to secure it for a wedding at such short notice was nothing short of a miracle, or perhaps a reflection of how powerful Finn's reputation as the Prince Charming of Rugby League really was, especially since the Knights' championship win two years ago. Izzy was well aware that although Finn and Cara hadn't invited media to cover their wedding, palms at the winery had been greased with the promise to release a single shot of the two of them at the venue in their wedding clothes. She couldn't blame them though – it was stunning.

She'd give her left tit to secure it if she was looking to get married, let alone a teeny-weeny photograph.

Not that getting married was on her radar. She couldn't even secure a proper date for this thing.

As the thought crossed her mind, movement inside the winery doors caught her eye. Zac had appeared sometime within the last minute while she admired the building. He leaned one shoulder on the doorframe, hands in his pockets, silvery eyes on her.

Relief nearly knocked Izzy off her heels. "You're here."

He watched her steadily. "I said I would be."

Her heart fluttered. "But you are."

He looked incredible too, wearing a dark green suit over a black shirt, unbuttoned at the throat.

He didn't answer, just leveraged himself off the door and walked towards her. His long legs ate up the distance, crunching over the pea gravel until he stopped right in front of her.

"You look incredible."

Heat climbed Izzy's cheeks as her gaze dropped to his chest. A pounamu pendant glistened against the exposed sliver of his tanned chest and she reached up to touch it, the cool slide of greenstone under her fingers settling her rioting emotions.

"I like this."

"Thank you."

"Who gave it to you?" According to tikanga, Māori protocol, greenstone needed to be gifted, not purchased for oneself.

"My mum, for my twenty-first." He cleared his throat. "I was thinking about what you said about home."

"Yeah?"

"Yeah."

They stood like that, cocooned in the amber rays of late afternoon light, everything green and gold and black. Izzy's heart thumped in her chest and she raised her eyes again. Zac was looking at her like he could see inside, like he could read the confusion and nerves rolling to an unfamiliar boil in the depths of her chest. She'd needed a casual date, and somehow she'd ended up here with her boss, a man she'd disliked intensely and there was nothing casual about it. Not about the way he looked at her, not about the pull that urged her closer to him, the desire to spread her fingers and explore the warm, hair-dusted skin of his chest, not about the way her heart leapt when he covered her hand with his and linked their fingers, squeezing gently as he moved back, their joined hands swinging between them.

"Cara's coming," he murmured, his eyes flicking over her shoulder. "We'd better get up there."

Izzy nodded, unable to speak as emotions clogged her throat. She let him lead her up the stairs to the rooftop patio and down the aisle, past his teammates and her extended family, guiding her into the first row of chairs beside her parents. She didn't miss the sharp look Finn shot the two of them, but she kept his hand tight in hers, anchoring her. Music swelled in the air above them, an instrumental version of The Chicks 'Easy Silence' that made her grin at how perfectly the lyrics fit the couple, while incorporating Cara's love of country music, and the celebrant asked them to stand. Izzy watched her sister walk down the aisle, glowing with happiness as she stepped up beside Finn and out of the corner of her eye, she saw Zac watching her.

~

THE WEDDING WAS FINE. Good, Zac supposed. Finn and Cara said lots of lovely things to each other, there was a bit of paperwork and then Finn kissed Cara, wrapping her up in his arms and pulling her off her feet, their lips locked, as the Gulf sparkled sapphire behind them.

Zac clapped dutifully, but Izzy bounced beside him, giddy with joy. It was infectious when she turned to him, dark eyes shining bright, her full pink lips smiling widely, and he found his own lips pulling upward.

He followed her as she bopped up the aisle after the newly-married couple and waited in line to shake Finn's hand and kiss Cara on the cheek. The latter shot him a suspicious look but accepted his congratulations gracefully and then it was onto cocktails.

The guests mingled in a garden area dotted with tiny doll-like wrought iron tables and chairs. Several of the Knights and their partners gathered around a giant chess set. They'd kept the guest list small, Zac noted. Aside from the team and coaching staff and Finn and Cara's parents, there were only about a dozen other people in attendance. That was significantly more than he was comfortable with though, especially given the way the wine was flowing and the speculative looks the strangers were lobbing at him and Izzy.

"I'm going to get a drink," he murmured in her ear and he didn't miss the way she shivered as his lips brushed her hair. "Do you want anything?"

"Bubbles, please," she requested, turning to face him. In her heels she was eye to eye with him and he loved it, loved the way her breath whispered across his lips.

He nodded and moved to the outdoor bar, accepting a glass of sparkling wine and a water from a staff member.

He returned to Izzy to find her talking to a dark-haired woman in a blue dress.

"Thanks," she smiled up at him, accepting her drink. "This is my cousin Andie."

"Nice to meet you." The other woman smiled, and though she was older than Izzy and had different colouring, he saw their genetic connection in the curve of her smile and the warmth of her eyes.

"You too," he managed, and watched the sun descend slowly towards the horizon while Izzy and Andie chattered away, Andie's husband Mike joining them after a while. The last wedding he'd been to had been Frances's. It had been miles from this, from the luxury that dripped effortlessly from each element of Finn and Cara's union, but it had been beautiful, his sister bubbling over with happiness and hope for the future. And then her world had shattered, leaving her alone with two young children and a hole in her heart. Zac could count on one hand the number of times he'd seen Frances smile since.

A light touch on his elbow brought him back to the present.

"Are you okay?" It was Izzy, peering at him, the golden hour light gilding the side of her face, turning her hair to honey. Behind her, Andie and Mike trailed after the other guests making their way down to the winery building.

"I'm fine," Zac lied. She shot him a look that told

him she knew he was lying. "Is it time for dinner?" he asked.

She let him off the hook. "Yeah. We've only got a few minutes to get seated before the newlyweds arrive back from photos. Are you ready to go in?"

That right there. That kind of care. That's what Finn had meant when he said Izzy made life better for other people. That she could see the strain that being around large groups of people had on him, and rather than berating him or writing him off as a grumpy bastard, she checked in on him. Gave him grace, and time, and breathing room to gather himself and his thoughts. That was what set Isabel Holt apart from other people.

She was amazing.

He inhaled deeply, the scent of lavender tickling his nose, as well as the citrusy-cedar scent of his body wash, which Izzy was definitely wearing as well, and nodded. She didn't pull away when he reached for her hand as they headed down the garden steps, nor when they paused in the doorway to the main dining area. French doors lined one wall, and light spilled across the rows of white-clothed tables, dancing across glassware and flashing on cutlery.

Izzy surveyed it all, and Zac surveyed her, so he saw the deep breath she pulled in, heard the phrase she whispered under her breath, so low he would have missed it if every fibre of his being wasn't specifically and meticulously tuned to this woman.

"Once more into the breach."

"You don't like weddings?" It surprised him. Despite her quick run of unsuccessful dates, she seemed like the kind of woman men would drop to their knees in front of. Not him, obviously, no matter how good she looked in that temptation of a dress and how high and tight her tits were, and holy shit he could not get an erection merely talking to a woman at a formal event in front of all of his teammates.

Izzy twirled her champagne glass, watching the golden liquid swirl and swish, catching the light from the chandelier above.

"Let's just say recent events have shaken my belief in the institution of marriage." He followed her gaze to the parents' table where Mr and Mrs Holt sat next to each other, staring in completely opposite directions.

"Ah." He'd heard in the locker room that the Holt parents were divorcing, but he'd dismissed that info, as it didn't make any difference to his own life. Watching the way Izzy's mouth turned down as she marched them towards another table, he reassessed that judgement. If her parent's separation was causing Izzy distress he was suddenly a lot more interested in how he could make her feel better about it.

They'd barely taken their seats when Dom McQueen, who was acting as MC for the event, had them back up standing to welcome Cara and Finn, who beamed as they weaved their way through their guests to a tiny table set for two in a little alcove.

"They look so happy," he overheard Andie exclaim to Izzy, and he had to second that. He'd never seen Chalmers smile so widely.

The food was delicious, and more importantly, plentiful.

"Cara ordered fifty percent more than the actual guest list," Izzy told him when he commented while reaching for his third helping of roast spuds.

"Something about all these massive league players bankrupting her with carbs."

They sat awkwardly through the Father of the Bride speech, and even more awkwardly through the Father of the Groom one, which turned out to be more of a critique of Finn's decision not to pursue a career in law than a celebration of his love. At one point Zac was fairly certain he saw Cara mouth a firm 'Move on' to Mr Chalmers, at which point he promptly did.

Zac could relate. Only a fool would fuck with Cara Holt. Chalmers. Whatever.

Then the floor opened for speeches. As Cara's boss Denise espoused the narrative that they'd all known Finn and Cara would end up together, Zac leant over to whisper in Izzy's ear.

"Are you going to give a speech?"

There went that shiver again. He loved it. It made him want to sink his teeth gently into the curve of her neck to see how she reacted.

She shook her head, soft blonde waves caressing his jaw and he stopped breathing.

"I don't do public speaking. Cara knows that. I wrote everything I had to say in their card." In lieu of gifts, the newlyweds had requested cards and donations to a local animal shelter in honour of their dog, Ted.

Zac toasted dutifully with his orange juice as Denise wrapped up her speech, and had turned back to Izzy when a familiar voice crackled over the speaker.

"I'd like to say a few words."

*Fuck.*

He met Rangi's panicked gaze across the table. This couldn't be good.

"Stop him," the younger man hissed, and Zac turned in his chair to see Matt Hollis standing directly behind him, microphone in hand.

"Oi, Matt. Give it here." Zac reached for the mike, but Hollis jerked it out of reach.

"Fuck off, Fearon," he muttered, the low profanity echoing to the high ceiling.

Matt cleared his throat hurriedly. "Sorry about that, folks."

Zac leaned back in his seat. *Shit.*

They were done for. The bachelor party incident had actually been the tamest run in Hollis had had with anyone since his wife kicked him out months ago. His usually polarising personality was edged with a sharp new aggression that was doing wonders for him on the field and exactly nothing for him in keeping friends off it. Behind Matt, Zac caught a glimpse of his estranged wife, Lauren, a horrified expression on her face as all eyes turned to her ex.

"For those who don't know me, my name is Matt Hollis." A titter went around the room. Hollis had captained the Knights for four years before stepping down this season. There wasn't a person in Auckland who didn't know him. "I'm honoured to be invited to celebrate Finn's marriage to Cara today. Marriage is a lot like league, actually. A lot of people think getting there is the issue. That once you've got that ring on your finger, the deal is sealed." A pause. "Those people are wrong."

"Jesus." Rangi muttered, reaching for his glass.

"Marriage," Matt continued, "like league, is a commitment. You need to work for it. You need to train yourself every day to be a little bit better for your partner. To anticipate how you can support them best. That looks different for everyone, so it's up to you to study your partner, learn their patterns and plays so you can defend them against the challenges they come up against."

Zac leaned back in his chair, exhaling. This wasn't so bad.

"But by far the most important factor in a successful marriage," Matt continued, "is communication. Telling your partner what you need. How you feel. Your fears, your history, your hopes, your frustrations. I'm not an expert on marriage–" his gaze slid towards Lauren, then back to the happy couple so quickly anyone who wasn't looking would have missed it "- but one thing that I've always admired about the two of you is your openness with one another. The way you look to each other for support, for companionship, the depth of your friendship that goes beyond surface attraction. It's impossible for anyone who has seen the two of you together to miss it. And that's why I'm certain you'll have a long and happy life together." He lifted his glass, and Zac noted the water in it. "To the bride and groom."

"To the bride and groom," the guests echoed.

CHAPTER 11

*I*zzy leaned her head against the wall of the toilet stall and sighed her exasperation out. Her exasperation sounded like a wounded elephant. Despite Zac's presence – and boy, in that suit, he was a presence; her ovaries were singing his praises like they were the gospel – she'd still managed to get cornered at the dessert table by her Aunt Cathy, whose sole concession to Izzy's tall, dark and monosyllabic date was to switch her usual refrain of concern at her niece's single status to pointed and nosy questions about how long she and Zac had been together and could they expect another family wedding on the horizon?

*Not one you'll be bloody invited to,* Izzy had thought, but she'd pasted a smile on, made a vague comment about seeing what the future held and escaped to the toilets.

"Jesus," an accented voice said in the stall next to her. "You okay, hun?"

Izzy let her eyes drift shut. "Yeah," she replied. "Just catching some feelings I'm not too keen on."

"Thoughts and prayers," the other woman

replied. "I'm trying so hard to catch feelings I'm gonna pull a muscle."

"Yeah?" Izzy liked other people's drama. Other people's drama was safe - you could observe it from a distance, like an animal at the zoo, offering advice and solutions. It was a lovely distraction from self-reflection. Izzy hated self-reflection. "What's up with that, then?"

"It's my boyfriend," the voice said gloomily, and through her champagne haze Izzy managed to pinpoint the accent. South African. "He's such a good guy. He's nice and funny and he buys me little gifts."

"What a fuckhead," Izzy offered when the other woman trailed off, and she heard a muffled laugh from the stall next door.

"It's me. I'm the fuckhead. I just can't fall in love with him. I've tried everything, but there's no spark."

"Apparently, sparks are anxiety advertised as romantic," Izzy reported loftily. She'd read it in the relationship column of a magazine once and since she was having regular fights with her boyfriend at the time, she'd decided it was an excellent explanation for their terrible relationship and dumped him.

Upon reflection, their relationship was likely terrible because of his failed dreams of being a DJ, his coke habit and the fact that he'd introduced her as 'my mate Izzy' to his mum despite the fact they'd been together for a year and once spent an entire week naked in Lanzarote subsisting only on room service cocktails, fries, and chocolate body paint.

"Maybe," the voice sighed. "But I think I need them."

"Get out now, then," Izzy shut her eyes again.

She was definitely switching to lemonades when she scrounged up the energy to return to the reception. "No point wasting your time with someone who doesn't meet your needs."

*Zac would meet your needs*, a traitorous voice inside her head whispered, and she waved a loose-wristed hand around her head as if to bat the thought away.

"Maybe," the voice sighed. "What are you going to do about yours?"

"Ignore them and hope they go away," Izzy replied honestly.

A snort came from the stall next door. "Good luck with that."

"Cheers."

Izzy flushed and stepped out into the main bathroom area. It was fancy as fuck, marble and polished wood everywhere, a velvet chaise in one corner, designer soap products and dried floral arrangements on every surface. Izzy had lived in worse places than this bathroom. She washed her hands with the cinnamon scented soap and was drying them with one of the thick cotton hand towels when the other stall flushed and the occupant stepped out.

Izzy's heart dropped. "Oh shit."

International plus-size supermodel Storm Erasmus eyed her as she moved to the sink. "You said that out loud."

"I did?"

"You did."

"Shit."

"It's alright." The other woman met Izzy's eyes in the gilded framed mirror above the sink. "It happens."

"Does it?" Izzy joked. "Do random strangers in the toilets tell famous people to break up with their boyfriends often?"

Storm swung her long, dark hair over her shoulder and grinned. "More than you'd think. What is the women's bathroom if not a sacred space to shit-talk men and fix each other's makeup?"

"Well, yeah," Izzy conceded. "When you put it like that."

"Speaking of..." The model fished a lipstick out of her abundant cleavage and held it out. "Try this."

It was the Lisa Eldridge shade she'd bequeathed to Cara after her hens do.

"My precious," Izzy breathed, slicking on the familiar dark pink shade and studying herself in the mirror.

"What's your name?" Storm was leaning against the sink now, arms crossed over her slinky copper dress.

"Izzy. I'm the bride's sister. Who are you here with?"

"Dom McQueen."

"Ah," Izzy nodded. She'd watched enough of Finn's games to recognise the big blond second rower's name. He was popular with the fans and commentators, who always seemed to have good things to say about him despite him being one of the older players on the team. "And that's not going great?"

Storm lifted a shoulder and waved away the lipstick Izzy offered back to her. "Keep it. I don't want to talk about my mess of a relationship. Are you here with someone?"

"Oh yeah," Izzy breathed. "The feelings, remember?"

Storm smiled, slow and wicked. "Fuck them all, Izzy. You and I? We're going to drink and dance, and for the next hour men do not exist. You in?"

Izzy didn't hesitate. "I'm in."

That was where Zac found her an hour later, lemonade held high – even Storm hadn't been able to convince her to keep downing alcohol – as she swayed to the popular local band Cara and Finn had booked, along with her sister, Storm and Andie.

"Hey." He'd had to lean in to be heard over the music, and his breath brushed her ear in a way that sent shivers down her spine. "How are you going?"

"I'm tired," Izzy confessed. "And my feet hurt." She wasn't about to pace around this extravagant venue barefoot, but despite the wide heel and soft leather straps, her shoes were definitely more suited for looking pretty while she sat than holding their own through a dance marathon on an uneven parquet patio.

"Come on," he said. "Let's get out of here."

The temptation was too much. She followed him off the dancefloor and skirted around the few tables scattered at the edge. He paused at the edge of the gravel path that would lead them across the carpark and through the small gate to her cottage.

"Are you going to be okay in those shoes?"

Izzy scoffed. "Of course. Besides, what's the alternative? You're going to carry me?" She went to move past him, but a strong hand on her arm stopped her. A second later the ground disappeared from beneath her feet and she was swept up in Zac Fearon's arms.

Izzy's temperature skyrocketed, heat twining around her links.

"Damn," she muttered. "This is even better than the glasses."

"What was that?"

"Nothing."

Zac harrumphed, and started along the path. Above them, the stars twinkled and the lights of Auckland's downtown shone across the water, casting a kaleidoscope of colours into the night sky.

"It's beautiful," Izzy said, staring across the water.

"Yeah," Zac replied. "It is." But when she turned back to him, those silver-grey eyes weren't fixed on the harbour lights or peering up at the velvet sky. They were looking at her.

Heat climbed Izzy's cheeks. Heat, and arousal too. She didn't try to wrestle it aside, try to push it down. Perhaps the alcohol had loosened her inhibitions, or the endorphins from seeing her sister so happy, but the admission came easily to her.

"I want you."

Zac blinked slowly, like he wasn't sure he'd heard her correctly. "Excuse me?"

"I want you," Izzy said, louder this time. It echoed above them, her confession spinning off into the dark corners of the car park, and it would be as easy for Zac to ignore it and write it off as tipsy ramblings as it would be for him to look down at her and see the truth she knew was painted all over her face.

He did neither. He merely tightened his grip on her and walked faster, leaving her carpark confession behind them as he strode up the little garden path to the cottage and deposited her on her feet.

Izzy swallowed her disappointment, and it

trickled down inside her, a sticky black residue clouding the glittery silver desire that had buoyed her into making such a reckless statement.

"Say it again," he demanded.

Izzy huffed as she gave him her back and fished the cottage key out of her pocket – yay, pockets!

"I don't think so."

"Isabel." Zac's voice was silkily dangerous. "Say it again."

"Whatever you hope to achieve–" Izzy started, pushing the door open and turning to face him "-it doesn't matter–"

She stopped. Zac's face was inches from hers, his gaze pinning her in place. As her breath caught in her throat, he lifted his arms and pinned them on the doorframe to either side of her head.

"Say. It. Again."

"I want you."

He nodded slowly. "Now like you mean it."

"Fuck's sake! I want you, Zac. I've wanted you since Agatha's and every day since. If you don't feel the same way, it's fine, but stop messing around–"

She broke off when he claimed her mouth with his, his fingers tunnelling through her hair, cupping the base of her skull and pulling her closer, until their bodies collided. Lust coiled in her stomach as they kissed, lips clashing and tongues tangling in perfect tandem.

"Dreamt of this forever," he breathed against her skin as he kissed and nipped his way down her throat.

Izzy arched her neck to give him better access. "Didn't feel like it."

"No?" Zac ground his erection into her stomach and she gasped out loud. "Didn't feel like you were driving me crazy with those tight little outfits every morning on the porch, drinking the coffees I made you and watching the sun come up with me?"

She gasped as he scraped his teeth against a sensitive bundle of nerves. "Maybe."

"Maybe that's why none of your dates worked out," Zac ground against her skin as one hand travelled down and round, slipping inside the slit of her dress, grabbing her leg and hooking it around his hip. "Maybe you knew what was waiting for you at home but you were too scared to come and get it."

His hand on her other hip urged her up, and she wrapped both legs around his waist, grinding against him through the layers of their clothes.

"Maybe *you* should try telling a girl how you feel sometimes."

"You knew," he panted, rocking forward against her. "You've known the whole time."

"Maybe it's time we do something about it then," Izzy whispered and Zac's groan echoed through the night. He stumbled forward, kicking the door shut behind him. They made it to the bedroom in seconds, and then Izzy was flying, landing on the bed with an inelegant thump, and she would have been indignant if Zac hadn't followed immediately, his lips settling back on hers like they belonged there, his hands learning every inch of her skin.

"I need inside you, baby," he groaned. "Can I have you? I'll eat you later, I promise. I'll finger you until I get arthritis, but right now I need inside. Let me in, baby."

"Yes," Izzy gasped, her knees falling open as he sat up to unbuckle his belt. "Fuck, yes."

They stripped in moments, clothes flying everywhere. There were a couple of seconds where

Zac stood and toed off his shoes, removing hers with infinitely more gentleness, pressing a kiss against the compass tattoo on the inside of her left ankle. Then he was back, kneeling between her thighs as he studied her in the soft glow of the bedside lamp, fisting his erection.

"You're perfect," he murmured. "Now roll over."

Izzy rolled over eagerly, lifting her hips. Behind her came a rough groan.

"This arse. I've lost days thinking about this arse." There was the crinkle of foil, his fingers swirling in the heat at her centre, spreading her desire across swollen skin, and then the blunt head of his cock against her entrance.

"Ready, baby?"

"Please," Izzy sobbed, her cheek pressed against a pillow, desire stringing her muscles together like taut wire. One touch and she'd surely snap. "Zac, please."

Zac pushed into her slowly, feeding her his dick one inch at a time until she was giddy with the sheer decadence of having him inside her. Once he was fully seated, his hips pressed against the curve of her ass, he gathered up her hair, lifting it off her neck and tugging the thick mass gently. Izzy's scalp came alive at the pressure, thousands of nerve endings lighting at the slight pressure. Not enough to be painful, just enough to be perfectly, deliciously aware. For several long seconds they remained like that, her arse in the air, his cock thick and perfect inside her in that delicious stretch, her scalp singing, and she laughed, joy and excitement swirling out of her because he was filthy, drawing it out like this, building the anticipation exquisitely until it twisted and glittered inside her, all sharp edges and bright colours. Just *filthy*. And already that made it better than she could have hoped. Then he began to move, a slow, indulgent slide in and out, his cock stroking her walls, pressing down for an extra beat every time he bottomed out again. Izzy arched her back and Zac let out a tortured groan behind her, one big hand palming her arse cheek.

"Look at you," he said, so softly she wasn't even sure he was talking to her. "Look how sweetly you take me." He thrust again, a little more force behind it. "Look how perfect you are on your hands and knees, giving me everything."

She hadn't expected pretty sentiments, not from Zac, who held his words close, doling them out like candy on special occasions. But there they were, floating in the air around her, and she gathered them up, letting them flood her brain and weave their way into her blood, all that sparkling praise and desire settling over her, cranking her desire higher, higher, her nipples tightening further as he told her how pretty she looked, how tight and lush she was around him.

He leaned forward and pressed a kiss into her shoulder, licked up the line of her spine and she shuddered, reaching up and back to grasp at his neck, holding his head closer to hers.

"Up, baby," he whispered, and gathered her to him, pulling her torso up to meet his, one thick arm banding her ribs so they knelt together at the top of the bed. Izzy reached out with her free hand and grasped the velvet covered headboard, gasping as Zac skated one hand down her stomach and teased her clit.

"You feel so good," he muttered and she whispered it in return, passing her pleasure back to him, their words fading into the shadows that surrounded them, into the push and flex of their hips, the sweet sound of her desire as he moved in her, strong and steady and controlled, winding her up with each thrust, each pulse of his hips, each biting kiss along the line of her shoulder and firm pass of strong fingers over the bud of her clitoris.

The pressure built slowly, looming through her, stretching its reach through every one of her limbs until she couldn't see, couldn't feel anything but the rising tide of desire, the twist and ache of that heavy, heady tension and she cried out.

"Almost there, baby?" Zac's voice rumbled against her ear, wrenching her higher.

"Yes," she gasped, blind with it now, with the need to scratch and bite and fight her way through to her climax.

He never stopped the movement of his hips, the motion of his fingers sliding her wetness through and across that bundle of nerves, but his other hand moved higher, and then there it was, the sharp pinch of her nipple, all the stunted passion inside her zooming towards that little bite of pain that sparked and zipped through her, mixing with the pleasure he was delivering so sweetly and she bucked against him, once, twice, his fingers holding her there, never letting go, letting the pinch carry through and she exploded.

"That's my girl," she heard dimly as her body clenched and shook, her mind spiralling through the dark, every piece of her broken and whirling through stardust, silvery magic pouring through her as she was put back together, reborn in stages. "That's my fucking girl."

She fell forward, dizzy, both hands on the

headboard, and Zac dropped his hands to her hips, his pumps jagged and loose now, the liquid echo of her release mimicking his movements and tumbling together with his satisfied groan as he held her in place, burying himself in her over and over again, thick and hot and deep, every stroke lighting up her internal nerves, sending residual shivers running through her, until he buried his head against the crook of her neck, panting, and sealed them together with an agonised moan.

They stayed like that for long moments, the harsh saw of his breath hot against her skin, Zac's fingers gripping and releasing her hips in tiny incremental grasps.

Then he nuzzled her jaw and she turned her head, catching the flicker of his mercury eyes in the dark as he pressed a light kiss high on her cheekbone.

"Incredible," he murmured. "Tell me we can do that again."

# CHAPTER 12

Zac felt as light as a feather when he woke the next morning in a bed that probably cost more than his entire house. Though the things he and Izzy had done in it made this particular piece of furniture priceless in his eyes. Maybe he should buy it off the winery. Have it bronzed and placed in his backyard as a modern art tribute to the best night of his life.

He reached for Izzy – keen to start his day the way he'd ended last night, his head between her thighs – but the sheet next to him was cool. Slowly he roused, checking his surroundings. All her stuff was still there, her gown jumbled on the floor with his own clothes, her hair products strewn across the vanity in a startling resemblance of the way she'd organised her things in the bathroom at home.

Zac rolled out of bed and pulled last night's pants on commando. He'd checked into a small boutique hotel down the road when he arrived on the island yesterday and hadn't brought a change of clothes to the winery. He only hoped he didn't see any of his teammates on his return today. Strolling out to the living area he took a moment to appreciate the view through the French doors; a blue sky dotted with puffy white clouds stretched above the ocean, the emerald hills of Waiheke reaching down to cradle the island's bays and coves. There were two comfortable looking loungers beyond the doors facing the sea, but when he moved closer he could see they were empty as well. Turning back towards the kitchenette area, he spotted a note.

*Morning!*

*My mum stopped by to see if I wanted to get breakfast, and you were in such a deep sleep I didn't want to wake you. I figured you needed it. I also figured you might not want my mum to know you were naked in my bed. Come over to the bistro when you wake up!*

*I x*

ZAC'S HEART tumbled over in his chest at the little x at the end of the note. Looked like his teammates were going to catch a glimpse of him in last night's clothes after all. He swung by the bedroom to pull on his shirt, then stopped in the bathroom to perform his morning ablutions and use his finger to brush his teeth using Izzy's toothpaste.

The bistro sat a little apart from the main winery building, crafted from reclaimed bricks and heavy wooden railway sleepers. Izzy sat by herself at a table by the window in a floaty looking blouse and jeans, looking fresh faced and gorgeous, freckles dusting her nose.

Glancing around, Zac took the seat next to her. "Where's your mum?"

Izzy snorted and gestured to a man Zac recognized as her father chatting to one of the waiters. "Dad showed up, so she left. Bonus, she already ordered. Hope you like waffles."

Zac loved waffles.

One of the waitstaff came over and Zac ordered a cappuccino. Izzy shook her head against another drink, gesturing to her half-full beverage.

"Orange juice?" Zac asked, as the server moved away.

"Mimosa." Izzy eyed him carefully as she lifted her drink to her lips. "It doesn't bother you that I drink?"

He shook his head. "Alcohol in general doesn't bother me, except for the smell. That... well, you've seen how that takes me back sometimes. I don't enjoy being around groups of drunk people if I can avoid it because they're unpredictable and I can't read how they'll react. Large groups can change direction in an instant. I see it sometimes with work. I'm never going to make someone feel bad about having a few drinks, but it's not something I do myself."

"You weren't thrilled with that glass of wine I had with Mrs Purdy," Izzy countered.

Zac rolled his lips inward. "I was being a twat," he admitted. "You'd just moved in and I was trying like crazy not to notice how attracted I was to you. Behaving like an arsehole seemed like a good way to get you to avoid me."

"What if I got drunk one night?" Izzy asked and there was no challenge in her eyes, only curiosity as she studied him over her champagne glass. "Like, really drunk?"

"Then I'd take care of you," Zac replied simply. If there was anything the hyper-awareness of growing up with a dysfunctional alcoholic had taught him, it was how to read people, to anticipate their actions and to listen to his gut. Izzy might indulge in a few too many at times like anyone else their age, but she wasn't reliant on the bottle. He could feel it. The same way he could feel the wafer-thin tipping point that sat inside others, the way they could go one way or the other depending on the time of day, their mood, the wind, or the stars or Mercury in retrograde or whatever the fuck it was that made addiction rear its ugly head in some people and not others.

Izzy waved at someone at the juice bar, and Zac looked up in time to see Dom's girlfriend blow a kiss at Izzy, who pretended to catch it and tuck it inside the silky folds of her bodice.

"You're friends with Storm Erasmus?" He tried to keep the surprise from his voice. Dom's girlfriend was a global superstar. She'd moved to New Zealand at sixteen and quickly signed with a talent agency, before moving into international runway shows. All of which was information Zac had acquired completely against his will. Dom was very proud.

"I am now."

Zac wrinkled his brow. "How do you do that? How do you become friends with someone overnight?"

Izzy shrugged. "It's a gift. Plop me down in a room of a hundred people and an hour later I'll be friends with ninety percent of them."

"What about the others?"

"Can't please everyone." She grinned up at him and his heart tumbled in his chest for the second time that morning. "I used to hate it. Everyone told me all their problems. That easy connection makes for some weak boundaries, but as I've become older,

I appreciate it more. Real life connections aren't easy to make in this world anymore. If someone wants to tell me about their sick parakeet or their daughter's dance recital or their crap relationship, it's the least I can do to listen. They'll feel better afterwards."

Zac eyed Dom's girlfriend again, noting the single plate she carried and the way she took the last seat at a large table with a group of the other WAG's.

"Crap relationships, huh?"

The doors opened, and Dom himself appeared. His normally cheerful face was drawn, with heavy bags under his eyes and his hair was scraped back off his face in a half-bun. He looked at Storm's table and his mouth tightened before he caught sight of Zac and headed across.

"Hey, Little Holt," he said, pulling out the chair across from Izzy and plopping down in it. "Nice to officially meet you. Zac here–" he tipped his chin in Zac's direction "-didn't introduce us last night. And speaking of last night, guess what happened? My girlfriend broke up with me."

"That sucks," Izzy replied calmly, leaning back as a server placed a platter of Eggs Benedict in front of her. Zac mirrored her movement, keeping a wary eye on Dom as his waffles made their appearance. Spiced pear, it looked like. With mascarpone, honey and walnuts.

"Do you know anything about that?" Dom continued, green eyes boring into Izzy, who calmly sliced into her toast. All of Zac's protective instincts went on alert.

"Dom–" he started, but Izzy's hand on his arm stopped him there.

"I know that if you and your girlfriend are having problems, you probably need to talk to her about it instead of interrupting my breakfast. I also know that if she broke up with you, it's possible that you going around being a dick about it is unlikely to make her reconsider."

Dom stared at Izzy for a beat and Zac glanced back and forth between them, tension prickling at his temples. Dom might have a reputation as an easy-going guy off the field, but he could be a fucking beast on it, and if he thought Izzy had something to do with Storm breaking things off with him...

"Ah," Dom sighed. "Damnit, I didn't want to like you, but you're alright, Little Holt."

Izzy smirked at her eggs. "Call me Izzy. I'm sorry about Storm."

"Not your fault." Dom reached out to grab a piece of bacon off Izzy's plate and she sliced through the air with her knife, barely missing him. "We've been on the rocks since Valentine's Day."

"You forgot?"

"Nah, I remembered. Planned a whole celebration." He was quiet and Izzy bugged her eyes out in the universal 'so what then' expression.

"There was a bit too much celebrating maybe," Dom admitted, popping his stolen bacon in his mouth. "Let's say when the time came to show our love, the spirit was willing, but the flesh had a touch of whisky-dick."

Zac closed his eyes against that mental image, but not before he saw Izzy wince. "Rough," she sympathised.

"Aye. Anyway," Dom gestured between her and Zac with a fork, "How long has this been going on? Does Chalmers know?"

"None of your business," Zac snapped, all too

aware that Isabel had just adopted another friend that he would have to be nice to, because not doing so would make her upset. "And it's none of his bloody business either, so don't go telling him."

"A secret romance?" Dom's eyes lit up. "Fun. And what about you, young lady?" he asked Izzy sternly. "What are your intentions with our Zachary? He's not an easy man to love, you know. Barely speaks. Always frowning. I saw him make a small child cry once."

"Fuck off you did," Zac mumbled around a mouthful of waffle.

"And that charm! Could give a snake a run for its money. What do you say?" Dom leant forward on the table, chin propped on his hands. "Are you going to be the one to save him with luuuurve?" He drew the word out like the wanker he was.

"Probably not," Izzy replied and it was only that Zac was watching her so closely that he saw the way the corners of her mouth tightened. "I'm leaving the country in a few weeks."

Zac's stomach dropped. It wasn't that he'd forgotten, but... he'd forgotten. He'd been so wrapped up in Izzy, in the way she made him feel, that he'd pushed aside the reminder that this was a temporary stop for her.

That *he* was temporary.

It wasn't that he thought a single night would be enough to get her to stay, but the easy way she brushed off the idea, like last night was barely a footnote in her life story burned all the way down his throat, cramping his stomach, tightening his chest. He stared out the window and tried to control his breathing. It wasn't as if he'd expected forever. Hell, he knew better than that. He didn't have anything to offer. Izzy wasn't interested in a house, or kids, or the dreary monotony of his life. She was too free, too focused on living life to its fullest. His money didn't matter to her. She'd be as happy in a tent or a caravan, something she could pack up and move on to the next place with.

And why was he even surprised she didn't want to stay? Nobody did. His father didn't. His mother barely came to visit, so consumed with her own life and toxic relationship. Even Frances had jumped ship, after the way he'd wrapped his life up in hers, making sure she wanted for nothing, that she was supported in every step of her journey. Where was she now? Nowhere he knew about.

"Ah, a fling." Through the rush in his ears, Zac saw Dom nod sagely and he wanted to take the other man's head off. "How scandalous. I'm proud of you," the big second rower told Zac, who bit back the sour tang of anger that burbled up his throat in response. He grunted instead and shoved another forkful of waffle in his mouth, ignoring the fact that it tasted like sawdust.

Izzy sank back in the leather seats of Zac's rental Volvo as he turned into their street. The pohutukawa trees along the promenade swayed gently in the breeze and she rolled her window down, breathing in the crisp, clean air.

Zac squeezed her knee and she smiled at him, loving the way he looked in the driver's seat, eyes covered by sunglasses, hair mussed. He looked relaxed. For the first time since she'd met him there were no stress lines bracketing his full lips. He'd rung Mrs Purdy after breakfast to check on the kids and come back into the bistro reporting that they'd had a great night's sleep and were off to the aquarium for a tour and lunch. Apparently the former teacher was amping at the opportunity to get Otis and Hazel into a learning environment.

Zac was still in last night's clothes. He'd stopped by the small hotel he'd checked into only to grab his bag and check out on their way to the ferry. During the fifteen minute boat ride from Waiheke Island to Devonport, he'd kept a hand on her at all times, when tucking a strand of hair behind her ear as the wind whipped it loose on the open-air deck, on the small of her back as he guided her onto the debarkment ramp, linking his fingers through hers as they wandered to his rental car. Mrs Purdy had his one because of the carseats in the back.

It was like a switch had been thrown within Zac. One where his issues around touching had suddenly been thrust under a spotlight and his response was to make up for lost time. Not that Izzy was complaining. She'd always been physically affectionate, but there was a certain kind of tender pride that pulsed through her knowing how difficult Zac had found the experience in the past, and seeing how much he was working to rectify it. With her.

She wasn't the only one to have noticed either.

"Good for you, dear," Aunt Cathy had said when she cornered Izzy outside the bistro, souring the buzz the morning mimosas and her post-coital proximity to Zac had given Izzy. She'd half expected him to run this morning, or at least revert to his grunting stand-offish persona, but he hadn't. He'd sought her out at breakfast and sat with her eating waffles, looking like sex on a stick, wearing last night's clothes in public. He'd even saved her the last bite of his breakfast, a truly noble gesture. She was giddy with pleasure.

"Good for me, what?" Izzy had asked, watching how Dom gestured wildly at Zac while recounting some story from a previous game and Zac stared at him expressionless in return.

*God, I love him.*

The thought hit her like a truck. Love? *Love?*

No. No, that couldn't be right. She shook her head, trying to dislodge the thought. Maybe she loved things he *did*. Like how he clipped pegs to Hazel's pink overalls because she found it hilarious to wiggle around and make them shake. Or how he sat quietly with Otis, building an obstacle course out of Lego and then bopping tiny Lego people around it in a sort of Lego Olympic race. Perhaps it was the way he watched Hazel dig up all the stones along his garden paths and then solemnly complimented the 'fossils' she proudly claimed to have found in them. It could be the way he saved every picture Otis drew and filed them all in his office, or how he had a coffee waiting for her on the porch every morning, or that he'd agreed to watch the BBC version of *Pride and Prejudice* after they knocked off their rewatch of all available *Bridgerton* seasons.

No, she realised, her heart glowing as Zac turned his attention to her and blinked once, his eyes warming as they raked across her from thirty feet away. No, it was him. Every grumpy, sweet, socially awkward and touch-averse part of him.

She was in love with Zac Fearon.

She'd beamed at him, sure it was written all over her face.

"Well, good for you that you've followed in your sister's footsteps, of course," Cathy had said, and the ludicrous statement had pulled Izzy's attention from the object of her affections and back towards the older woman.

"How so?" she'd asked, already tensing against the answer. Anything that compared Izzy with her sister was bound to find her wanting.

"A rugby league player." Aunt Cathy nodded approvingly. "Not the friendliest one, clearly, but surely you can overlook a few personality defects with that kind of salary."

Izzy gaped at her aunt. "You must be joking."

"Financial security is important," Aunt Cathy sniffed imperiously.

"So are *manners*, Aunt Cathy. Jesus Christ, what's wrong with you?"

Her aunt had huffed her indignation and stormed away, no doubt to narc Izzy off to her dad, and Izzy's own anger had been greatly reduced after Zac took one look at her rage-filled face and dragged her back to the cottage where he ate her out like a starving man at an all-you-can-eat buffet despite the amount of waffles he'd put away at breakfast.

He was giving her the same look now as they pulled into the driveway.

"What?" Izzy asked.

"You," he replied, leaning forward and capturing her lips. They kissed like that for a minute. Soft and sweet, letting the hunger build until Izzy pulled back, breathless.

"You're dangerous," she laughed, opening her door. "The things you could get me to do…"

"The things I'm going to do to you," Zac countered, opening his own door and stepping out, rounding the car to pull their bags out of the boot. He handed hers over and she slung it over her shoulder grinning up at him.

"Yeah?"

"Yeah." He kissed her again, short and sharp. "Get inside and get your pants off. We're on a deadline, baby." He swatted her arse as she turned towards the gate that led up to the front porch and she giggled, putting a little extra shimmy in her step as she climbed the porch steps.

Her giggle died a swift death on reaching the top.

"Can I help you?"

The woman on the porch swing looked at her with open hostility.

"Who the fuck are you?"

"Who the fuck am *I*?" Izzy's eyebrows hit her hairline. "Who the fuck are *you*?"

"Frances." Zac's grim tone came from behind her. "What are you doing here?"

The other woman stood and faced them, hands on hips. Closer up, Izzy could see the similarities, the tanned skin, the high cheekbones. Frances' eyes were brown, but she shared Zac's height, his athletic frame. His 'don't-fuck-with-me' expression.

"I'm here to see my kids. Care to tell me where they are?"

"They're with a sitter." Zac moved past Izzy and dropped his bag on the porch swing. "I had an event to attend last night."

"An event? Is that what we're calling it now?" Frances shot a hateful look at Izzy over her brother's shoulder. "Surely your event has a name, Zac? She looks like a Tiffany to me."

"Hey–" Izzy started, stepping forward, but Zac held up his hand and she paused, uncertainty shimmering across her skin.

"This is Isabel. She's an au pair and she's been looking after Otis and Hazel for the last month."

"A *nanny*? You're screwing the nanny? My god, Zac, could you be any more of a cliche?"

"Frances." Zac's voice was low in warning, which Frances apparently chose not to heed.

"Like it's not bad enough to come back and find you've handed my kids off to some random girl, you're boning her as well? How do you think that's going to end, Zac? What do you think that's going to do to Otis and Hazel when she leaves you, or worse, when you marry her?" Frances raked her eyes over Izzy again. "She looks like she could use the money. Hope you're wrapping it up."

"Holy shit. Listen here," Izzy stepped forward, again, pushing Zac's arm away when he tried to reach out for her. "Your brother is an amazing uncle to those kids. He has been nothing but incredible with them since you dumped them on him and disappeared. How dare you come back and accuse him of not doing right by them? I haven't seen you here taking care of them this last month."

Haughtiness drew Frances up to her full height, which was still a couple of inches shorter than Izzy's own six feet. "This is actually a family matter. I'm not interested in opinions from the help."

"You miserable–"

"Izzy." Zac's voice was soft behind her. "That's enough."

"What?" She turned. Surely she'd heard wrong. Surely he wasn't going to let his sister talk shit like that about him – about *her* – right in front of him?

"Frances is right. We need to sort this out between us. It's a family issue."

*It's a family issue.*

*A family issue.*

*A family.*

The realisation stole Izzy's breath. She'd done it again. Goddamn it, she'd done it again. Gone and fallen in love with a family, only to be deeply, explicitly reminded that she didn't belong. That she wasn't part of it. That the family she'd poured her time, her energy, her care into, only saw her as an employee. Only this time it wasn't just the family who she'd fallen in love with. It was Zac too. She'd gone and lost her heart to him, and here he was dismissing her because a member of his family – a family he most definitely did not consider her a part of – said to.

A dark hole wrenched open inside Izzy, filling with darkness.

*Not again, not again, not again.* The words whirled in her head, like a cyclone, lifting her and tossing her round until she fell, the crack echoing in her ears as she blinked and came back to herself.

So this was Oz. It wasn't Munchkins and poppies and yellow brick roads. It was champagne headaches and too bright suns and a porch swing that mocked her as it drifted back and forth. Empty. Like the loneliness that yawned inside Izzy.

She nodded slowly.

Yes. This was her Oz. She'd landed here by mistake, and everyone who met her knew. They knew she didn't belong. And now she knew it too.

"Right." Her voice was faint, like it was coming from far away. "I'll let you get on with it."

She moved past Frances, letting her bag hit the

other woman on the way past because even through the fog she was a little bit of a petty bitch, and slid her key into the front door lock.

*Slow down*, her brain reminded her. *Don't do anything rash. You love him* – Jesus, the cramp that thought brought to her stomach almost crippled her – *you have to at least give him a chance to explain.*

Izzy stepped inside her bedroom and slumped against the wall. One chance, she promised herself. He gets one chance to explain that shitshow away.

And then she pulled her suitcase out of the closet because if there was one thing she'd learnt in years of childcare, it was to always be prepared.

# CHAPTER 13

Zac watched her go, gritting his teeth.

"That was out of line," he snapped at his sister as soon as the front door banged shut.

Frances jutted her jaw out. "She was out of line. Who does she think she is, talking to me like that? Those are my kids."

"Yeah, well she's raised those kids for the last month while you've been fuck knows where with fuck knows who." He was dangerously close to shouting so he made an effort to lower his voice. The last thing he needed was nosy Annabel Whatsherface from next door coming out for a casual eavesdrop.

"You were supposed to be doing it," Frances said petulantly, kicking at the driveway with one booted foot, and Zac almost went blind with rage.

"How? How was I supposed to be doing it, Frances? I start training in the city at eight in the morning. I'm not home until four in the afternoon most days. I'm away from the house all day Saturdays and sometimes all weekend if we're not playing at home. How the hell did you think I would manage by myself? Who would take the kids to school? Who would pick them up? Who would watch them for hours at a time while I'm getting slammed into the ground up and down a league field every week?"

"I thought maybe you could take a leave of absence."

Zac raked his hands through his hair, close to pulling it out. "No, you didn't, because if you'd thought that, you would have realised that there wouldn't be any money coming in to pay your rent. Or for Otis's school fees, or for the expensive Montessori preschool Hazel goes to. You didn't think at all."

His sister stared out at the ocean, her jaw tight.

"Frances," Zac tried, gentler. "We can't keep doing this. This dynamic we have, it's not good for us. Wherever you've been–"

"Rehab," Frances interrupted. "I've been in rehab."

"Rehab. Right." Zac nodded, even as his stomach dropped and the chorus echoed inside his head. *You've failed, you've failed, you've failed.*

"I started drinking too much after Ben died," Frances shrugged, like she wasn't giving voice to Zac's deepest fear right there on the red brick drive. "Then pot. Not every day at first, but after a while, yeah."

"I didn't see it." Zac's words were like razor blades in his throat.

"I didn't want you to," Frances said, meeting his eyes. "People who grow up like us know how to hide it, you know?"

Zac nodded, his breath sharp.

"Anyway, a couple of months ago I was at a party. It was right after Ben's birthday and I was struggling.

Grieving for him, grieving for the future we were robbed of. Someone there had a needle. I didn't know what it was, but they said it would help me feel better." Frances paused and Zac swallowed back the rising bile to ask the question that hung over them, dark and ominous.

"Did it?"

Fair play to Frances, she didn't look away from him. "Yes."

Zac closed his eyes, the Greek chorus of failure growing louder in his mind. His ribs tightened, squeezed, pressure climbing up through his chest.

*You've failed, you've failed, you've failed.*

"It made me feel too good," he heard Frances say from far away, and he rolled his lips inward and nodded, trying to fight back the tears. Goddamnit, this fucking family and their fucking curse.

Addiction.

His father's was obvious, seeping out of his pores when he rolled home, written in the trail of vomit and urine that lead to his unconscious body, it stank and swore and shouted, taking up every breath of air in their home until everything revolved around it. His mother's was no less potent for its lack of substance. Hers was his father, the roiling toxicity of their life together that she mistook for love, that she neglected her children, her friends, her good sense, her honour, holding that seething mess high above everything else she should have made a priority, time and time again. And now Frances.

"Zac? Zac, are you listening?"

He exhaled, hard. Inhaled, trying to control the rush of moisture in his eyes, then exhaled once again.

"Yeah, Frances." His voice was as weary as his

heart. "I'm listening."

"That's why I went away. I knew if I stayed, if I didn't break the cycle right then after a single incident there would be more. I wouldn't be able to help it. Whatever this thing in us is, it would have taken over if I let it."

"Your kids, Frankie..." Exhaustion let her childhood nickname slip from his lips.

"I know." Then she was there in front of him, reaching for his hand. He moved it out of the way, not ready for that, not after her betrayal of everything they'd worked for their whole lives. "Zac, I know. That's why I didn't tell you where I was going. You've done so much for me, and for them. I didn't want to see the disappointment in your eyes."

"I could have helped. Could have paid for a good place..." He trailed off helplessly.

"It was a good place," Frances assured him firmly. "And I needed to do this on my own. I realised there I need to do a lot on my own. I've been relying on you too much, especially since Ben died."

"We're family–" Zac started and she shook her head, a sad smile playing at the corners of her mouth.

"Just because someone is related to you doesn't mean you let them hurt you. I can't ever thank you enough for what you did for me when I was younger, bringing me here and helping me out with Otis. But the best way I can thank you is to stand on my own. I'll always love you, but I don't want to always need you. I want to be able to handle things myself, to show my kids that they can as well."

"What about when you need help?"

"Then I'll call you, but give me a chance to try to fail by myself first, okay? You've protected my peace all this time. Now I need to protect yours, even if it's from me."

Zac trailed into the house fifteen minutes later, frustration riding a hard edge on his nerves. Frances had promised to come back tomorrow after he'd had time to talk to the kids and prepare them for her arrival. He understood where she was coming from intellectually, but his stomach was still a mess over her revelations.

Izzy was sitting on the couch, typing into her phone. The fact that she didn't throw it at him seemed promising, so after grabbing one of his emergency cans of full-sugar cola from the fridge, he flopped down beside her.

"So..." he began, and she raised her eyes from the screen to look at him. "That was Frances."

"She's delightful." If sarcasm was a barbell, he'd be pinned under it gasping for air with the way it weighted her words.

"She was a bit rude," Zac acknowledged. "But these are her kids. She has a right to know who's looking after them."

"I'm not bothered about that. Honestly, she should have shown an interest before now, but that's addicts for you, isn't it?" She turned back to her phone, casual as anything and her relaxation meant it took a moment or two for the words to hit him. Anger flared in his gut.

"That's not fair."

Izzy shut her eyes, huffing out a breath. "Yeah, well, life often isn't, Zac." She paused. "Is that it?"

"Is that what?"

"Is that all you have to say about what happened out there?" She looked at him, and something flickered behind her eyes. Hope, maybe? The fire inside him on Frances' behalf dimmed to a smoulder. She was angry, of course she was. Frances had been a bitch, and Izzy was too proud to take that well, but hope was a powerful tool, she'd see sense soon and they could, well, maybe not laugh about it, but work out a plan to stop it happening again. Maybe if she went ahead into the house if Frances turned up in the future. Something that would prevent them coming face to face, lobbing harsh words at each other that would only make it harder for the kids.

"I mean, I guess?"

The light in her eyes flickered and disappeared, and she stared at him with brown eyes that suddenly looked a lot less warm. Panic crawled up his throat. No, no, no, that wasn't good.

"What I meant to say," he scrambled out, "Is that Frances shouldn't have talked to you like that."

"You're apologising for Frances?" Izzy's voice was cool.

"Yes."

"Not for anything else?"

"What?" Zac frowned. "No. She was an arsehole though."

Izzy nodded, slowly at first, then gaining speed, her eyes fixed on the pink nail polish stain Hazel had left on the carpet after the last time she'd gotten into the bathroom cupboard despite the baby lock.

"Okay."

"Okay?" Zac grasped at the word desperately.

"Okay." Izzy turned back to her phone, her face scarily blank and unlocked it. She hit a button on the screen and then stood and exited the room. Zac watched her go, the uneasiness in his gut doing nothing to deter him from eyeing the sweet curve of her backside in her jeans as she left. The visual feast had barely turned into the hallway when his phone pinged with an incoming email. Glancing down distractedly, he caught the sender's name - Isabel Holt, and the subject line. *Resignation.*

*What?*

Mind zapping into focus, he stabbed at the notification, opening the email on the screen.

*Mr Fearon,*

*Thank you for the opportunity to work in your employ as a nanny for Otis and Hazel. Unfortunately, I am unable to continue in this role. Please accept my resignation, effective immediately. No reference will be required.*

*Regards,*
*Isabel Holt*

*What the fuck?*

"What the fuck?" Zac muttered, then louder, "Izzy!" He stormed down the hallway to her bedroom and rapped on the door. "What the hell is this?" There was no answer, so he grabbed the handle, but it wouldn't budge. "Izzy!" He pounded on the door. "Open the goddamn door! You're acting crazy!" The door whipped open so quickly he almost fell in.

"Thanks a lot," he groused, the words dying in his throat when he saw the half-packed suitcase on her bed.

"Izzy," he tried again, aiming for softness despite the sharp anger behind his ribcage. "What are you doing?"

"Packing," she said calmly, like it was obvious. Like it made any sense at all.

"Iz, come on. You're not leaving."

Izzy arched a brow, the coolness in her gaze turning to ice. "Oh, but I am. I'm leaving tonight."

"You still have a month on your contract."

"What contract?" She huffed out a bitter laugh. "We didn't sign a damn thing, Zac. I was here to help out and I'm no longer able to do so. I sent you notice in writing and I'm vacating the premises. What leg do you think you have to stand on here? Are you planning to lock me in? Keep me here against my will? I can't see that ending well for you."

*No shit.*

"What about the kids?" he tried, and her expression softened.

"I'll say goodbye when they get home," she said. "I wouldn't leave them like that. But I am leaving."

Frustrated, Zac raked his hands through his hair. "I don't understand."

"I know you don't." She didn't bother explaining it to him though, just turned back into the room and emptied another drawer.

"Hey!" Zac snapped, stepping through the doorway. He ignored the incredulous look she shot him. "You can't do this, Isabel. Whatever you've got your knickers in a twist about, tell me and I'll take care of it."

"You can't take care of everything, Zac. And the state of my knickers is no concern of yours anymore." She threw a handful of brightly coloured underwear in her suitcase as she spoke.

Anger spiked in his blood. "Stop shutting me out."

It was the wrong thing to say. She whirled on him, dark eyes flashing.

"Me? You're the one who shut me out. 'Oh, it's so great to have you here, you're part of the family,'" she mimicked in a low tone before switching back to her normal voice "But your bitch sister shows up in your driveway after being gone for months, while you've been raising her kids, while *I've* been raising her kids, and you let her talk to me like that? Like I'm a piece of shit on her shoe?"

"Baby, come on," Zac tried. "She's their mother."

"I know that," Izzy said tightly. He watched her take a deep breath. "I know that," she said again, quieter. "I'm not trying to be their mother, Zac. I'm not trying to be any sort of parent at all. But I am part of their lives at the moment. I'm the one who's been here, cooking for them and doing their laundry and cleaning up toilet accidents and reading them stories. I'm not nobody to them, and that's how you made me feel."

"Baby–" he started, and reached for her, but she shook her head, holding up a hand to stop him.

"No. A lot of this is my issue, I know that. But there's a line. I can't keep giving everything to people and getting nothing in return. It's not healthy for me."

"So that's that, then? You've decided it's not working and you're leaving?"

"I'm sorry."

"Bullshit." He spat the word out, rage making him dizzy. "That's bullshit, Isabel." He threw his arm wide, gesturing to the suitcase on the bed, full of rolled outfits he'd never once seen her wear. "You never even finished unpacking. You've had one foot out the door the whole time."

Her face paled. "That's not true."

"Isn't it? You haven't committed to a damn thing, you said so yourself. Not the length of time you'd stay. Not me. Not the kids. You've been ready to walk out on us at a moment's notice and now that moment is here and you think you get to play the victim in all this?"

"Why would I stay somewhere I'm not wanted?" Izzy shouted. "You've made it clear that I'm not a priority. And why would I be? You've got your career, you've got your family. I'm the nanny." Her voice turned sour, dripping with poison. "I'm just the nanny."

Zac's gut dropped. "If that's what you really think, then nothing I say will change your mind. But I do want you, Izzy–" he stopped, because she was shaking her head again, dejection and rejection painted over her tanned skin.

"Fine," he said, relenting. He pushed back the swell in his mind that told him this was wrong, bad. She had to listen, she had to stay. He was being left again. In all of his grimy, gritty childhood, he'd never once begged someone to stay with him, to choose him, to love him. He sure as shit wasn't going to start now. It didn't matter that the numbness he knew came from being abandoned was already spreading through him, a cold wash over his limbs. He'd be fine without her. He had been for twenty-eight years. And he would be for another twenty eight, and twenty eight beyond that. Frances was back, the kids would go home with her tomorrow and his life would return to how it was before. Calm. Controlled. Quiet.

Just how he liked it.

# CHAPTER 14

It took Zac approximately three days to realise how badly he'd fucked up. Otis and Hazel had been devastated by Izzy's farewell. He'd hidden in his room like a coward while she told them, and he could hear them sobbing through the wall as she hugged them goodbye. They were thrilled to have their mother back of course, but the way they'd looked when they'd piled onto his bed with him after Izzy closed the front door behind her haunted Zac.

It wasn't the only thing that haunted him. The spectre of Izzy hung over his morning routine on the porch, reclined beside him on the couch when he tried to finish *Pride and Prejudice*, shimmered through the air when he showered. He'd had to buy new shower gel because the old one reminded him of smelling it on Izzy and he'd had the deeply unfortunate experience of a sad boner.

"Zac? Your front door is open."

Zac didn't move from where he laid on the couch staring up at the ceiling, with a half-eaten bag of carrots on his stomach. It was the closest thing he had to snacks in the house, since he'd already eaten all the cookies Izzy had left behind and he couldn't bring himself to go to the supermarket to buy food that would fuck up his training regime no matter how mopey he was.

And fuck, he was mopey.

Frances bustled in and stopped dead when she saw him.

"What on Earth is the matter with you?"

"Nothing," Zac pulled his attention from the ceiling to glare at her. "I'm resting."

Frances flicked her eyes around the living room. His cookie plate from two days ago was still on the coffee table covered in crumbs, there were coffee cups and water glasses scattered around and he was wrapped in the comforter off Hazel's bed. It had unicorns all over it.

"Oh, Zac," his sister sighed. "What happened?"

"Nothing happened." He went back to looking at the ceiling. Maybe he should replace the crown moulding. A new project might help fill the gaping hole inside him.

*Lies.*

Clinking sounds came from the kitchen. He didn't lift his head to see what was happening, but a mug of tea was plonked in front of him on the coffee table a minute later.

"Drink this."

"I don't want tea."

"I don't care," Frances replied bluntly. "Sit up and drink it."

Zac glared at her again. "This is my house, you know."

"Stop being a baby, Zac." She eyed the mess again. "You haven't been drinking, have you?"

That got his attention. He snapped upright at once. "Of course not."

"Good. Then drink your stupid tea and tell me what's going on."

"Fuck off, Frances."

"You fuck off, Zachary," she replied cooly, glaring right back at him. They held it a minute before his lips tugged upwards reluctantly and they were grinning at each other, the tension between them falling away.

"Why are you here, anyway?" He reached for his mug and took a sip. Ugh, green tea. She was trying to detox him. God knew from what. Too many carrots maybe.

"I came to apologise," Frances admitted, settling back in the brown leather chair across from the couch. "I was an absolute bitch the other day. I was so excited to see the kids after being away. I knocked on the door but nobody answered, and when you turned up without them, I just saw red."

"I already told you, they were at the aquarium with Mrs Purdy."

Frances waved a hand. "I know, I know. Hazel's been chasing me around the apartment with her new stuffed stingray for days. I don't actually have a problem with it. I was just being pissy and immature and I wanted to say sorry."

"Say it, then."

She rolled her eyes before meeting his gaze dead on. "I'm sorry, Zac. You were right about everything you said the other day. I had my reasons for going to rehab and I'm glad I did because that shit could have got really bad, really quick for me. But I was selfish to go about it the way I did and it wasn't fair on you or the kids. I especially wasn't fair to your nanny, and was really hoping she was here so I could apologise to her in person. I took all my anger out on her when I should have been directing a bit more of it inwards."

Zac leaned back against the couch arm. "She's not here," he confessed. "She left that day."

Frances sighed, setting her own tea down on the floor by her feet. "I'm not surprised," she admitted softly. "Do you have her number?"

"She's not picking up," he said. "I think she's blocked me. We had a fight after you left."

"Because you didn't stick up for her?"

Zac gaped at his sister. "How did you know?"

She looked at him like he was crazy. "Because it's the most obvious reason in the world? Trust me, if Ben had stood by while someone talked to me like that, I'd have left him too."

"You would never have left Ben," Zac muttered, and his sister laughed.

"Of course I would have, if I felt like he didn't respect me. You and I spent too much of our lives watching that dynamic in play to put up with it ourselves."

"But you loved each other," Zac protested.

"Deeply," Frances responded. "But that doesn't mean we didn't have problems. Our life together was wonderful, but it wasn't perfect. No marriage is. We had two young kids and money was tight. I'm chock full of issues and he was taking on the dad role to Otis out of nowhere."

"He was a great guy."

Frances smiled softly. "He was the best. But he also drove me to distraction sometimes."

"How?" Their relationship had always looked picture perfect to Zac.

Frances thought for a second. "He left the butter out after he finished making toast."

"So?"

"Every morning, Zac. Every single time. I'd come out after being up all night feeding Hazel and there would be the butter and a knife sitting on my kitchen bench without fail. He let Otis watch him play Call of Duty, and he forgot Mother's Day the first year after I had Hazel."

"That's not too bad."

"Of course not," Frances shrugged. "All the kinds of normal annoyances or issues every couple has. It's nice to be able to talk about them, actually," she smiled. "Whenever I talk to his parents, it's all about what a great man he was. He *was* a great man, I'll never dispute that. But it's nice to have a whinge too. Not that I wouldn't take dirty knives on my benchtop every day for the chance to just see him once more."

"How are you doing with all that?" Zac asked carefully.

"It's shit," Frances shrugged. "It's never going to not be shit and some days it's shittier than others. But I take a great deal of comfort in knowing that he loved me and the kids. That he died loving us and knowing we loved him. I'm glad I never let those dirty knives get in the way of the love we had for each other. That's the thing," Frances continued, eying him speculatively. "You have to ask yourself, if you knew you only had days or weeks or months left, who would you want to spend it with?"

He knew the answer before he spoke it into reality. "I'd want Izzy."

"Then go get her."

"She's leaving," Zac muttered. "It would never

work, anyway. She doesn't want to stay here and my whole life is here."

"Why?"

"What?"

"Why is your whole life here?" Frances asked, and he sputtered at her. "Because of me, right? Because of the kids?"

He nodded slowly.

"Screw me and the kids. We don't want to hang around you when you're a heartbroken mess because you put some idealised version of big brotherhood above your true desire. Maybe you'll stay here, maybe you won't. You can go anywhere with your career. If you're choosing to play for the Knights then I'm happy for you. If you're doing it because you don't want to abandon me then stop. Go where you want, live where you want, love who you want. We'll adapt."

"It's not that easy," Zac protested and Frances let out a frustrated groan.

"Love isn't easy, Zac. It's messy and frustrating and real. It's sacrifice and compromises and sometimes it's paper-scissors-rocking your way to decide who's cooking dinner. But God, when you're doing it with the right person, it's worth it."

Zac swallowed hard. "That sounds terrifying," he admitted.

"Yeah." Frances grinned. "A control freak like you? You're going to hate it. Do you love her?"

"Yes."

If that was what love was, he'd loved Izzy since their first morning together on the porch. He'd wanted her long before that. The concept gave him the willies, but the reality was like sinking into a warm bath. His name was Zac Fearon, he was twenty-seven years old, and he was in love with Isabel Holt.

He stood up, the bag of carrots falling to the floor.

"I have to go."

In the car he called his agent Scott and instructed him to put out feelers in other clubs.

"How far south?" Scott asked.

"Not south," Zac replied, checking his mirrors and merging lanes off the Harbour Bridge. "West. I want to know what's on offer in Australia, the UK. Even the States. Find out what my options are."

There was shocked silence on the other end of the line.

"Scott?"

"I'm here," his agent said. "Are you sure? You've always been clear about sticking around locally."

"That's still my preference," Zac said, "but I want to know what else is out there."

"Okay." In the background he could hear frantic typing. "Okay. Well, if nothing else, this should put a fire up the Knights to offer an extension if they're looking at keeping you."

Zac disconnected and navigated his way to Izzy's old flat in Epsom. He banged on the door, and a pretty Samoan woman who looked to be in her early twenties answered.

"Can I help you?"

"Is Izzy Holt here?"

"No." Her gaze raked him up and down and he could see it the moment recognition hit her.

"You sure? She used to sublet a room here and I thought maybe she would have moved back."

"She hasn't," the girl shrugged. "Sorry about it."

Zac tried her phone again on the way back to his car. No connection.

He drove to Finn and Cara's place, but when he asked if Cara knew where Izzy was living, she laughed and slammed the door in his face.

"Come on, Cara," Zac begged through the door. "At least give me a suburb."

"Piss off before I tell Finn you violated his favourite sister-in-law," Cara yelled back, which was bullshit because Izzy was Finn's only sister-in-law.

"That's some patriarchal nonsense," he blustered.

"Good line. Tell him that while he breaks your nose."

Zac sighed and pressed his forehead against the big wooden cathedral door. Honestly, it was a miracle Cara had managed to shut it on him. She must have the upper body strength of an ox.

"At least tell her I'm looking for her?"

"Fine. I'll tell her. But don't come back looking for her, or it won't be Finn you have to worry about. If she wants to talk to you she knows where to find you."

So Zac went home and waited. He waited for three weeks, the truth growing more vivid every day, pressing down on him like a cold weight.

He was in love with Isabel Holt.

And Isabel Holt wanted nothing to do with him.

# CHAPTER 15

ne month later

"OF ALL THE gin joints in all the world…"

Izzy turned towards the bar and grinned, a half dry glass in her hand.

"It could be the last gin joint in the world and I still wouldn't go out with you, Ken."

"Shame," Ken, who was approximately four hundred and eighty years old, sighed. "I'd better settle for a pint instead, then."

Laughing, Izzy grabbed a pint glass from under the bar and pulled Ken's usual, a thick stout that settled with a wide creamy head.

"Here you go. Much more reliable than a woman."

Ken chuckled, revealing several missing teeth. "Ah, you're a good girl, Izzy."

"Even more reason to stay away from a heartbreaker like you, Ken. I'd never recover if you cast me aside." Izzy blew the regular a kiss and he caught it in the air and slapped it to his cheek.

Grin splitting her face, she turned to the till to input his dinner order - roast of the day with an extra side of broccoli. She'd been working at the bar for a month, living in the staff rooms upstairs, and Ken was one of her favourites. His wife had passed recently, and he came to the pub every night around five for dinner, a pint and conversation. All of the bartenders had a soft spot for him, and the owner Pete drove him home each night in the courtesy van so he wouldn't trip and fall in the dark.

Izzy had been sceptical of the Ponsonby bar when she'd applied. The decor was pseudo-highbrow, all books and globes lining the walls, and it had the nerve to call itself a gastropub, which seemed the epitome of wankery. But by the end of her first week she'd realised that the gentrification was surface level. A pub was a pub was a pub, anywhere in the world, and like any other pub, this one was the heart of its community. In the short while she'd worked there, she'd seen parties and fundraisers, wakes and proposals. Fights were few and far between, and propositions rare, with the exception of Ken, who'd declared his open adoration for her after she successfully pulled his pint correctly the first time.

*Not a euphemism.*

The front door opened as she punched the order through to the kitchen, letting in a blast of chilly air and the raucous laughs of a group of men.

Great. The after-work office crowd was usually pretty tame but the bartender in her preferred the smaller groups of three or four to ones like these, at least eight men spilling in the door, ties already loosened, sleeves rolled up. She made her way back to Ken while they rolled in a slow-moving wave towards the bar, pulling out today's newspaper, already folded with the crossword out and slid it across the polished wood to him with a pen.

"You're a doll, Izzy."

"Don't tell anyone, yeah? I've got a reputation to uphold." She grinned at him and moved back towards the crowd at the bar. *Beers and vodka*, she predicted in her head, a little game she played with new customers. *Twenty nonexistent bucks to you they order beers and vodka.*

She looked up and stopped dead. Zac stared at her from across the bar, the skin around his dark eyes tight with shock. Her stomach rearranged itself, vital organs twisting around one another as realisation filtered in. Zac was here, in her bar and holy guacamole, he looked good. Like an arsehole who'd grind her heart under his heel to appease his snake of a sister, but good nonetheless. His hair had grown out a little, the dark tips brushing the collar of his shirt, stubble darkening his jaw, somehow emphasising the taut angles of it rather than hiding them. His shirt was open at the collar and she could see the tender skin of his neck, the press of a collarbone under the tan skin of his throat and she wanted to press her nose against that spot, inhale him, wrap her arms around his big body and make herself a home in the strong planes of his body.

"Hey." Fingers snapped in front of her eyes, bringing reality flooding back to her, along with the burning desire to break those fingers. "Hot girl, can we get some drinks?"

*Wowwwwww.* So this was how she'd end up on a Dateline special featuring female murderers. She opened her mouth, but –

"Don't talk to her like that," Zac growled,

actually growled, and the group of men turned to look at him. "Use your goddamned manners," he added, and the tension in her chest relaxed. He liked being polite to waitstaff, she remembered. It was general civility, nothing to do with her. He'd do the same for any bartender.

"Sorry," the finger-clicker, whom she vaguely recognised from Cara's wedding, offered meekly. "Can we please get some drinks when you have a second?"

Izzy stared him down. "What do you want?" One by one they rattled off orders - *beer and vodka* - until they got to Zac. "Lemonade." His voice was rough still, and she nodded, keeping her focus on his left earlobe, which should by all rights be a sexless appendage, but it looked so soft and sweet, the pink curve of it framed by the dark stubble of his five o'clock shadow. She wanted to bite it and hear the hitch of his breath echo in a dark room.

"Do you... are you sure you can remember that?" Finger Clicker was looking at her doubtfully and it would be a miracle if she didn't castrate this man tonight. She glared at him and he shrank back a little. "Five beers, three draft lagers, two bottled Heineken. One vodka, lime and soda, one Ciroc on ice, and a lemonade."

"Right," Finger Clicker's voice wavered. "That's... that's great. Can we start a tab?"

"Credit card." She held out a hand, continuing to glare at him as he fished it out of his wallet and slipped it into her palm, his fingers brushing across hers gently. He was Māori, so good-looking he could almost be called pretty, and she was positive her failure to fall at his feet in a pile of simpering goo was disconcerting him.

*Good.*

"Rangi," Zac was growling again. Perhaps he'd been possessed by a wolf. "Go get us some seats."

"Roger." Finger-Clicker faded away, followed by the rest of the group. Except Zac. He stayed, and the way he looked at her might have been enough to sway a weaker woman. Like a nun.

But Izzy was not a nun. She didn't need God on her side to resist Zac Fearon. She had another all-powerful voice in her head that damped her lust every time it threatened to engulf her. Her own.

*He doesn't love you like you love him.*

A sobering reminder. If these *were* Biblical times she'd have engraved it on a stone tablet, but they weren't so she'd written it on a Post-It and stuck it on the mirror in her little room upstairs instead. Every night when her inconvenient feelings raised their ugly heads and she thought about calling him, she looked at that Post-It and repeated it like a mantra until the urge went away.

It wasn't dignified, but it was effective.

"I looked for you."

Her heart leapt but she didn't speak. What was there left to say? He'd made his feelings perfectly clear the day after the wedding.

"I thought you might have left Auckland by now."

"Two weeks." Her reply was clipped, and she kept her attention on the pint she was pouring, angling the glass just so, to get the perfect head on it.

"Ah."

He didn't say anything else as she assembled his group's order on a tray on the bar top, but stopped her when she went to pick it up, lifting it himself instead.

"How are the kids?" She didn't mean to ask, but she couldn't help it, the words bursting out of her. God, she missed them. The memory of Otis's silent tears and Hazel clinging to her leg while she tried to get through the front door haunted her. She *ached* to see them again, to wrap them in her arms, to tell them she loved them, that wherever she was in the world she would always be there for them. But that wasn't her place, and it definitely wasn't the right thing for them. Both kids had been through too much, and had lost too many people already. They deserved better than her and her flighty dreams. As much as it broke her heart, she understood why Zac had made the sacrifices he had. That had been the hardest thing for her to reconcile when she'd left. Neither of them were wrong. They'd both made poor choices that last afternoon together. She could definitely have handled it better, but the outcome would always have been the same. Him, here, supporting his family. Her, there, doing anything to avoid hers. The inevitability of it hollowed her stomach, left her dry-mouthed and drained, but it couldn't be fought. It was what it was.

Zac swallowed hard. "They're good. They miss you."

She bit her lip to keep from blurting out that she missed them too.

"How long have you been working here?"

God, why wouldn't he leave? She'd thought for sure that by working in a bar she'd be safe from any potential run-ins with him.

"Zac, what do you want?"

He eyed her solemnly. "You."

Her heart leapt but she schooled her features into an impassive mask. "You can't have me."

"Doesn't stop me wanting you."

"It should." She thunked his lemonade on the tray full of his table's order. "Drinks up."

He nodded quietly, picked up the tray and disappeared.

Izzy made eye contact with the other bartender who, along with Ken, was studying her with interest.

"I'm going on a smoke break." She didn't smoke, but she'd worked enough short-term hospitality jobs to know that you were more likely to get a break if people thought you needed a smoke than not.

She made her way to the short hallway that snaked around the back of the bar, under the stairs that led to the owner's apartment, when a hand shot out of the dark office door and yanked her inside.

"What the hell?"

"Shhh." Zac pressed a finger against her lips. "Don't yell. It's me."

"What do you think you're doing?" Izzy hissed. The last thing she needed after that scene at the bar was someone catching them in the office together. Her coworkers seemed nice, but Izzy didn't know them well and she wasn't interested in relaying the whole, tortured tale of how she'd ended up the subject of a rugby league star's fickle interest.

"I can't believe you're here. I tried to find you when you left, but Cara wouldn't tell me anything. Izzy..." Zac pressed his forehead against hers. "The way you make me feel..."

"Shitty? Used? Like a convenient employee fuck?" Izzy kept her voice hard even as her body melted, her hips rolling forward, seeking his. "Is that how I make you feel?"

"Like fire," Zac said hoarsely, running his thumb

across the base of her throat. "That's how you make me feel. Like I'm on fire and the only thing that soothes me is my hands on your skin." He dropped a kiss to her collarbone, by the edge of her black cotton shirt embroidered with the bar's name. "You balance me, Iz."

"How nice for you," she responded tartly. "You shouldn't be here, Zac. Go back to your friends."

"I don't want to sit with them. I want to stay here with you and beg you to forgive me with my words and my tongue until you come screaming on my face and then I want to tuck you into my bed and feed you chocolate covered strawberries until you fall asleep and watch you while you dream."

"Too bad," she gasped as he sank to his knees in front of her. "You had your chance."

"I need another one. Please, baby?" Zac's finger toyed with the button on her jeans. "Let me make it up to you."

She was weak, so weak. He looked up at her like that with those pleading grey eyes in the dim light filtering through the office door, and he was beautiful, a deviant angel on his knees, the shadows cutting across his face, picking up the golden glints in his stubble. She couldn't help it, even though she knew it made her weak, because her traitorous heart still cared for him too deeply, still throbbed in her chest when he caught her hand and pressed his lips to the fleshy part of her palm.

"Yes," she moaned and he closed his eyes, mouthing something she couldn't decipher before he went to work. He sawed the zipper of her jeans down, the sound echoing like a gunshot in the quiet office. He pulled off one of her canvas sneakers and peeled denim and lace down her legs, throwing one of her thighs over his shoulder and licking a hot stripe directly up her centre. No hesitation, none of the teasing torment he'd delivered so thoroughly the last time he performed this act, bathed in golden lamplight. Zac ate her like he was possessed. He lapped at her clit, fingers tunnelling through her wetness and arrowing directly up into her, stretching her wide. Izzy gasped, and grabbed at his hair, twisting the thick strands between her fingers.

"Mmm, that's it, baby. Tell me when it gets good." Zac's voice was muffled but every atom in her body focused on him, on his mouth in particular, so she heard him.

"It's good," Izzy choked out, only to be met with a low chuckle.

"No, when it gets *really* good."

Zac reapplied himself to his task, and she let pleasure roll over her in a thick, hot wave, washing away the tension that had taken up permanent residence between her shoulder blades since she'd left his house in Devonport, washing away her sore feet from standing all evening, the smell of beer and fried food that clung to her clothes, washing away everything until there was nothing but Zac's mouth on her, the way he sucked her clit into his mouth as he curled his fingers inside her, repeating the dual rhythm again and again. He didn't stop when she tightened her grip in his hair, didn't stop when she bucked against his face, kept going until she broke, tightening around his fingers as she came, biting her own fist to keep from screaming.

Then he lifted his head, dropping a kiss on her mons, on the top of each of her thighs, helping her put herself back together again. It wasn't until he went to kiss her mouth and she ducked away that she saw realisation pass over his face.

"Are you serious?" Zac's voice was incredulous, and his genuine shock sent irritation skittering across the base of her skull.

"Of course I'm serious. What do you think this changes?" Izzy didn't like the way she sounded but what was the alternative? Another two weeks of orgasms that made her see through time and space and then she walked away again? She had plans, damnit, and so did he. And not one of his plans included her. He'd made that clear enough. She could not – *would not* – twist herself into a pretzel for someone who was okay tossing her aside.

"I'm still leaving and you're still staying. You'll always put your family first. There's nothing wrong with that, but for me to take a chance on someone I'd have to feel like I was going to come first sometimes, too. And with you I'd always be number three. After Frances and the kids, and after the game."

"It's not like that." His voice held a pleading note. "My relationship with Frances has changed since she got back. She's stepped up. I'm not watching the kids as much..."

"Uh huh. And was that her decision or yours?"

His silence was answer enough.

"That's what I mean, Zac. If she called you this instant and she needed you, you'd go. I'm not trying to make you feel bad about it. Good for you, you're a great big brother, but there's no space for anyone else in your world right now. You're not willing to make that space."

"Izzy..."

"Go home, Zac." Izzy turned and opened the

office door, checking the hallway outside to make sure the coast was clear. It was, and she took a deep breath, harnessing the strength she needed for this next part.

"There's nothing for you here."

THE CLATTER of steel and raucous laughter echoed through the Knights' locker room. Zac sat in the midst of it all, an island. He'd been shit at practice today. Harro had reamed him out in front of everyone, but he just... didn't... care. For the first time in as long as he could remember, he didn't care about the game. What did it matter? It was only a game, after all. A bunch of guys throwing a ball around, smashing into each other in stunning displays of culturally-sanctioned violence that other people could salivate over like a regulated, human version of dog-fighting.

Zac would rather face the dogs, honestly. At least there'd be no artifice there. No pretty words and gentle touches before they ripped him apart and left him bleeding out on cracked concrete, cold and alone as he watched his life slip through his fingers.

He was used to being alone.

No matter what Izzy thought about his relationship with Frances, that had always been the goal, for his sister to be okay without him. And now she was, truly was, maybe for the first time ever, he was slowly realising that he wasn't that okay without her. That maybe some of their closeness since she moved to Auckland was the result of him being too afraid to let her go, because if he wasn't stepping into that parental role for her, what else did he bring to the table?

He wasn't fun. He wasn't silly. He didn't play dress ups with the kids or take them to laser tag. He built them savings accounts, and paid for their school fees and watched them occasionally, always searching for signs of trauma in them, always looking for confirmation he was doing the right thing, that Frances was. That Otis and Hazel would have it better than they had as kids.

All he'd done in trying to shoulder all of their burdens was turn into a grumpy old man, stretched too thin to play and run and wrestle with them.

He hadn't been good enough. Not for them and not for Izzy.

And that was the rub, wasn't it? Because even now, after he'd drunk her down and begged her on his knees to take him back, even after she'd told him she wouldn't be his final priority, his first thoughts were still of how he'd failed other people, before he considered his failings with her.

*Shit. She's right.*

He'd thought that Izzy's departure and the kids' return to Frances would have been a blessing in disguise. All that lovely quiet at home, his serene, controlled environment restored. Instead, he'd spent the last few weeks rattling around the house, not able to focus on anything. Not books, not his watchlist full of documentaries, not the alpine rock garden he was working on for Hazel in the shadowy corner of the backyard. Everything felt wrong. Even the golden hour mornings on the porch watching the sun rise were edged with a melancholy shadow, something that lurked in the corners of his mind and told him he was missing something, twisting like fog when he tried to catch it.

He knew, though. He couldn't admit it to himself in the still of the mornings, but here surrounded by metal and hard lines, here where destinies were shaped and warriors forged, he knew.

He missed Izzy. Not only missed her. His soul longed for her, every piece of him, blood and bone and tendon, stretching out, seeking her and finding nothing.

The bar had been a mistake. Up until that point he'd thought she was angry but would come around. He'd cocked up, he knew that. Shouted and raved instead of reassuring her. Fallen right into the fucking patterns of his fucking father. He might not have had a drop of alcohol in his system but that hadn't made a difference in the end. He'd been as much of an arsehole as John Fearon any day of the week. So when he'd seen her there behind the bar, blonde hair shining in the light, hope had leapt in his chest. He'd been wrong. He knew it. She knew it. He could apologise and they could move on.

But they hadn't.

He'd missed her so much, *ached* for her, for that sense of peace that fell over him the moment she touched him that he'd lost his senses. He'd tongue-fucked her up against the wall in a bar back office, a cruel mockery of their first meeting and how far they'd come since then. Then, when it was over and she'd soaked his chin and flooded his heart, when he'd been seconds from begging her to come home, she'd told him there was nothing for him. That they'd never be together.

He hadn't believed it until then. Words shouted in anger didn't count. Passion was a fickle beast, it could switch from side to side like a cha cha dancer, driving anger with the same spittling intensity that it fuelled lust. But when she'd said it like that, so sadly, her voice weary with resignation, how could he not believe her?

He groaned and buried his head in his hands. Around him the locker room quietened.

"You okay, Fearon?" Chalmers' worried voice reached him.

"No," Zac mumbled into his fists. "I've fucked up."

There was a pregnant pause. Then...

"Is this about the woman from the bar?"

"Shut up, Rangi."

It was too late. "What woman? Chalmers demanded.

Zac snapped his head up to glare at Rangi but the young scrum half wasn't even looking at him.

"We went to the pub near my place after that charity thing last night. Me, Fearon and a few of the others." Rangi flicked a quick glance at Zac and hurriedly looked away. "I was kind of surprised Fearon agreed to come when we asked him, because he doesn't drink and he hates everyone, but we got there and there was this scary blonde behind the bar and her and Fearon had a weird vibe."

Chalmers' mouth tightened and he looked at Zac as if seeking confirmation. Zac nodded reluctantly. Finn would know where Izzy was working. He'd know it was her.

"Christ," Finn muttered, scraping a hand across his jaw. "How long has that been going on, then?"

"Since your wedding at least," Dom piped up.

"Shut up, McQueen!"

"Well it has." The big man spread his arms wide.

"You think we like doing this, Fearon? You think we sit around and plot the day we can stage an intervention for your crotchety arse? No, we don't, but you don't tell us anything about yourself, ever. I've been on this team for six months and I don't know if you play video games, if you have pets, when your birthday is or what you like to eat after a game. All I know is that you look at Izzy Holt like you want to have candlelit lady-porn sex with her and you weren't so much of a miserable bastard for a few weeks there, but now you are again."

Silence descended on the changing room again.

"I don't hate everyone," Zac muttered finally, because everyone was staring at him expectantly.

"You do a good job of acting like it then," Rangi said, then grunted as Victor Hewitt elbowed him in the ribs.

Zac ran a hand through his hair. "I don't... I don't really know how to talk to people. All I've known for so long is this game and how I can use it to take care of my family. I don't know what to do with all this–" he gestured around the room "–interest in me." He met Dom's gaze. "I play video games occasionally, but I'm shit at them and I prefer reading. I don't have any pets. My birthday is September first and I get Chinese food from a dodgy looking noodle bar near my place after every home game."

He looked at Rangi. "I don't drink or go out much because my dad's an alcoholic. I usually avoid bars because they remind me of him. He used to spend all our money at them and I'd get a call from the staff to go pick him up after he'd get shitfaced and start abusing people."

He swallowed hard. "I'm from a small town. Growing up everyone knew our family's business, knew what it was like for us. I hated it. Hated feeling judged all the time. That's why I'm not really a sharer, don't do the magazines and that bullshit. If people don't know that much about me, they can't use it against me or the people I care about."

"Makes sense," Dom said, and there were murmurs of assent from around the locker room.

Fuck, he hated this. It was like pulling his skin back, inviting people in to pick and pull at the wounds he'd worked so hard to layer over.

"And Izzy?" Finn's eyes were still hard. He wasn't off the hook there yet.

"I screwed up," Zac admitted. "It looked like she was going to run and I didn't say anything to make her stay. I might even have said stuff to push her away."

"Why?"

Zac shrugged. "I figured she was leaving anyway. And I guess I was angry at the idea that she would find it so easy to walk away."

"And now?" Jesus, he had not counted on this interrogation when he got up this morning. Not from their good-natured captain.

"I miss her. I want her back, but I've got no chance. I can see Izzy forgiving me once for bailing on her, but not twice. It took me a month to find her, and then when I did... Let's just say I didn't adequately express my apologies." He wasn't going to go into detail about what had happened in the bar.

Finn rolled his eyes, catching his drift.

"Why should she forgive you?" his captain asked, sinking onto the bench next to him.

"Because I love her. I'd do anything for her." He realised it was true as he said it. He would. He'd leave the game for her, leave Auckland for her. Frances had told him she and the kids would be okay, and he had to trust her. He had to trust *himself* if he had any chance of happiness.

"Have you told her?"

Zac buried his face in his hands. "No," he admitted, frustration leaking out through his fingers. "She won't listen to me now though, not now I've made such a balls up of it all. It'll be a miracle if she hasn't already banned me from the bar." He peeked at Finn. "You know it's true."

When Chalmers acknowledged that with a grimace, Zac figured stubbornness must be a family trait in the Holt women.

"So," Dom said from above him, and when Zac looked up, the whole Knights team had circled around his locker. "You need a game plan." The big lock rubbed his hands together, a gleeful look on his face. "Let's make a game plan, boys."

CHAPTER 16

"*E*xcuse me, but are you Cara Holt's sister?"

Izzy eyed the sophisticated blonde woman suspiciously.

"Who wants to know?"

"I'm JJ," the other woman offered. "I'm a sports journalist. I have a league podcast."

"Sorry," Izzy shrugged unapologetically. "I'm not really a sports girl."

JJ sighed. "Sometimes I wish I wasn't so much either." She leaned forward, elbows on the bar. "You know Zac Fearon, right? I was wondering if you had a few minutes to talk about the rumours he's looking at signing with an Australian team next season?"

Izzy's heart leapt. *He's leaving?*

No. There was no chance. He wouldn't leave Otis and Hazel, not with their lives in so much upheaval already.

*His Knights contract does end soon, though...*

"Isabel!" Her name was hollered from the doorway and every person in the pub swivelled to see a giant blond bear of a man as he marched towards the bar. Izzy's heart - the tattered remains of it anyway - sank.

"So," Dominic McQueen dropped his phone on the bar and stood with his hands on his hips and surveyed her with startling green eyes. "This is where you've been hiding."

"Dom," Izzy tilted her head in acknowledgement.

"That's it? No hug? No explanation? No undying declaration of love?"

"I don't love you."

"Well, you should. It's extremely poor taste on your part to refrain. My fragile self-esteem might never recover."

"You'll be fine."

"Perhaps." Dom sighed dramatically. "Or perhaps I'll never recover from having my new best friend ripped away from me without a word in the shadow of the night, ignoring my calls, no note, nothing to hint as to her whereabouts until Rangi told us about a terrifying blonde bartender Fearon couldn't stop staring at last night."

Her heart jumped. "Could have been anyone."

Dom scoffed. "Darlin', it could *only* have been you." He turned to JJ who was eyeing him with trepidation. Smart woman. "You'd pine if you lost this one too, wouldn't you? Sulk? Stare at her? Become even more monosyllabic and make the lives of everyone around you hell as you regret ever letting her go?"

JJ looked at Izzy who grimaced in return.

"Yeah, probably," JJ answered, and Dom whooped in victory.

"Told you so. Now, to make up for leaving me without a word, you vicious wench, I'd like a beer.

On the house." He turned back to JJ as Izzy rolled her eyes and grabbed a pint glass from under the bar. "I know you," he said, eyes trailing up and down her slim form.

JJ's mouth tightened, her eyes growing cold under Dom's inspection.

"I don't think so."

"No," Dom insisted. "I definitely do. What's your name?"

JJ sipped her drink before answering. "JJ Conway."

Dom snapped his fingers. "Ah, the journo with the podcast."

JJ's expression grew even stonier. "Yup."

"I've seen you at the press conferences."

JJ inclined her head. "I'm allowed in as long as I behave myself."

"Well where's the fun in that?" Dom leaned one elbow on the bar and gave JJ a lazy grin. She looked at him like he was shit on her shoe.

"Leave her alone, you lunatic." Izzy said. "What are you even doing here?"

Dom looked offended. "I'm here to claim you. Everyone picks a side after a breakup. I want to be on yours."

Izzy stared at him, incredulous. "You're Zac's teammate."

"Irrelevant. I'm your friend now. We're besties. I'm gonna get us matching bracelets. Also, on top of coming here to lay my sword at your side, I've got a meeting."

"So you're here for a free beer before your meeting?"

"Pretty much." Dom looked up. "Here he is now. Grab us that beer, would you, darlin'?"

Izzy resisted the temptation to glass the cocky blond bastard.

"You want anything else?" She asked JJ, but the other woman was rigid, her face deathly pale as she watched the dark haired man in the fancy suit swaggering towards Dom.

"There he is!" The newcomer boomed, drawing attention from Ken and a couple of the other regulars.

"Tony," Dom shook the man's hand firmly. "Good to see you."

Tony's eyes slid past Dom, over Izzy, who resisted the urge to shiver and landed on JJ.

"Look at this, then. Here I am to have a chat with one of the game's most talented locks about what his future looks like." Tony smiled with an easy charm that probably fooled most people. "And I find him already in cahoots with my wife."

"Ex-wife," JJ said quietly, and Izzy shared a surprised look with Dom.

"Yes, of course." Tony chuckled. "Lovely to see you as always, Jacinda." He moved as if to kiss her cheek and it happened.

JJ flinched.

Every nerve in Izzy's body went on high alert and she knew. She *knew*. Silence settled like a heavy cloud over the small group.

Tony straightened, a practised smile fixed in place. "Well, Dom. Shall we?"

"No." Izzy had never heard Dom's voice so cold.

"Excuse me?"

Dom straightened, his giant body filling the space in front of the bar, shifting so that the petite sports journalist was partially hidden from her ex-husband's view.

"There's no need for a meeting." Dom's normally open, sunny face was shuttered, his jaw tight. Deep grooves furrowed his brow. "My future doesn't include the Cobras. Not under their current leadership."

Tony's smile faded. "You're making a mistake," he sneered, all of his sophisticated charm gone.

"I don't think I am." Dom tilted his chin towards the door. "There's no need for you to stay."

The team owner's mouth twisted. "Perhaps I'll stay and have a drink. Catch up with Jacinda for old time's sake."

JJ looked at Izzy, her eyes pleading, knuckles white around the stem of her wineglass.

"No, you won't." Izzy blurted before Dom could respond. "Get out."

Tony's eyes narrowed on her. "What did you say to me?"

Izzy glared daggers at him, letting him see every speck of her rage and disgust.

"Get. The. Fuck. Out." She enunciated, venom dripping from her words. "You're trespassed. If you come back in here again, I'll call the cops."

"You can't do that," Tony blustered, and Izzy shot him a smile dripping with malice as she pointed without looking to the sign above the bar.

*Staff may refuse service at their discretion.*

God bless Pete, the grumpy old bastard who ran this place. He didn't have a lot of patience for bullshit and he'd told Izzy her first day here that he didn't expect her to have to put up with it either.

Tony levelled her with a venomous glare and she narrowed her eyes in response. A tense moment brewed before he spun on his heel and stalked out.

The tension dissipated immediately, evaporating with a pop.

"Thanks for that." JJ's voice was small, and Izzy shot her a quick smile as she poured Dom's beer.

"No worries."

For his part, Dom acted like nothing had happened. "Are you coming to my game on Saturday?" he asked, accepting the pint from her and swallowing half of it in one go.

"No."

"Why not?"

*Because I broke up with your team's winger and I'm emotionally distraught?*

"I have to work."

"Rubbish. Hey, blue eyes," he summoned Izzy's co-worker Sarah with an easy grin. "Are you working Saturday?"

Sarah almost dislocated her head shaking it.

"Can you cover Izzy's shift by any chance? She's got something real important to take care of. A family emergency."

"Sure," the other girl answered faintly. "I can do that."

"You're a legend." Dom blew her a kiss and Sarah wandered off looking dazed. Izzy tracked her progress carefully to make sure she didn't wander into a tray of glasses in her lust-drunken stupor.

"Problem solved," Dom said, rubbing his hands together with satisfaction. "I'll leave tickets for you at the front office. You can bring a friend. What about you?" he asked JJ. "You want to watch from the family box instead of the press one?"

"No," JJ replied flatly.

Dom shrugged. "Suit yourself."

"Why are you doing this?" Izzy pleaded. "Is this

revenge for the Storm thing? I told you I was sorry about that."

Dom stilled, his eyes meeting hers sombrely. "It's not about that. I thought you might want to come. I meant what I said about us being friends, but Fearon's my friend too, even if he'd never admit it. He's hurting, Izzy. I'm new to the team this year, but everyone who's known him longer than me is worried. Chalmers, Katu, Hewitt. Come see him for yourself. If you think he's doing okay, I'll never mention it again, Scout's honour. Besides, it's a big game for me. My first one against my old team." He flashed her a grin that had probably dropped panties from Cape Reinga to Oban. Izzy wrinkled her nose at him instead. "I could use a friend there."

"Fine," she relented, because Saturday evening shifts were full of city wankers hitting on her and the events of this week had her nerves strung so tight there was a chance she'd eviscerate one and lose her job entirely. But mostly because she'd already thought about the future, and come to the conclusion that if Zac stayed with the Knights her ability to avoid him long term was zilch. Her closeness with Cara and Finn meant the team would be part of her life when she was in Auckland. She might as well practise seeing him. It couldn't be any worse than last time, and at least she could leave knowing she'd done it. Enjoy herself overseas without the awful anticipation of their next meeting hanging over her. "I'm not talking to him, though. I'm there for you."

Dom's happy grin almost blinded her. "I'm honoured, darlin'."

He wandered off with his beer while Izzy filled orders and sterilised glasses, making conversation with JJ, who for a sports journalist didn't look in Dom's direction once. In fact, the other woman seemed almost determined not to look at him as he lounged in a booth, playing on his phone.

"So," JJ eyed Izzy speculatively. "Zac Fearon, huh?"

Izzy felt the heat climbing over her cheeks. "What about him?"

The other woman leaned forward, elbows on the bar. "Look, I have to ask…"

Izzy braced herself.

"Do you not just think of Zac Efron every time you hear that name?"

Izzy burst into laughter. "Yes! Every time!"

"Thank goodness," JJ sighed. "I thought it was just me and my childhood obsession with High School Musical making it weird."

"Definitely not," Izzy assured her.

"How do you know him? Through Cara?"

Izzy's smile slipped, and she studied the other woman. "Off the record?" You couldn't be too careful with journos, everyone knew that.

JJ shrugged. "Of course."

"I nannied for his niece and nephew."

"Oh, cool. So you're a nanny?"

"I was." Izzy said. "Now I'm a bartender. After this, I'll be working on a cruise ship."

"Busy lady."

"Yeah," Izzy sighed. For the first time in forever, thinking about the stop-start unpredictability of her life made her feel tired rather than excited. "Busy is one word for it. I haven't stayed in one place for more than two years since I was seventeen."

JJ gave a low whistle. "And how long have you been doing this now?"

"Eight years."

"You like it?"

"I used to." Perhaps it was because JJ was a stranger, but somehow Izzy could voice the idea that had been nagging at the back of her mind for the last few weeks. "Lately, I've been feeling like it's more of a habit than anything else."

"Sounds like you're burnt out."

Izzy had heard of burn out, obviously, but it had always been in the context of other people's jobs, linked with bustling offices or creative roles with no knock-off time, part and parcel of the hustle culture that demanded people access their work emails on their phones and respond to messages as soon as they received them. Not to jobs where you often had several hours a day to do laundry and cleaning, and weekends where you could pop off to Portugal and sip an Aperol Spritz by the ocean.

"Maybe," she hedged.

"Definitely," JJ stated firmly. "If you could do anything, anything at all, what would it be?"

Izzy closed her eyes and let the veil of possibility settle over her. The pub chatter and clink of glasses faded away as she let herself imagine for a moment what she would do if she wasn't restricted by mundane things like money and visas and obligations.

When she opened her eyes, it took her a couple of blinks before the fuzziness receded from the corners of her vision. JJ was still watching her, eyes curious over her wineglass.

"I'd probably do something like this," Izzy admitted. "I'd still travel because I love it, but I'd like to do it with people who matter to me as well. Have a job where I wasn't likely to end up covered in vomit. I'd keep making jewellery because I'm really enjoying that, but maybe I'd write poetry or sell sourdough bread at farmers' markets, or crochet blankets for premature babies. Something that brought other people joy, but didn't drag it out of me in return. I'd watch the babies my sister is bound to start popping out and maybe have one of my own so they could grow up together, and I'd get up early each morning and watch the sun rise over the ocean. I'd have a simple life, full of love and laughter and happiness. That's what I'd do if I could do anything."

"Who would you want to do that with?"

Izzy's heart echoed in her ears, Zac's name freezing in her throat. She wanted all of that with him. With the man who had rejected her, pushing her aside when his real family needed him.

*With the man you pushed aside when he tried to apologise*, a small voice in her head whispered and the truth of her loss hit her like a brick. He had, he'd tried to make amends. He'd come to her bar and he'd attempted to make it up to her with his words and his body, but she'd been so hurt, so bitter about his actions that day in his Devonport driveway, she'd rejected him in turn.

*What if I hadn't?* Where would she be now? Snuggled up on Zac's big brown Chesterfield with her head in his lap while he read a book wearing his fuck-hot professor glasses? Sitting on the porch swing with a cup of coffee, watching the world go by in their own little bubble? Spread out across his sun-warmed sheets while he blew her mind and stitched her ragged heart back together at the same time?

*Shit.* She wanted that. All of it. And she'd blown

it, her stupid pride pushing its way to the front when she was hurt and telling Zac there was nothing for him with her. Who was she kidding? He could have *all* of her. Not because she was weak, or needed him, but because she *wanted* him. Because she felt better when she was with him, when he looked at her with those molten silver eyes, a half-smile tugging at his lips and *saw* her. All the messy, terrified pieces of her that had set her on a path at seventeen and kept her there until twenty-five, running, running, running from the truth.

She wanted to be loved.

And Zac Fearon loved her. He'd told her, in a million little ways. Maybe he hadn't said the words yet, but looking back, Izzy knew it in her bones. Her man wasn't good with words. He showed people how he felt. He showed his team how important they were to him each week when he laced up his boots and played his heart out for his brothers on the field. He showed Otis and Hazel how much he cared by listening to them, treating them as individuals, making time for them both and encouraging them to follow their own passions.

And he'd shown Izzy he loved her. Every steaming mug of coffee he'd made for her to sip on the swing in the golden light of dawn was a declaration. His willingness to attend her sister's wedding as her date. The way he'd placed his hand on her back, supporting her with his very presence. Replacing her dulce de leche, letting her choose what they watched at night, even the way he held her after they'd made love. He'd been showing her the whole time, only she hadn't been looking, blinded by her own ignorance and fear.

"Shit." This time the word spilled from her lips.

JJ raised her brows. "Sounds like you know."

"I know," Izzy admitted. "I just don't know what I'm going to do about it."

~

ZAC WAS SUFFERING. It wasn't a new sensation. He spent half his life being smashed to the ground by men as big and tough as he was, but today was different. The sun burned brighter, the ground was harder, and the hits? Well, they kept on coming.

"You okay?" Chalmers asked as he hauled Zac up from the ground again. They had seconds before the turnover brought play back their way, no time to sit around and chat about their feelings, but Zac appreciated the gesture anyway. He grunted and ran back into the line.

They were playing the Giants, a team that had robbed them of a championship chance the season before, and the sole focus of the team in the pre-game locker room had been beating the Giants to such a degree that nobody would doubt they were the better team today. They were playing tight, unforced errors at a minimum, but Zac was having trouble finding his stride. Everyone else was having a banger of a game – they were up by fourteen points – but he was too quiet, not seeing enough of the action and finding himself face down on the turf more often than not when he did.

It could be the knowledge that Izzy was watching from the box. Dom had announced his success at convincing her to come to the game for the planned halftime surprise, but rather than spurring him on, the fear of another rejection held him back.

"On me," Dom yelled as he streaked past, ball tucked safely under his arm after a turnover, and Zac fell in behind him, following the big man's lead as he swerved across the field, ducking defenders.

Zac saw the Giants' player approaching, saw Dom reach out a hand to fend him off, but he went too high. The Giant dropped a shoulder, angled his head down and drove forward.

"Fuck!" Zac raced forward. There were no arms there, ready to wrap in the tackle – none. It was a pure shoulder charge – vicious, violent and completely fucking illegal.

Dom stumbled back, the ball falling from his hands, and Zac was right there to see it, the way his body twisted as it fell, his leg pinned at an unnatural angle under the opposition player's body.

Dom's hoarse roar cut through the boos of the Knights' supporters in the stands, and Zac's fury found a target. He ripped the Giants player off Dom, holding him by the collar as he drew back and punched him right in the face. The player stumbled, then shook his head and drove forward, blood pouring from the fresh cut above his eye.

The return hit clipped Zac on the jaw, the sweet sting a perfect opportunity to unleash, and he leaned into it, swinging again even as both teams swarmed them, trying to pull them apart and take their own shots in equal measure.

"Fuck you, Fearon," the Giants player yelled as his captain pinned his arms behind his torso. "I hope you get the clap."

Zac, equally restrained, spat at the other man's feet. "Fuck *you*, Evans. If I do get it, it'll be from your wife."

He had no idea what Evans' wife got up to in her

spare time, but the taunt served its purpose. Evans turned a mottled purple and tried to kick him.

The whistle sounded sharply.

"Captains!"

"Ah, shit," Chalmers muttered from behind Zac. "Stay here and don't say a word. Don't even look at anyone." He marched off towards the referee, already yelling a defence and gesturing at Dom, who was still in a heap on the ground with the Knights' medics next to him.

The referee flashed a yellow card at Zac and he stomped off towards the sidelines, looking up at the stadium screen in time to see Evans receive a red one.

*Good. Smarmy prick.* He made a wanking motion at the other man from the shadows of the tunnel and Evans flipped him the bird and mouthed something about his mother.

"Harro wants you in the locker room," the assistant backs coach said.

"What? There's only a few minutes left in play." He'd be sidelined for the beginning of the next half too.

"He doesn't care." The assistant coach tapped his earpiece. "He said to get your head out of your arse and into the locker room before he gets down here."

Zac shook his head stubbornly. "No way. I've got something happening at half time."

The assistant coach gave him a long look. "Look, mate. The best advice I can give you is to follow these instructions. Whatever you think you have going on, you need to get a check over after that fight, anyway."

Zac sighed, and headed straight for the

changing room, his sprigs clattering on the concrete. Could nothing go right for him today?

Once in the locker room, he ripped off his sweat-soaked shirt and collapsed on the bench in front of his locker, feet splayed and head back against the cool metal door. He closed his eyes and inhaled deeply, working to get his breathing under control.

It wasn't the first time he'd been carded in his career, but it was the first time it had happened because he'd lost control of his emotions. All the other incidents had been minor mistakes because he was fixated on the play; failing to protect the player in the air, an accidental head high when the ballrunner ducked in a direction he hadn't anticipated. Fighting? That wasn't his style. Nothing about this game had been usual for him. Nothing about his *life* was running usually for him.

Izzy was watching, and here he was, scrapping like a bloody amateur on a club team instead of the professional he was. He'd paid over a grand to have a declaration of his love shined up on the big screen during halftime and instead of being on the field so he could see it, see *her*, Harro had relegated him to the locker room.

"Zac?"

He was hearing her everywhere lately. Snippets of her laugh, of her voice, even her music seemed to be haunting him. He'd turned off the car radio last week when the third country song in as many days made its way onto his classic rock station. The only place he didn't hear her was the house, where the very lack of her resulted in a silence so powerful it almost overwhelmed him.

"Zac?"

Someone touched his cheek gently and his eyes

flew open. Izzy stood over him, eyes wide and worried.

"Are you okay?"

He swallowed thickly. "What are you doing here?"

She dropped her hand. "I was in the family box with Cara. Dom invited me, and... I wanted to see you."

"You did?"

"Yeah." She dropped to the floor, her hands settling on his knees. "I need to tell you I made a mistake at the bar."

He opened his mouth, but she held up a hand. "Please let me say this, okay? I'm really nervous and I have a whole speech thing planned."

Zac closed his mouth, because he couldn't deny her anything, and she took a deep breath before continuing.

"I was scared. It's always been easier for me to run than to face hard things, and nothing has ever been harder than loving you. I don't mean it like that," she hurried on when he clenched his teeth. "Loving you is easy, too easy. It's the most natural thing I've ever felt and that's why it scares me so much, because the idea of you not wanting me, the idea of being rejected or cast aside by you..." her voice quavered, "That's what's hard. Taking a risk by giving you my heart and knowing you could break it."

"I wouldn't," Zac swore, sitting up, cupping her cheeks in his hands. "Izzy, I wouldn't. I messed up that day at the house, but if you give me another chance, I promise I'll show you every day how much you mean to me."

"I know," she nodded, a tear slipping from her

eye. He brushed it away with his thumb. "I know you would. You always have. We both made mistakes that day. I was too defensive, too stubborn to try to see things from your perspective. The things you do for others." She let out a heavy breath and closed her eyes. "Zac, you're the best man I know. Being with you, it's worth the risk. Can you forgive me for not seeing it sooner?"

Zac's heart leapt. "Baby..." He leaned forward, dropping feather-light kisses on her eyelids, her temples, her cheekbones. "There's nothing to forgive. This is new for both of us. We're going to make mistakes. But at the end of the day, as long as we're willing to work through it, we'll be okay. I can guarantee it."

"Yeah?"

"Yeah."

Her hands travelled up his body, over his arms and across his pecs. He let her, lips parting on a soft moan as she traced across sinew and bone, her touch spreading life back into him.

She paused when one of her hands reached his heart. "What's this?"

Zac looked down as her fingers brushed his tattoo.

"It's for you," he admitted. "I meant to show you in the bar, but... you know..."

Izzy ran her fingers down and across, following the lines of the compass. "It looks like mine."

"Almost." He reached for her hand and moved it down. There, where the S would be on a normal compass was an I instead. None of the other points were marked. Her intake of breath echoed in the locker room as she saw it properly, realised what it meant.

"You're my Southern Cross, Isabel. You're my guiding light. I didn't realise I'd been living in darkness until you arrived and lit me up from inside. My ancestors used the Southern Cross to navigate new waters, to lead them here to Aotearoa. To where they belonged. That's what I'm doing too. You want to travel, baby? I'll follow you anywhere because I'm following my heart, and my heart has led me straight to you."

Izzy's eyes welled with tears and he brushed them away with his thumb.

"I've missed you so much," she whispered.

"Me too," he admitted. "You have no idea. The house has been so empty without you. *I've* been so empty without you. I tried to find you right away but you were gone, and then when I found you again, I was so relieved I messed it all up. I need you, Izzy. I need that sparkle and joy you bring to my life, and I need you in the quiet moments too. The times that will be hard for us both. If I've got you, I can handle anything."

"You have me," she declared fiercely. "And I've got you."

"You'd better fucking believe it, baby. I'm yours. Forever." He tilted his chin, capturing her mouth and the rightness of it flooded him like a tidal wave. Finally. *Finally.* His girl was back in his life, back in his arms. The shadowy greys of the last few weeks were obliterated in a shower of technicolour as he sank to his knees, pressing their upper bodies as close as possible. He wanted to feel her everywhere.

And that's how his teammates found him moments later, on his knees, hip to hip and lip to lip with the love of his life in the middle of the Knights' changing room.

"Christ's sake," Harro shouted from the doorway. "We're down to twelve players on the field and you're in here pashing up some woman?"

"Hey!" Chalmers protested. "Don't talk about her that way."

Zac pulled back and looked down into Izzy's eyes, shining with joy. "What do you say, baby? Should we lock this one up and head home?"

"Sounds good," she grinned up at him.

"Done." His voice was thick with satisfaction. "They'd better watch out, though. I'm on a winning streak here."

*hree months later*

Izzy stepped onto the tarmac and inhaled deeply. There it was. No place on Earth smelt like Aotearoa New Zealand. That special blend of freshness that danced through her nostrils even through the haze of aviation fuel.

*Home.*

She'd been gone a little over three months, undertaking a short training course in Sydney with the cruise line to guide her on the requirements of childcare work on board a ship, then a two-month contract sailing the Cairns to Hong Kong route via The Philippines and Indonesia on a sixteen-night schedule. Zac had been supportive of her desire not to renege on her commitment to the line.

"I'll miss you like crazy," he'd told her as they lay tangled in his bedsheets after the Knights beat the Giants, Zac running in two tries once he got back on the field in the second half. "But I'll be here when you get back. I've waited my whole life to find you,

Izzy. I can wait another few weeks while you do what you need to do to come back to me without any guilt or regret."

In return, she'd requested the shortest contract the line offered. Cruise ship work was hard work, no doubt about it, but on the few shore leave excursions she had over the course of her time she found herself wishing Zac was there with her. She'd taken a zillion photos of herself on a boat trip through the limestone caves of Puerto Princesa, on a stroll through Rizal Park, sending them to Zac with messages that told him how much she wished he was there with her.

He'd messaged back, telling her how much he wished he was with her too. They spoke most days, working around her schedule and his training, and she streamed all his games. In many ways, the fact they needed to spend so much of their early days communicating by phone and messages had solidified their bond. Izzy was more confident about their future than she'd ever been, after all the late night conversations sharing their hopes, their fears, their plans for the future.

She hustled through customs and immigration, smiling at everyone she spoke to along the way. Unlike the last time she'd landed in New Zealand, nerves stretched tight in the wake of the news about Cara's stalker and her parent's separation, she moved quickly, thankful she'd only taken a small carry-on suitcase with her. The ship's uniform and the routes through tropical climates had meant she could travel light. Along with her beading equipment, which had been a godsend for her in long hours between shifts, she'd taken only workout gear, her bathing suit, a couple of pairs of shorts, a few tops, a maxi skirt and long sleeved blouse for temple visits and a single pair of jeans and lone sweatshirt that she wore now to combat her return to New Zealand's winter. She was returning with a lot more beads than she'd left with though. The local sights and materials had sparked her inspiration.

Izzy dragged her case across the gleaming tiles, eyes locked on the large green Arrivals sign lit up like a beacon above the automatic doors that would usher her home.

*Home.*

She would never have thought she'd call Aotearoa home again, but she'd also never have predicted she'd fall head over heels in deep, soul-baring love with a taciturn introvert who took the weight of the world on his shoulders and still managed to make sure every day that she knew where she stood with him. Her phone was filled with messages from Zac over the last few months, some achingly beautiful, some simple heart emojis. He'd sent photos of himself and the kids, links to songs that made him think of her, and the titles of books he thought she'd enjoy. He'd even gone so far as to reach out to the friends she'd made on staff and arrange for little treats to be delivered to her room, like slices of chocolate cake when she was on her period or a face mask from the on-board salon when she'd mentioned that she was rundown from the long hours.

Izzy sped through the double doors, out of the artificial lights into the main terminal, lit by floor-to-ceiling windows. She scanned the crowd, searching for her man. Searching for her future.

It was the commotion that got her attention at

first. People whispering and pointing towards a pillar nearby. She followed their gazes, and there he was. Zac. Tall and lean, hands shoved in his pockets as he watched her, dark hair longer and hidden beneath a backwards Knights cap. Their eyes met and he smiled, that wide, open grin he saved just for her.

*Hi baby*, he mouthed, and the first tear fell. She ran towards him as he opened his arms, and she dropped her suitcase handle and leapt. He caught her, wrapping her up in those big arms. Izzy buried her face in the warm skin of his neck and inhaled, breathing him in, the citrus-cedar scent of him, her heart thudding heavy in her chest as it slowed and settled, finding true peace for the first time since she'd kissed him goodbye at the same airport three months ago.

"I missed you," she whispered, kissing his temple and tasting the salt of her tears from where they ran down his skin.

"I missed you, too," he replied. He lifted his head, catching her lips in the softest kiss. A *hello* kind of kiss. A *you're wonderful* kind of kiss. A *forever love* kind of kiss.

She kissed him back, telling him the same without words. They'd said the words before, and they'd say them again, but in this moment they pressed those promises into each other's lips, lost in the hazy relief of being together.

When they pulled apart Izzy finally became aware of the whispers and clicks echoing nearby.

"You're famous," she smirked, rubbing her nose against Zac's.

He shrugged, unconcerned. "It's been a good season." Despite Dom McQueen being ruled out for the remainder of the year because of a torn ACL, the Knights were on a hot streak, looking set to finish in the top four before the championship rounds started in a couple of months. Zac's performance on the field had been phenomenal, causing Izzy's shrieks of excitement and pride to echo around her stateroom as she streamed the games or highlight reels on her phone between shifts. It had certainly been enough to earn him a three-year extension on his contract, which he'd happily accepted after checking with Izzy that she would be okay keeping Auckland as their home base for a few years once she returned.

"I can't believe the attention isn't bothering you," she murmured, as he lowered her to the ground, keeping one of her hands firmly linked with his and grabbing her suitcase with his other.

"Are you kidding? I've got my girl home with me. Nothing could bother me today." Zac pressed a kiss against her temple. "The kids are pumped to see you too. There were genuine hysterics when they found out they couldn't come to the airport. Expect them to be round within forty-five seconds of us pulling into the driveway."

Excitement bubbled in Izzy. "I can't wait to see them either." She'd video-chatted with Otis and Hazel several times since she left, and two weeks ago she'd sent a box of gifts she'd collected for them during her travels to Zac's for unpacking when she got home. She'd even spoken to Frances a couple of times. In the weeks after the Giants game, before Izzy left New Zealand, Frances had apologised for her behaviour the night they met and both women had made an effort to get along. Edith Purdy had finally convinced Marvin to downsize, and Zac had talked them into a private sale. Frances, Otis and Hazel now lived next door to his Devonport villa, and according to Zac the kids happily bounced back and forth between houses, both places full of love.

Izzy couldn't wait. Though she had mentioned to Zac they'd need a lock on their bedroom door with the kids popping up so unexpectedly. He'd sent her a picture of a newly installed one later that day. The current plan was for Izzy to work on her fledgling beading business – she'd had several requests for pieces after Cara and Finn's wedding photo was released, crediting her for Cara's earrings – and picking up the kids on days Frances or Zac worked late.

"There may be an ice-cream sundae party planned," he warned her as they stepped out of the terminal into the winter sun. "The dulce supply has been raided in preparation."

"Oh, my dulce," Izzy sighed longingly. "How I've missed it."

"Uh huh," Zac replied dryly. He stepped up to the line of taxis and handed her bag off to a driver. She hadn't understood why someone as private and controlled as Zac would come and pick her up in a taxi when he'd mentioned it and he'd simply laughed through the phone, that low, sexy chuckle that sent a zing straight through her body.

"Because," he'd purred. "I haven't touched you in three months, and I'll be damned if I'm taking my hands off you for one second once I get you back."

He kept his promise too, holding her hand across the backseat as the taxi pulled out of the rank and headed towards the motorway, the sun shining over the familiar suburbs and rolling green fields that led towards the city proper.

"Speaking of things you've missed," he said, the thumb of his free hand busy on his phone. "I bought you something."

"A present?" Izzy squeezed his hand. "I love presents."

A small smile played at the corners of Zac's full mouth. "Kind of."

Izzy's phone pinged in her sweatshirt pocket.

"You should check that," he suggested.

She shot him a suspicious look as she dug the device out, and checked her notifications. A forwarded email from Zac Fearon.

"If this is one of those good luck chain letter things..." Izzy grumbled good-naturedly as she opened it. It wasn't. It was a confirmation of return flights for two adults to Zimbabwe in November.

Shocked, she met Zac's eyes. He shrugged. "I've always wanted to see Victoria Falls, and Cara said you've never been. I thought maybe once the season is over we could have our own adventure. Together."

"You really want to travel with me?"

"Izzy," Zac gripped her hand more firmly. "I want to do everything on this earth with you."

Another tear streaked down her cheek as she raised their linked fingers and kissed the back of Zac's strong hand.

"I'd like that," she smiled up at the big man who'd stolen her heart not long after he'd stolen her underwear. "But for now, the only place I need to be is home."

*Home.*

Zac closed his eyes at her words, a smile settling across his features and she knew he'd misunderstood her. She'd tell him later, after she'd hugged the kids, and eaten ice cream with them, once their house had cleared of the excitement and energy that came with their messy, beautiful family, once they'd retired to the bedroom and greeted each other again with touches and kisses and pleasure they cried out into each other's mouths as their bodies found heaven in one another.

She'd tell him then that her home wasn't a place. It was him.

THE END

# ACKNOWLEDGMENTS

Is it even a Courtney Clark Michaels book if I'm not kissing up against a deadline like my life depends on it? The biggest thanks to my incredible husband for his unwavering support when I disappear for days on end and only communicate in grunts during the drafting process - very Zac of me! To my kids and my parents, one for the inspiration and one for watching the inspiration while I work. My ongoing gratitude to Barbara DeLeo for always being the first to wade through my messy, misspelled drafts. I am eternally thankful to Ray Collins and Phillipa Kitchin for their incredible eye for editing detail, meaning that a good portion of that mess and those misspellings were eradicated before Off His Game went out to the masses. Any mistakes are mine alone. To Kate and Sally, who are always willing to read my work and offer feedback on my characters and their actions. My writing groups, who give me space, sanity, advice and encouragement, as well as a swift kick up the arse when required - The Blenheim Girls and Wordmakers, this book would not have made it on time without you! Finally, but most importantly, thank you to everyone who has purchased Off His Game! I appreciate you spending some of your limited free time with these characters in this world of mine - I hope you've enjoyed watching Izzy and Zac wrestle their way to their HEA as much as I did!

# ABOUT THE AUTHOR

Award winning author Courtney Clark Michaels has been reading and writing romance since she first pilfered a novel out of her mother's bedroom at the tender age of thirteen. While her newly discovered writing hobby didn't endear her to her teachers, it did make Maths more interesting for her friends. Ironically, after gaining degrees in Criminology and English, Courtney now teaches high school students and spends a fair bit of time bemoaning their off-task behaviour. Karma is indeed a bitch. Courtney's passion for writing strong, independent heroines and smart, sexy men is equal only to her passions for travel, online shopping and patting other people's dogs. She is lucky enough to live in the heart of New Zealand's winemaking region with her own alpha man, a few gorgeous children and a hyperactive poochon named Kevin.

**Also by Courtney Clark Michaels:**

Pacific Passions Series
Pregnant by the Prince
Rooming With Royalty
Protecting His Princess
Christmas in Paradise
Ginger Kisses

Hot Rugby Knights Series
Game Changer

Sign up for my free newsletter at my website: www.
courtneyclarkmichaels.com for updates, giveaways
and exclusive content.